In the Greenwood He Was Slain

Dorothy Bodoin

A Wings ePress, Inc.
Cozy Mystery

Wings ePress, Inc.

Edited by: Jeanne Smith
Copy Edited by: Christie Kraemer
Executive Editor: Jeanne Smith
Cover Artist: Trisha FitzGerald-Jung

All rights reserved

Wings ePress Books
www.wingsepress.com

Copyright © 2020 by: Dorothy Bodoin
ISBN 13: 978-1-61309-562-1
ISBN 10: 1-61309-562-7

Published In the United States Of America

Wings ePress Inc.
3000 N. Rock Road
Newton, KS 67114

Dedication

In loving memory of my mother, Helen Bodoin,
my first reader.

One

Snow lay heavily on the ground, and the silence of early morning held the land in a death grip. If I listened carefully, I could hear the proverbial pin drop.

Balancing the heavy pot of stew in both hands, I followed the cleared walkway out to Jonquil Lane—my destination the yellow Victorian house where Camille, my aunt by marriage, lived. Camille, usually so vibrant and energetic, had been felled by a bout of influenza. I was doing all I could to help her, including taking care of her two dogs along with my eight collies.

In the first week of February, winter showed no signs of moving on. It was difficult to believe in the fragrant yellow jonquils and daffodils that would spring up from the thawed ground on either side of the lane in a few more months.

But believe I must if I were to survive the endless winter.

In any event, in any season, I couldn't be living in a better place. The yellow Victorian and my green Victorian farmhouse were the last houses on the lane. In imaginative moments, I fancied that I lived at World's End, happily isolated from the rest of Foxglove Corners, blessed with the peace and quiet of country living.

Suddenly, it wasn't so quiet. The approaching hum of an engine insinuated itself into the stillness. I waited and watched as a silver car came into view, swerved on an isle of ice, then righted itself.

The windows were partially covered with snow and ice, obscuring the driver's vision. He must have figured he'd be unlikely to encounter another vehicle on this lonely stretch of roadway.

That might be true, but what of the animals?

Wishing my deputy sheriff husband, Crane, were with me to see the condition of the driver's car and take note of his speed, I stepped onto the lane and looked northward.

The car had stopped alongside one of the most sinister places in the county. Here a man's vision of elegant French chateau style houses had died when he went bankrupt and fled from Michigan, leaving the unfinished houses to deteriorate. A ghastly, ghostly place, it attracted vagrants and ne'er-do-wells and had been the scene of more than one dangerous encounter in the past.

The driver lifted a large box out of his car and dropped it on the ground. He was tall and burly and dressed in black with a hood over his head. Dressed for stealth, I'd say, and up to no good.

Out of the box tumbled four bundles of golden and white fluff. They stood still, stunned for a moment. Dogs. Puppies. They looked like collie pups. One tried to climb back into the box; one roused itself and padded into the woods; one...

"No," I cried. "Don't do this."

The driver didn't turn or give any indication he'd heard me.

Sadly, it wasn't unheard of for an unscrupulous, heartless person to dump unwanted dogs in the country, either thinking someone else would give them a home, or not sparing them another thought. But it was unusual to catch such a despicable person in the act.

Not that I'd caught him.

A little one tried to crawl back into the box. The man lifted him by the scruff of his neck and flung him into the air. Into the woods. The puppy landed in a nest of snow-covered branches.

The next instant, the man was in his car, driving away.

I set the pot of stew down on the snow. The puppy had made its way back to the box, no doubt searching for his lost security. Winding my scarf around my mouth and nose, I set out hurriedly up the lane, unmindful of the cold, thinking only of the puppies, hoping they wouldn't wander too far from the scene of their abandonment.

The lane was unplowed, its surface marred with ruts and ice which made walking hazardous. I should have taken the time to drive the short distance, but I was almost there, at the box.

The puppy cowered inside, trembling on a soiled blanket. It was a sable collie baby, as I'd thought, perhaps ten or twelve weeks old, with nicely tipped ears and a wide white ruff. I spoke softly to her and reached inside to gather her in my arms before she could bite me.

"Come," I said. "I'm Jennet, rescuer of collies. You're in good hands."

The little mite bared her teeth and burrowed further into the blanket, regarding me in defiance. Such a pretty new set of teeth. Such spirit for a baby.

I reached for her again and scooped her into my arms.

I had one, but I had seen four. Where were the others?

The lane stretched out before me, with dark, uncompromising woods on either side. The puppy lay in my arms, her resistance melted away, her body as hard as stone.

Little pawprints led into the tangle of dead vegetation and grasping branches that formed the edge of the unfinished development. The close-growing trees and falling structures stared back at me coldly, issuing a challenge and a warning.

I would return, of course, but first, I had to take my small rescue to Sue Appleton, the president of the Lakeville Collie Rescue League. Her horse ranch was too far for walking in this weather, so I headed back home, down the lane. I'd take the car and maybe see the other puppies on the way. My original errand, and the stew, slipped out of my mind.

~ * ~

Jonquil Lane ends at Squill Lane where Sue's horse farm is located. The man had to have turned right here as the other direction would have taken him to a cornfield and a currently untenanted cottage. In other words, no outlet.

After that, he could have gone anywhere. All I could tell anyone was that he'd been dressed all in black with a hood and had neglected to clear the windows of his car which looked like a Honda. Possibly an older model, an Accord?

This wasn't much to go on, but as I glanced at the puppy shivering in the passenger's seat, I resolved to find the others. Resolved, not for the first time, to do the impossible.

~ * ~

Sue's horse farm drowsed in the cold morning sunlight, like the rest of Foxglove Corners steeped in snow. If it weren't for three horses idling under their blankets in the corral, I might have come to a place that lay under a spell of enchantment.

A spiral of gray smoke coiled up to the sky. Sue opened the door before I could knock. She wore a long white bathrobe, and her strawberry blonde hair tumbled over its Mandarin collar.

Had I arrived on her doorstep too early?

Her collies, all of them rescues, kept their distance at her command, but not their silence. They were used to canine newcomers and visitors, accustomed to barking their welcome.

Sue smiled as she spied the puppy in my arms and extended her palm for her to sniff.

"Who is this little one?"

"Our newest rescue," I said. "She was dumped on Jonquil Lane."

"Did you take a day off from school?"

"We're on winter break. I need a week off. My classes this semester are wild."

"It's fortunate you were there to find her." Sue took the puppy from me. "How pretty. She's just a baby. Little Goldilocks."

I told Sue about the man who had driven away, leaving four puppies to fend for themselves, likely four littermates.

"Diabolical," she said. "Where are the others?"

"They could be anywhere. They scattered. This one went back to the box he brought them in."

I ran my finger gently over her soft head. She was so good. So quiet. So unlike wriggling, adventurous puppies I'd seen in the past. As she trained her eyes on me, I frowned.

"What's wrong, Jennet?"

"Look at her little eyes. I don't think she feels well."

"You're right. After I give her a drink and a little food, I'll call Doctor Alice."

Alice Foster took care of all our dogs. A trip to the animal hospital was at the top of Rescue League's list for new arrivals.

"Diane will take her," Sue said, referring to one of the high school girls who helped her on the ranch. "They're on winter break, too. I'm glad for the help. I went to bed early, but I feel like something drained all my energy during the night."

The vampire flu.

"Don't get sick," I told her. "You have animals who need you."

"What are we going to do about the other three puppies?" she asked. "They can't stay out there in this weather."

We? Sue wasn't going anywhere today. What was *I* going to do about them?

"Find them, of course," I said. "They ran into the woods. How far can they go on those little legs?"

Foolish question. By now they could be long gone.

"I'll do my best," I said.

Two

I had to do better than my best. The collie babies would never survive the cold and lack of food. Even worse, what if all four littermates were sick? The man who had dumped them so unceremoniously on the lane had given them a death sentence.

I didn't see the missing puppies as I drove home, neither on the lane nor at the edge of the unfinished construction site. Even the box was gone, its whereabouts a mystery.

I regarded the area with trepidation. Venturing into this forbidding stretch of wilderness would be tempting fate. I could easily fall over roots or branches covered by snow and freeze to death; and no one would know where to look for me.

That wouldn't happen, I told myself. In any event, I didn't have a choice. Three little lives depended on me. I had to come back. I would leave a note for Crane, change into clothing suitable for tramping through woods, and take one of the collies with me. Probably Misty, my tri-headed white who had proved a stalwart companion on past adventures.

We would find the rest of the puppies and save them from a slow, certain death. Now to visit Camille briefly. I heard my own dogs barking inside the house. They'd be gathered at the side door, clamoring their frustration that I'd gone out and hadn't taken them—and, moreover, that I wasn't coming inside.

I parked the car and looked for the pot of stew. It was where I'd left it, only now resting on its side, the contents gone. A spill of gravy stained the snow and tracks led across the lane and into the woods that adjoined the yellow Victorian.

Coyote tracks.

Darn! It was all for nothing—cutting the chuck roast into bite-sized pieces, browning it, all the chopping and stirring. All the time wasted cooking a savory meal—for wildlife. I didn't have anything to give Camille now.

I should have known better than to leave food unattended outside. Still, when I'd seen the plight of the puppies, I hadn't stopped to think.

I felt like kicking the pot. But what would that accomplish? Instead, I trudged across the lane and knocked on Camille's door. Twister, her Belgian shepherd, and Holly, the tricolor collie who had once belonged to me, began to bark.

You'd think any coyote who valued his health would stay far away from our houses, but they had moved into our territory long ago and didn't intend to move out.

Camille, like Sue wearing a long robe, opened the door and brushed her lightly silvered blonde hair back from her forehead. Holly dashed out to the porch and sniffed my boots frantically. *Where's the other dog?* she must be thinking.

I stepped inside, missing the traditional smells of baked goods that usually wafted through the house. Camille looked wan and fragile, her usual radiance seriously dimmed.

I said, "I was going to bring you stew for dinner, but some wild thing intercepted it. I'll make another batch tomorrow."

"That's sweet of you, dear, but I have no appetite. Gilbert has been bringing take-out for himself."

Camille's husband, Gilbert, was Crane's uncle, their marriage having made my first friend in Foxglove Corners my aunt.

"I'll bring some by tomorrow for him," I said. "Shouldn't you be in bed?"

"I've been in bed for fourteen hours." She stepped back. "Thanks for checking on me, Jennet, but I don't want you to catch whatever I have."

"Neither do I, but I can't live in a bubble. Let me make you a cup of tea."

"I couldn't drink it."

"Weak tea. Sure you can. You don't want to get dehydrated."

I made myself at home in Camille's blue and white country kitchen, admiring the way morning sunlight bounced off the cobalt bottles that lined the windowsill, turning them into blue fire. Even without muffins or fruit breads cooling on the counter, this was a pleasant, welcoming place.

From my first days in Foxglove Corners, I had brought many a problem to Camille in this kitchen and come away with a clearer understanding of the matter and determination to act.

Camille sank into a chair, her dogs lying at her feet. With a sigh, she said, "I hate being sick. I don't like drinking water. Even fruit juice loses its taste."

While I poured our tea, I told her about the collie puppy I'd rescued and the three littermates who had wandered into the woods.

She grew even more agitated if that were possible.

"Oh, Jennet, you have to find them," she said. "It's going to be even colder tonight through tomorrow. Puppies that age need nurturing. They'll die," she added.

"I'm going back to look for them," I assured her. "And I'm going to find the man who dumped them."

Camille moved a teaspoon languidly through her cup. She had yet to take even a sip of her tea.

"How?" she asked.

At the moment, I didn't know. But this was something I had to do.

I imagined myself hunting for a silver Honda-like car with ice and snow on the windows. How many vehicles fit that description?

"I'll find a way," I said.

She removed the spoon, set it on a napkin. "I wish you could go someplace warm and wonderful for your winter break."

Sunshine. Fragrant breezes. Palm trees. Many of my senior students had gone to Florida. Crane's schedule and the dogs tied me to my home. Not that I minded. I wouldn't enjoy myself without them.

Besides, if I'd gone on a vacation, I wouldn't have been in the lane to see that horrible man dump the puppies, wouldn't have been able to rescue one of them. It was enough to be able to stay in my quiet home and not deal with constant classroom strife familiar to every high school teacher in the land.

"Annica and I are going antiquing and out to lunch one day this week," I said.

Annica, my friend and sometime partner-in-detection, attended Oakland University and worked as a waitress at Clovers, my favorite restaurant in Foxglove Corners, to supplement her scholarship money.

"That'll be nice," Camille murmured, trying to hide a yawn.

"You'd better drink your tea and go back to bed," I said.

"I'm not really sleepy. Just drained."

"Rest, then," I said.

I needed to begin my search for the puppies. I hoped it would be a search and rescue mission.

~ * ~

As I stooped to retrieve my pot from the snow, I had a strong feeling that someone was watching me from the thin woods behind our house. The man?

Unlikely. Why would he return to the scene of his crime?

Something then. Some evil thing.

I stood, holding the pot as if it were a weapon. I wasn't afraid. I was close to the side door and, once again, all of the collies were inside barking. Also it was mid-morning, no time for an assailant to be abroad. Still, preparedness is essential when you live in a remote area.

I saw him then at the wood's edge, a large, scrawny coyote staring at me, motionless, challenging, and too close for comfort.

"You!" I said. "You're the one who ate my stew."

He didn't deny it.

I knew coyotes usually ran from noise. In the house, I had a jar filled with pennies I could shake if I encountered a coyote while walking the dogs, which hadn't happened yet.

It wasn't like a coyote to come so near to the house, to stand and watch as if contemplating its chances of overcoming me.

The jar was out of reach, but I had a pot with a lid and my voice, and dogs' frenzied barking on the other side of the door.

"Go away!" I yelled. "Get!" I banged the pot and lid together several time. "Get out of here!"

The creature turned tail and headed into the woods. Crisis averted. Only I'd dented the rim of my pot. It wasn't enough that their infernal yapping often woke me at night; they had to steal my good stew.

Coyotes are hungry, too.

At that moment, I remembered the collie babies. Like kittens and small dogs, to the coyote predator, they'd be tasty little bites.

Not if I have anything to say about it.

Three

I unlocked the door and stepped into a tidal wave of excited, yipping collies. Could anyone hope for a more enthusiastic welcome home? Candy, my wild-child tricolor, tried to open the storm door with her nose, most likely wanting to chase the coyote. Quickly, I secured it.

"Show's over," I said. "Who wants a biscuit?"

They were keyed up from the knowledge that a wild creature had been so near their home with them inside, unable to drive it away it. In other words, they were quite a handful. But biscuit was a magic word.

Of my collie brood, all but my tricolor, Halley, the first collie I'd raised from a puppy, were rescues. They circled around me as I reached for the Lassie tin, tricolor Candy going so far as to nip at my ankle.

Velvet and Misty, one black and one white, vied with each other for the spot nearest the counter. Gemmy and Star, both sables, wagged their tails, eyes bright in anticipation. My shy, once-abused blue merle, Sky, waited patiently on the fringe like the lady she was, with black and white Raven at her side.

I poured fresh water, distributed biscuits, then hurriedly changed into heavy wool pants, a turtleneck sweater, and higher boots. I remembered to fill a plastic bag with puppy-sized treats and added left-over Christmas cookies from the freezer. They would soon thaw, and what puppy could resist them?

I wrote a note for Crane and dropped my cell phone and house key in my pocket, after which I surveyed my faithful helpers. Eight good dogs, but Misty was the one best suited to accompany me. I attached her leash to her collar and led her to the side door. Back into the frigid air.

"I'll be home soon," I said to the others, hoping, as always, that it would be true.

~ * ~

The woods are silent, dark, and deep...

"And cold."

Misty glanced up at me. Hearing no command, she shoved her nose in a snow drift, wagging her tail. Something irresistible hidden in the snow called to her.

"Misty," I said. "Heel!"

She left her snowdrift with some reluctance, then nudged my pocket where I'd stashed the treats.

I entered the abandoned development warily, stepping across a two-by-four that had no doubt been intended for one of the houses.

At first I was able to follow a trail of tiny pawprints as they zigzagged through the snow. The puppies must have stayed together for a while. Moving deeper into the woods, I lost them in a tangle of other depressions. Deer and smaller animals had run through the trees, and coyotes...

I didn't want to think about coyotes.

The winter winds had been unkind to the structures that would have been elegant mansions, with the wilderness that surrounded them divided into neatly landscaped parcels. Bits and pieces of it lay between young trees that had returned, encouraged by the departure of man and his machines. Here wood, here broken glass, there most of a wall and nails. Everywhere downed branches of all sizes. Everywhere danger.

Perhaps the finished development was never meant to exist.

I kept my eyes trained on the ground, all the time calling to the puppies while Misty, wild with excitement, pulled on her leash and barked. I wished I knew their names. A person who could throw them away wouldn't have bothered to name them.

My voice only served to warn the denizens of the woods to hide themselves. The wind forced its way through the trees, and the temperature dropped drastically, or seemed to. In spite of my fleece-lined gloves, pain jabbed at my fingers; and snow and scattered debris hindered my progress. I knew the exact moment when I needed to abandon my quest.

Turning around, I resolved to return another day, hoping it wouldn't be too late. Maybe, if luck favored the lost puppies, some kind human would see them and take them inside. After all, who could resist a puppy in distress?

It depended on how far they wandered on their little legs, if they reached a populated area.

God protect them, I thought; and to Misty, I said, "Let's go home."

Once there, I didn't intend to leave the house again until the following day.

~ * ~

I crumpled the note I'd left for Crane, who took a dim view of any activity that might result in harm for me, and glanced at the clock. I'd been in the woods longer than planned, but I had time for a hot shower. I'd kept enough of the ill-fated stew for our dinner and only had to make a salad and biscuits.

But time has a way of slowing down or racing ahead at will. Today it flew by at warp speed. By the time I'd changed into my green corduroy dress, most of the day was gone. My failure to find the puppies lay like a ton of lead on my heart. I no longer had faith in the kind Samaritan who would rescue my little orphans. *I* was that Samaritan, and I'd had to give up. For now.

I was putting biscuits in the oven when I heard Crane's Jeep. He opened the door, allowing a gust of icy wind to blow into the kitchen.

The collies advanced on him in unbridled joy, each one demanding individual attention. I had to wait my turn.

Crane is the perfect man, the best-known and, I'm sure, best-loved deputy sheriff in the county. Tall with handsome, rugged features, blond hair sprinkled with silver and frosty gray eyes, he is like a force of nature bringing light and energy to the quiet house.

My turn for a greeting came with an ardent kiss that tasted of snow and smelled of balsam fir.

"How was your first day of vacation, honey?" he asked in a voice that retained a hint of a southern accent.

"Busy," I said as he locked his gun in the cabinet set aside for weapons. "I'll tell you about it later. How was yours?"

"Run of the mill," he said, eying the apple pie I'd baked this morning. "A few speeders. A fender bender. What smells so good?"

"Biscuits and stew," I said. "Take your pick. Later I'll tell you a story about the stew."

There was a lot to tell: Camille, the puppies, the silver car, the stolen dinner, the coyote...We sat in the living room over coffee and pie, all of our collies safe from the elements. Lively flames danced in the fireplace, scenting the air with applewood. The woods and their hazards seemed far away.

"What are the odds of finding the man?" I asked.

"Let's see. A man in black, a silver Honda...By now the sun will have melted the snow and ice. You didn't see his face or license plate. Not good."

"He was too far away. I just saw him spill the puppies out of the box. What do you think of their chances?"

The look in his eyes confirmed my fears. "Even worse. Unless somebody picked them up."

"What that man did was criminal. He should be made to pay for it."

"I agree, but you're not the world's avenger."

I refilled his coffee cup. "You'll watch for them as you drive around, won't you?"

"I'm always on the lookout for abandoned dogs and cats," he said. "Especially after the holidays when unwanted Christmas presents wear out their welcome. I don't like a coyote coming so near the house," he added. "Be sure to take the jar with you when you're out."

I said I would, knowing I'd probably forget unless I was walking the dogs, in which case I would be safe. No coyote in its right mind would challenge three large collies.

"I've never known a coyote to come so close to me," I said. "It's scary. They're getting bolder."

"And hungrier."

"This one gobbled up my good stew. I hope he won't be back for more. But mostly I'm worried about the puppies."

"I'll take a hike through the woods tomorrow," he said. "But I'm afraid they're long gone."

He didn't have to speculate on their probable fate. I'd already done that.

He drew me into his arms. "Remember you saved one," he said.

I had that knowledge to hold onto.

~ * ~

A call from Sue Appleton the next morning chipped away at my small victory. As I had suspected, the puppy was sick.

"Goldilocks has parvo," she said. "Doctor Alice is treating her."

I'd never experienced parvovirus with my dogs, but I knew how serious it was. Such a little sweetheart to have to fight for her life. I remembered the warmth and weight of her in my arms and felt like crying. She was indeed in distress. It was as if the saving of her had made her mine in a sense.

"Where is she?" I asked.

"Still in the hospital. When she's ready to go home, I'll keep her till she's cured."

"I'm guessing the puppies were from the same litter," I said. "They must have parvo, too."

"I assume so."

"That's why that horrible man dumped them."

"It sounds likely."

"Crane is going to search the woods for them today."

"I doubt if they're still there," Sue said, "but I wish him luck."

Four

I didn't sleep well that night. Coyotes woke me with their infernal yapping, and when I fell asleep again, they invaded my dreams. The puppies were running from them, desperately trying to evade their snapping jaws. My pot found its way into the dream sequence, too, filled again with stew.

One coyote stood in the middle of Jonquil Lane, a malevolent gleam in his eyes.

"I'm going to get you," he said.

The puppies had discovered the stew. They pounced on it, lapping up bits of beef and pieces of carrots until the pot was licked clean. They couldn't know it was a trap.

The rest of the coyote pack came slinking out of the woods, dark shadows come to life, taking canine form.

I tried to yell but couldn't make a sound. Couldn't save the hapless collie babies from the predators.

"It's Nature's law," someone whispered in the dark. "Eat or be eaten. Only the strongest can survive."

My voice returned. "I hate country living."

And the dream ended. I reached for my phone which I'd left charging on the nightstand. Eleven-thirty. All was well. Crane slept beside me, untroubled by outdoor disturbances. Halley and Misty, who considered our doorway their bedroom, didn't stir. The house was steeped in quiet as only a house can be when darkness falls, and I no longer heard the coyotes' eerie calls.

The puppies are safe, I told myself. *Go back to sleep.*

~ * ~

I prided myself on sending Crane off to his patrol of the roads and by-roads of Foxglove Corners with a good breakfast. This morning it was French toast with bacon and freshly squeezed grapefruit juice.

"Did the coyotes wake you up last night?" I asked, nibbling on a strip of bacon.

He drenched his French toast in maple syrup. "I didn't hear them. Are you going out today, honey?"

"Yes, with Annica. We're going shopping for antiques, then out to lunch in Maple Creek."

"Take the coin jar with you," he said.

"I'm only going out to the car."

"It's best to be prepared. I've been thinking. We should look into hiring an exterminator."

"To kill the coyotes?"

"To capture them humanely and relocate them. I hear we have three separate packs living in the woods nearby."

"That many?"

"They keep breeding," he pointed out.

Previously, we had talked about hiring a similar service as a group of neighbors, but the idea had fallen through. Surely I wasn't the only one bothered by them.

"It may come to that," I said. "Only...Three packs? That's a lot of animals to move."

"Better than letting them continue to multiply until they outnumber us. This time of the year is their mating season. Male coyotes can get aggressive."

"And bold," I added.

Here in our warm, safe kitchen with no wild animal to covet our food, only begging collies, I could afford to be charitable to my dogs' wild cousins.

Coyotes had to eat and feed their young. Developers stole their habitat and built houses. Humans moved in, forcing wildlife deeper in the woods. Where could the displaced animals go?

But the stories I'd heard haunted me. A coyote will lure a dog into the open, whereupon the rest of the pack emerges and overpowers him.

In my view, that implied a diabolical intelligence.

A fragment from my dream took shape in my mind. The coyote who had stared at me from the edge of the woods. Did he plan to draw me into a trap? If so, he'd met his match.

Or so I liked to think.

"Be sure to take the jar with you," Crane said again.

"I will and maybe some other kind of noisemaker if I can find one."

I didn't like to think I was under a siege on my own land, and the missing puppies were never far from my thoughts. I hoped Crane would find them before the coyotes did. But, if he didn't, as soon as possible, I'd launch another search for them.

In the meantime, I craved a brief respite from the trauma that had marred the start of my winter break. I needed that antiquing excursion and the company of my light-hearted friend, Annica.

~ * ~

The quaint little shops in nearby Lakeville on the street known as Antique Row held endless fascination for me, and none more so than my favorite haunt, the Green House of Antiques. Annica had her heart set on a pink Victorian lamp she'd seen in the Green House at Christmas. As for myself, I was always in the market for books to add to my collection of vintage series.

"This is fun." Annica pulled the hood of her coat over her red-gold hair and walked with her head down, looking for ice. "It's great to leave English novels and Clovers' specials in the dust for one afternoon."

"I agree. Along with lesson plans and papers to correct."

"You're lucky to have all week off," she added.

"And no place to go."

But that was all right. I loved my home and Crane and my collies. All I wanted was to be where they were.

"Look at the Valentines!" Annica exclaimed as we approached the Green House.

The window, always elaborately decorated, was an extravaganza in red and pink with splashes of silver and gold. From an artificial Valentine tree set up in the center of the window, lacy hearts of all sizes fell like leaves. They lay amidst storybook dolls, ruby and garnet antique jewelry, and delicate boxes made of bone china and crystal.

Annica pressed her nose to the glass. "I would *love* to have the earrings Cinderella is wearing. And those little heart boxes!"

The doll's earrings were tiny cards, whimsical mice holding faux chocolate kisses. Annica had an impressive collection of earrings. She was currently wearing her silver bells.

"What are you and Crane doing for Valentine's Day?" she asked.

"We're going out to dinner, and I'm baking a cake. I have a heart tin."

"I hope Brent will ask me out," she said.

Annica had a long-standing semi-relationship with Brent Fowler, Foxglove Corner's perennial entrepreneur, bachelor, and fox hunter. Each one appeared to be content with the status quo as Annica was passionate about her English literature courses at Oakland University, and Brent liked too many girls to settle down with one.

However, anyone could tell that Annica was his favorite.

"He will," I said.

"Well, what are we waiting for?" She was shivering. "Let's get out of this cold."

She opened the door to the Green House. A set of red heart chimes rang out a welcome as we entered a place of warmth, charm, and enchantment.

Five

A gentle explosion of pink and red greeted us. It was as if the owner, the same woman who decorated the window with so creative a touch, had placed every pink and red item in the store close together.

Crimson tapers in antique candleholders burned at every turn, sending out waves of warmth. To the left stood a cafè table set for tea and covered with china in a busy pink pattern. A two-tier silver server filled with tiny heart cookies invited the visitor to help herself and envision a similar set-up in her own home.

Annica took a cookie and headed for the antique jewelry counter, her search for the pink lamp temporarily on hold, while I stopped at a curious display of old tintypes priced at twenty-five cents for one, or three for a dollar.

Who, I wondered, would buy pictures of someone else's ancestors? Possibly another store owner wishing to create an evocative display like this one.

Set among the sepia depictions of somber faces and old-time clothing was a selection of vintage greeting cards and bric-a-brac, all of it Valentine-themed. A music box mounted on four tarnished silver legs captured my immediate attention. It looked like one of the Valentine cards had been pasted on its lid.

The picture was predictable but nonetheless charming. A golden-haired Cupid reclining on a nest of blue forget-me-nots. He held a heart bearing a traditional inscription 'Truly Thine.'

I turned the music box over, curious to see what melody it played, but the only information I saw was the price tag: Three ninety-nine.

Dollars?

"It doesn't play."

The person who had spoken stood behind me, so near that if I had backed up suddenly, I would have stepped on her foot. She was a tall, busty brunette wearing a pink sweater sprinkled with glittering hearts. Her dark eyelashes also glittered, makeup and outfit obviously chosen to coordinate with the shop's Valentine's Day motif.

"My name is Lola," she said. "The music mechanism doesn't work."

"Are you selling broken antiques?" I asked.

"It may not play, but you can scoop out the innards and use it as a jewelry box or to keep little stuff like safety pins in. Isn't it beautiful?"

Setting aside the image of spooning seeds out of a cantaloupe, I asked, "Do you know the tune it played?"

"Some love song, I guess. There's a story that goes along with it." She glanced around as if to see whether anyone needed her assistance. "Would you like to hear it?"

"Why not?"

"It belonged to a lady whose true love betrayed her. When he died, it stopped working, but she kept it all her life in his memory."

"The sentiment was obviously inaccurate," I said.

Lola looked at me. "Huh?"

"Well, if he betrayed her, he wasn't truly hers."

"The point is, he died." She lowered her voice. "There's a rumor that she killed him. I believe it."

I smiled. Lola reminded me of Annica as she was when I'd first met her working at the antique shop, Past Perfect. Annica had told stories about the antiques she sold, always dark and shivery tales that bordered on the impossible.

I'd never believed them. I didn't believe this story, but the nostalgic image on the lid and the accompanying sentiment had taken hold of my imagination. And, after all, how often do you wind up a music box? The vintage Valentines were priced higher than this little treasure.

"I'll take it," I said, "but I really want to look at your books."

"Ah, romances." The sparkle in her eyes rivaled the glitter of her makeup. "They're in a special case. We have *Gone with the Wind, Forever Amber…*"

"Old series books," I said.

"Then you're in luck. I was just going to set some out. Their dull covers don't fit in with our color scheme. I'm looking for some dark corner to hide them in."

I noticed the small box at her feet. It held perhaps a dozen books, none of them with dust covers. The three on top were Beverly Grays, my current favorite. One, I noted, was the incredibly rare *Beverly Gray at the World's Fair*. I had wanted to read that book for ages.

"How much for the box?" I asked.

"Don't you want to look at them?"

I could, but I knew I wanted the Beverly Grays. In case there was another Beverly Gray collector in the store, I didn't want to miss my chance to buy them.

"Our vintage books are on sale," she said. "There are twelve books here, so that'll be twelve dollars."

"Are you sure?" I asked, having paid that amount for a single Judy Bolton a few months ago.

"We'll be happy to unload them."

I doubted that but didn't plan to argue with her.

"If you'll hold on to these for me, I'll see what my friend is up to," I said and scanned the crowd looking for a girl with bright red-gold hair.

Annica was still browsing at the jewelry counter. She had set aside earrings similar to the ones on the doll in the window display and a pair of elaborate garnet teardrops.

"Did you find your lamp?" I asked.

"Yes, but it's marked 'Sold.' She held the teardrops up to her face. "How do these look with my hair?

"Perfect," I said, "for an elaborate occasion."

"That's what I hope Valentine's Day will be. Do you want to look around more?"

I considered. One unusual music box and a rare book. I'd been lucky today. "I'm ready for lunch, if you are."

When our turn at the check-out counter came, Lola pasted a large heart sticker on the box of books and wrapped the music box in a sheet of pink tissue paper.

"What tune does it play?" Annica asked.

"Nothing. It's broken."

"Why are you buying it then?"

Why indeed?

"For the picture," I said, and it made sense to me.

"Nobody will know it's broken unless they ask," I added.

~ * ~

We found a small restaurant in Maple Creek and ordered soup and sandwiches.

Annica said, "I'm in charge of decorating Clovers for Valentine's Day. I'm going to steal some of the Green House's ideas."

I nodded. "We need a red holiday to brighten up this dreary winter."

"Out with the poinsettias, in with carnations. Let's see, red roses and white carnations, or white roses and red carnations..."

The rippling notes of my cell phone sounded from the depths of my shoulder bag. It was Sue Appleton, whose calls invariably involved collies in need of help.

"Hi, Jennet," she said. "Are you at home?"

"I'm in Maple Creek having lunch. Why?"

"A collie puppy has been sighted on Jonquil Lane. It has to be one of our missing littermates."

Thank heavens. One had escaped the jaws of the coyotes. That left two unaccounted for.

"I spent half an hour driving up and down the lane but didn't see her," Sue added.

"She must have run into the woods," I said.

"Those woods." She shuddered. "They're a death trap."

Knowing what she was going to ask, I said, "I'll see if I can find her."

"Would you?"

"Definitely. As soon as we get back to Foxglove Corners."

I dropped my phone back into my purse and glanced at the bill. We could leave as soon as we paid it.

"Bad news?" Annica asked.

"Just the opposite," I said. "How would you like to join me in a winter adventure?"

Six

Jonquil Lane was deserted, as was usually the case. Not that I expected the puppy to be waiting for us. An older dog might have been watching for the car that had brought her to this lonely place, but not a baby.

The abandoned development glowered at me, bare black branches silhouetted against an ice-blue sky. The woods were in forbidding mode, broadcasting menace as clearly as if they had a voice.

I parked on the verge and scanned the area in my view, hoping to see a little golden collie, head tilted, curious to see who had breached her wilderness.

No flash of brightness, no movement at all, broke through the frozen still life.

"How large is this tract of land?" Annica asked.

"I'm not sure. Eighty acres. Maybe more. The developer planned to build seven houses on the property."

"We can't possibly cover all that territory."

"We won't. At least one of the houses is pretty much intact, and a few others are solid enough to attract a little runaway. We'll check them all out."

"It'll be fun," she said. "I was hoping our day out would last a little longer."

She tied her scarf higher around her neck and pulled her hood forward. We had both dressed for cold weather with warm hooded parkas and tall fleece-lined boots. I took the package of treats, and, on second thought, the coin jar, and we entered the woods.

"I feel like we're walking into a fairy tale," Annica said. "Enchanted woods where a witch lives—and wolves."

"Coyotes," I said. "Watch that board!"

It was long and snow-encrusted with exposed nails. Annica had almost stepped on it.

"We can look at it that way," I said, "but our main objective is to find the puppy. If she's sick like her littermate, she'll need treatment."

That she was still alive was encouraging. I could only hope the other two puppies were somewhere in the woods as well.

The first house in the development was in the worst shape. Snow-covered building debris surrounded it, and the three still-standing walls hardly looked stable enough to survive another winter.

On an impulse I dropped two cookies in the ruins. Maybe their scent would lure the puppy to the treats. She or another creature. I didn't delude myself.

Annica shivered. "If only it wasn't so cold…"

Constantly calling the puppy, we moved further into the heart of the woods, past the ghostly remains of structures that retained not even a hint of their might-have-been elegance. Gradually, my sense of direction slipped away. The straight line we'd been walking required many a twist and turn through the trees, and the woods were unnaturally quiet. Where had all the wildlife gone? I imagine scrawny coyotes dozing in their dens saving their howls for the nighttime hours.

Were we still heading north?

Finally, we came to the one house that had more or less defied the ravages of time, exactly the sort of shelter to attract a vagrant or a puppy. I had been inside it on previous occasions and knew what to expect.

"Let's get in out of this cold before I turn into an icicle," Annica said.

"It won't be warm inside," I pointed out.

"It'll be easier walking, though."

Unfortunately, the house was empty. I had so hoped we would find her here or evidence that she had nested within its walls. Well, we would have to wait for another sighting.

"I would love a cup of hot chocolate," Annica said. "Actually, a cup of hot anything."

Apparently, the woods had lost their magic for her.

~ * ~

Magic, like fate, is capricious. On the far side of the woods, we came to an unexpected clearing, a charming place where light, such as it was, created an oasis of luminescence. Suddenly it even seemed a little warmer, but that was my imagination. The air was as cold as ever.

A small Victorian cottage with weathered pink paint sat in snowdrifts alongside a frozen stream. In its center between twin gables, a window-sized red heart retained much of its deep color. The elaborate white gingerbread trim was reminiscent of a vintage Valentine card.

The little house conjured visions of strawberry and whipped cream. Magical images.

It might have been a playhouse built for a wealthy man's daughter. Or an illusion born of the cold. I blinked and looked again. No, it was real, a little forgotten house in an unexplored part of the forest. The stuff of fairy tales.

"Look!" Annica cried. "The witch's house! Too bad it isn't made of gingerbread."

"A Valentine House," I amended, glancing at the heart decoration. "I didn't know it was here."

I had never ventured this far into the woods. Certainly this charming little cottage wasn't part of the French chateau development, obviously predating it by several years. It appeared to be forgotten indeed, its owner having lost interest in maintaining it.

It needed only fresh paint to make it sparkle.

Annica said, "Shall we investigate?"

We could hardly do anything else. I could almost see a small puppy inside, alert and wary, waiting. Maybe the rest of the litter would be there, too. Or perhaps we would find something surprising and remarkable. I reached for a handful of treats.

"If it's unlocked," I said.

It was. Strangely I had to overcome a powerful sense of intruding on a place that was private and should have remained so, even though no one was near to challenge our intrusion.

We stepped inside, not surprised to discover that the interior was as cold as the woods.

It consisted of one large room. To the left, a twisting staircase led to an upper story. Four windows, strategically placed, allowed a modicum of light to enter the structure through tattered pink gingham curtains heavy with dust. Like the exterior, the walls were painted a light pink that had faded. The floors—and the entire house, for that matter—were relatively clean except for the ever-present cobwebs and dark, dried leaves from past seasons that had found their way inside.

What a delightful playhouse this must have been in its heyday! It could still be. I imagine a little girl playing house on long past summer days. The single room would be furnished, after a fashion, and there'd be a cafè table set for tea like the one displayed in the Green House. The child would have her dolls with her, or her plush animals.

"Let's see what the second floor is like," Annica said.

I tested the first step. The stairs seemed safe enough, but toward the top, the bannister was loose. We climbed up to find that the upper level of the little house was one large, empty room, like the first floor.

"I wonder why the owner painted a Valentine heart on the front of the house," Annica said.

"I have no idea, but it fits the house."

A sudden strangeness took hold of me. We had just been to an antique shop that overflowed with Valentine ambience. Now to find a Valentine cottage in the woods so near my home with February fourteenth a week away? It was uncanny.

Lucy Hazen, Foxglove Corners' celebrated horror story writer, believed the walls of a house could absorb emotions associated with certain events and pass them on to future dwellers if they were sensitive to otherworldly influences. Could this be true of the cottage?

Suspending extraneous thought, I stared at the pink walls, concentrated and tried to connect with that other plane that existed alongside our world. It was no use. All I felt was a sense of loneliness, which was to be expected in the circumstances. But then, I didn't have Lucy's talents.

Remember you're looking for a collie puppy, I told myself.

"This reminds me of a house in Maple Creek," Annica said. "It's known as Valentine Villa and is supposed to be haunted. It's for sale."

"Are you looking for a new house?" I asked.

"Just dreaming, but keeping up with the market, and looking at houses for sale is a hobby of mine. Some day…"

"One house at a time," I said. "I'd like to find out the history of this one. I don't think it's part of the land the developer owned, but I don't know."

"Someone will," Annica said.

I dropped three green-sprinkled Christmas cookies on the floor for the puppy if she happened to stop by.

"We'll leave the door ajar,' I said. "If a little snow drifts in, it won't hurt anything after all these years."

"I'm ready for this adventure to be over," Annica said. "I'm sorry we didn't find the puppy, though. Can we have hot chocolate at your house?"

"Sure," I said.

Her voice echoed in the empty space. And there was something else. I thought I heard a whisper embedded in the sound. Two whispered words: *Don't go.*

But the little pink house was as silent as it was empty. The overload of Valentine extravaganza had set my imagination into overdrive again.

Seven

Fortified by two cups of hot chocolate and several mini-marshmallows, Annica left for her late shift at Clovers. Faced with a few free moments, I examined the music box carefully, turning the mechanism in the hope that it wasn't broken after all. Turning... Waiting... The lever stuck. Nothing.

Oh, well, the picture on the lid had lost none of its charm. It seemed as bright and shiny as if it had just been painted. The sentiment, *Truly Thine*, reminded me of those tiny candy hearts that convey messages from the giver: *Be My Valentine*, *Heart's Desire*, *Forever*, and the like. Did they still make them?

I moved the music box so it stood between our prized heirloom candlesticks that had belonged to Crane's Civil War era ancestress, Rebecca Ferguson. Later, I'd add my collection of china heart boxes to the credenza and have a lovely Valentine display of my own.

Questions tugged at me. What was the real story of this enticing little antique? Love betrayed. Betrayal revenged? Murder unsolved? Could Lola's tale contain even a grain of truth?

It was remotely possible, I supposed, but like Annica, Lola most likely wished to add a touch of intrigue to her job while hoping to unload a damaged article.

But if a mystery were connected to the antique, it would add excitement to these dull, endless winter days.

Excitement aside, it was high time to slip into my other role as homemaker. I recalled promising Camille another batch of stew for Gilbert. That meant I'd have to triple the recipe if I wanted leftovers.

In the midst of chopping potatoes and carrots, my mind wandered back to another strange purchase I'd once made at the Green House, the television set that aired episodes from a long-defunct Western series at will.

Maybe I'd found another anomaly.

On the other hand, I'd might just have bought a pretty antique that was broken.

~ * ~

An hour later, with the stew bubbling merrily away on the stove, the dogs alerted me to a visitor. Glancing out the window, I saw a vintage white Plymouth Belvedere with long green fins parked behind my car.

Who but Brent Fowler made his appearance just before the dinner hour?

He opened the car door and closed it quickly but not before I saw a sable puppy face with pretty tipped ears and a wide white blaze in the window. A tiny paw raked down the glass, and high-pitched yipping carried to my collies' ears.

It had to be one of the missing littermates.

Brent stamped back to the Plymouth's trunk and took out a large shopping bag with a familiar logo, that of Pluto's Gourmet Pet Shop. Rays of late afternoon sunshine glanced off his dark red hair, and his forest green jacket gave the monochromatic vista a rare splash of color. Seeing me in the window, he waved.

I hurried to let him in, telling the collies to back up, for all the good it did. They knew treats were forthcoming and certainly heard the indignant barking of the puppy.

"Hey, Jennet," he said. "You'll never guess what I have in the car."

"I saw her." I took the bag, and he deftly avoided Candy's ill-manner lunge. "I've been looking for her. Annica and I covered almost every inch of the abandoned development. That's where they were last seen."

"They?"

As I told him about the unknown man who had abandoned four puppies on the lane, his face took on a rare stormy look.

"They're just babies," he said. "Is there any chance of catching the guy who dumped them?"

"I'm going to try, but I don't have much to go on."

"I'd like to get my hands on him."

"So would I."

The dogs had gathered by the window, their noses pressed to the glass, their attention on the small newcomer who hadn't been taken out of the strange looking car.

I set the Pluto's bag on the dining room table for later.

"She was right on the lane, chasing after a squirrel or groundhog," Brent said. "It was running for its life, so I didn't get a good look at it. When I slammed on the brakes, she ran up to the car, and I picked her up. I remembered about needing to get a rescue vetted before letting her mingle with healthy dogs," he added.

"That's right, and there's a chance this puppy has parvo. Her littermate is with Doctor Foster now. If you'd drop her off at Sue's, she'll take her to the animal hospital."

"From what you say, there should be two others," he said. "What about them?"

"I hope they're still alive. I wonder how long it takes an abandoned dog to turn feral?"

"Not long, but this cold weather will get them first."

"Or the coyotes will," I added. "Are you bothered with coyotes at your barn?"

"They're around," he said, "but I have big dogs and men with shotguns. They don't dare come too close."

"I have the same—big dogs, that is—but the other day, one of the coyotes stationed himself about three yards from me...after it ate the stew I made for Camille."

"What a waste of good stew!"

"I made more for tonight."

"You have to be careful," he said. "They're getting bolder all the time. Make sure you have a noisemaker with you, or scream at them. Pretend they're kids raising hell."

"I don't scream at my students," I said. "Words work better."

"Well, words won't work with a wild animal."

For a moment, Brent sounded like Crane in lecture mode, but he was right. Country living had its disadvantages. Snakes and poisonous plants in the summer, and coyotes in every season. Coyotes growing hungrier and bolder every day.

"I'll drop the little lassie off at Sue's horse farm and come back," Brent said. "What time is dinner?"

"As soon as Crane gets home, which should be in about an hour."

"Did you bake anything?"

"A chocolate meringue pie."

"Good. My favorite. All this rescue work makes me hungry."

~ * ~

My second batch of stew disappeared almost as fast as the first one. Soon only a spoonful of salad remained in the bowl, and all of the dinner rolls were gone. During the course of the meal, I related the story of our adventures in the woods.

Crane and Brent were both interested in hearing about the Valentine House with its fading pink paint and decorative red heart.

"It sounds like one of those tiny houses they're building these days," Brent said. "I wouldn't like to live in one myself, but lots of people do."

"It wasn't a proper house," I pointed out. "Just two rooms, one upstairs, one downstairs. There was no kitchen and no bathroom."

"So no one could have lived there."

"Not permanently. My first thought was that it was a playhouse, tucked away in the woods. You know how kids love to think they're all alone in the world when they play."

Crane was puzzled. "I don't know why I didn't see it. I never saw a clearing and had no idea that a stream ran through the acres."

"If the developer owned that land, he would probably have torn it down," I said. "That's what they do."

"We don't have to worry about him," Crane pointed out. "He's never coming back."

"I can't help wondering about the house," I said. "Who did it belong to? Who owns it now?"

Brent winked at me. "Look out, Sheriff. Jennet found another haunted house."

"It isn't haunted," I said. "Just sad. Like any house would be without its people."

But even as I spoke, I remembered the two words I thought I'd heard: *Don't go*.

I might have imagined them. On the other hand...

Brent and Crane knew me well. I'd found another place with a story to tell, perhaps a dark history. It might not be haunted, but it was certainly mysterious; and I knew I would be returning to the Valentine House as soon as possible, even while the entire area remained in the grip of snow and arctic temperatures.

Eight

The snow stopped by mid-day and the next morning the weather moderated slightly. The desire to go somewhere, anywhere, was strong. But the woods would be too hazardous for hiking today.

The Valentine House wasn't going anywhere, and the missing puppies...Well, I couldn't look for them today. Maybe they would turn up on the lane chasing prey for their dinner. It comforted me to think that, although I wasn't deluding myself. In the meantime, I decided to drive to Clovers.

Annica had decorated the little restaurant with a light touch. Red and white carnation centerpieces, white tablecloths with red napkins, and a chain of paper hearts strung above the counter dispensed a blast of happiness that more than compensated for the dreary February day.

I passed the dessert carousel, with its tempting array of cakes frosted with flowers and hearts. Seeing that my favorite booth, the one with the best view of the woods across from Crispian Road, was unoccupied, I seated myself. In a minute, Annica was at my side, pen and order pad in hand.

She wore a dark red midi-dress and the Valentine card earrings she had bought at the Green House of Antiques.

"Is this another 'no cooking' day at the Ferguson house?" she asked.

"It's a leftovers day, but I could be tempted to bring a dessert home."

"We have plenty to choose from," she said. "How does chocolate angel food cake sound? It has pink frosting. Or cheesecake with strawberry sauce?"

"I'd like a piece of cake and a cup of tea," I said.

"Good choice. I'll join you."

She sent a brief nod in the direction of her fellow waitress, Marcy, who was always willing to cover for her when I came to the restaurant. "Do you see that man sitting alone near the door?" she asked.

How could I have failed to notice him? He was exceptionally handsome, with roughhewn features and wavy black hair. At present, he was giving his full attention to his dinner. Although, he chose that moment to look up, just in time to see my scrutiny.

I looked quickly away. "What about him?"

"He comes in about three times a week and usually orders pie and coffee. He's been flirting with me."

"I'm not surprised."

With her bright red-gold hair and natural radiance, to say nothing of her sparkling personality, Annica must attract scores of admirers.

"His name is Colton Reeves," she said. "He's new in town. He comes from San Antonio, Texas."

"What's he doing in Michigan?" I asked.

"Something with batteries. His explanation went right over my head. Anyway, he plans to make his home in Lakeville."

"I wonder how he's dealing with our Michigan weather," I said.

"He says he likes snow. He's learning to ski." She paused. "He asked me if I'd go out with him."

Again I wasn't surprised.

"I told him it wasn't possible with my classes and my hours at Clovers," she added.

"You *do* have some free time," I pointed out. "You had a whole day yesterday. You spent it in the woods."

"I'm not really interested," she said.

"*I* would be."

She gave me an incredulous glance. "You're *married*, Jennet. You have Crane."

"Let me rephrase that. In your place, I would accept his offer."

"That's exactly what Marcy said."

"Well…" I knew, of course, where Annica's interest lay. But she shouldn't close down every opportunity that became available to her. She wasn't engaged or—gasp—married.

"You could get to know him better," I said, "and you could use a little diversion."

"I guess, but I'm not into horses and guns."

I stole a glance at Colton Reeves. Once again, he was intent on his dinner.

"Maybe he isn't either," I said. "Texas isn't the wild west anymore."

"You'd never know it to hear him talk."

"He must have other interests."

She cast him a covert look. "I'll think about it, but I won't have a free evening for a while."

~ * ~

That night I dreamed about the Valentine House. It sat proudly in its clearing surrounded by lush green grass. The exterior looked as if it had been newly painted. The white gingerbread trim gleamed, and the red heart between the gables glittered in the sunlight. Pink and yellow flowers blossomed around the foundation.

The stream wound its way into the woods and out of sight. I wondered where it ended.

The door was ajar, as I had left it. In the manner of dreams, I found myself transported inside without actually moving. The single room was furnished with a maple table, two matching chairs, and an antique china cabinet with what would be described as a distressed finish. On the table, a jar of pink flowers and a picnic basket suggested that someone was here or had been here. On the second floor, perhaps?

This was not the child's playhouse of my imagining.

A large silky scarf in rainbow colors had been tossed across one of the chairs, along with a single white glove. Where was the other glove? For that matter, where was the woman who had discarded them?

I lifted the cloth that covered the basket. Inside were sandwiches, blueberry tarts, and bottles of Coca-Cola, together with pears and apples. Everything looked fresh and tempting.

Suddenly hungry, I reached for an apple. Before I could take a bite, it dissolved in my hand, and the dream changed. I was outside now, standing in snow, still hungry and vaguely afraid.

Of what? What could more innocuous than a pretty little house tucked in the woods?

'The Witch's House,' Annica had said.

Obviously, there was no witch, no scarf, no glove. Nor was there a little girl with her dolls and stuffed toys. I had conjured them out of whole cloth.

But there was a mystery...

I had to get back inside the house. I wanted to climb the twisting stair to the upper level and see if that, too, was furnished. If the owner of the scarf and glove was there, unwilling to make her presence known.

There the dream ended. I woke and lay still, struggling to hold on to its images before they, too, dissolved. In that I was unsuccessful. The next moment, I was asleep again, and the moment after that, the alarm clock rang.

~ * ~

I planned on going back to the woods the next day until I looked out the window at the heavy snow falling. I'd be spending the third day of my winter break inside where it was dry and warm and safe.

But what of the two remaining puppies?

You can't do anything about them today, I told myself.

Perhaps they would turn up on the lane like the little one Brent had found. Maybe they would somehow survive the killing cold and the ravening coyotes and emerge in the spring running through the woods with their unfurling leaves. By then, they would be larger and stronger but still fluffy. Still puppies. Ferals.

What about parvo?

They didn't have it.

I could tell myself anything I wished until I knew what had happened to them.

Crane was already up, and Misty and Halley had followed him down to the kitchen. I heard the dogs barking. Crane would have let them out. I didn't want him to make his own breakfast.

By now, of course, my dream had fallen apart completely, leaving only impressions of scarves and sandwiches and an apple that turned to pulp in my hand.

"I'm glad you don't have to go to school today," Crane said when I joined him in the kitchen.

"And I'm sorry you have to go out in this snow. I wish you could stay home with me."

He kissed me. "Someone has to keep the Corners safe."

"I know."

"Don't go out today. Not even to Camille's."

"I wouldn't dream of it."

I saw no point in telling him about my desire to visit the Valentine House. It wasn't going to happen today, anyway.

After he left for his shift, I drank a second cup of coffee and cleaned the kitchen.

It was still snowing. Would spring ever come?

With my plan for the day derailed, I brushed the collies, vacuumed, thought about what to cook for dinner, and moved quickly through the house with a dust cloth.

Finally, with my work finished and a meatloaf in the oven, I glanced at the box of books I'd bought at the Green House. Now was as good a time as any to lose myself in another time and place. *Beverly Gray at the World's Fair* waited, and it was high time I saw what other treasures I'd bought for the ridiculous price of twelve dollars.

Nine

The books were dusty, which told me that nobody at the Green House had looked at them properly before offering them for sale at a pittance. One by one, I wiped them clean and set them on the credenza.

I had *Cherry Ames Student Nurse* and *Cherry Ames, Army Nurse*, three *Nancy Drews*, two *Dana Girls*, four Westerns, (the *X BAR X series)*, and one book that didn't conform to the size and shape of the others. It had a smudged blue cover and, strangely, no title or author's name. What on earth?

As I opened it, a wave of lavender scent drifted into the air along with a breath of dust. It was a diary, mixed in with the series books by someone who didn't know any better or didn't care.

But whose diary? The first page told me the answer. *Happy Birthday, Eva. With this little book you can tell the story of your life.* The entries were undated but prefaced with titles printed in large capital letters.

Writing covered the pages, a slanted script in turquoise ink that grew increasingly difficult to read as the writer neared the end of an entry.

To read? Of course I was going to read the diary.

For a moment, I hesitated. What was more private than a person's thoughts? On the other hand, the writer had obviously discarded it, and I seriously doubted that anybody in the antique shop wanted a dollar sale item returned.

I left my coveted Beverly Gray book on the credenza and took the diary to the living room where it looked old and sad in the lamplight. I couldn't think of a better way to spend a snowy winter day than by delving into the past.

~ * ~

EVANORA'S DIARY

RAIN, RAIN, GO AWAY—It's raining, again, and here I am in the middle of nowhere with nothing to do except read. That's all I've been doing. I wish we hadn't moved to the country, but I love my room. From the window I can see the woods. I like to think I'm so close to the sky I could reach up and touch a cloud.

SYBIL—We walked to the corner store for bread and lunch meat this morning. The woman behind the counter isn't very friendly. She's short and thin with white hair and black eyes. Sara says she looks like a witch. That's unkind, I told her. But thanks to Sara, from now on I'm going to think of her as a witch. I'll call her Sybil, but not to her face.

CALL OF THE WOODS—There are so many different kinds of flowers growing wild along the lane. I picked a bouquet of lilies-of-the-valley for my room. I'd like to go exploring in the woods, but Sara is afraid of snakes, and I don't want to go alone. I don't like snakes, either, and I'm afraid of getting lost. We'll wait for Dad and go as a group.

There's something about the woods. They fascinate me, but they also scare me, just a little bit. Especially at night. I'm glad our high fence holds them back.

BORING DAY—It's raining again. I got a new book for my birthday. Might as well read.

I wish something would happen.

~ * ~

I read a few more pages of the diary and decided that Beverly Gray's adventures would be more interesting than Evanora's. She wrote about clothes, a friend she missed from the old neighborhood, and her plan to go to school in the fall. She had loved her English classes in high school and wanted to major in English and become a teacher. She recorded the shade of nail polish she wore—another birthday present—and the progress of a dress she was making.

I closed the diary, planning to read more at a later time. It felt odd, a bit disconcerting, to have the diary in my possession, but reading Evanora's thoughts and impressions made me feel close to her. That was odd, too.

I tried to figure out how old she was. She must be seventeen or eighteen, a high school graduate, if she was looking forward to college. But what was the year? If I knew that, I could tell how the old the diary was.

Unfortunately, I couldn't know that as none of the books contained dates, only inscriptions. They had all belonged to Evanora. We had something in common, liking the same books. But did girls really used to sew their own dresses? How times had changed. Evanora was definitely not a product of the twenty-first century.

Evanora, I thought. *What a pretty name.*

~ * ~

Crane found the third collie puppy and took her straight to Doctor Foster's animal hospital. She was at the edge of the abandoned development watching the lane. The poor little orphan. No doubt she was waiting for the car that had brought her to the woods. Or for her litter sisters.

I wondered why the puppies hadn't stayed together.

"She was sniffing around roadkill," Crane said.

"Ugh. Did she look sick?"

"Not that I could tell. But she's skin and bones. She needs a bath."

"Alice will take care of her. That leaves one unaccounted for."

"There's good news on another front." Crane locked his gun in the cabinet and gave his shadow, Candy, a quick pat on the head. "We may have a lead on the guy who dumped the puppies."

Darn. I should have been the one to find him.

"How did that happen?" I asked.

"Fowler offered a five hundred dollar reward for information leading to his identity. A woman called about her neighbor. He had a collie and four puppies last week. Now he doesn't have any dog. He claims he sold them. She says she saw him load them into his car."

"The mother, too?"

"Just the puppies."

"What's his name?"

"Greg Blackwell."

"Does he have a silver Honda?"

"He does."

"That's the man," I said.

"It's a start."

Of course, Blackwell would deny any involvement in the crime, but maybe another witness would come forth, incensed with the cruelty of throwing away helpless puppies. Most people cared about animals and would want him punished. The reward was an added incentive.

"I didn't know Brent was going to do that," I said.

"Neither did I, but that's how he works."

"Now, if we could just find the fourth puppy."

"The one I picked up is a cute little thing," he said. "She'll make someone a good pet."

"So will the others, and they've proved they're hardy. I hope they're healthy. I'd like to see them," I added. "Maybe I'll stop by the animal hospital while I'm off."

"Wait for better weather."

"Ha! They'll be grown by then."

"Count the days till spring," Crane said. "No season lasts forever."

~ * ~

That was true, but it seemed as if this winter would be an exception. Every day it snowed, not heavily, but enough to turn the roads to skating rinks since often rain came with the snow, and it all froze.

Camille recovered but didn't leave her house for fear of a relapse. Most of the dogs preferred napping in quiet corners to playing outside, but Misty and Velvet had to be bribed with treats before they condescended to come inside. Crane patrolled the roads of Foxglove Corners every day in all kinds of weather, and I counted the days left of winter break. Before long, Leonora and I would be back in the classroom.

Every night I heard the coyotes howling. It sounded as if they were right outside our door.

One morning I saw *the* coyote too close to the yellow Victorian for comfort.

All of the dogs were barking, my eight and Holly and Twister across the lane. I yelled and shook the jar of coins which didn't faze him. He stared at me with blatant defiance as if to say, 'I'm here to stay. Deal with it.'

In his own time, he slunk back into the woods and disappeared from view.

I thought about the Valentine House deep in the woods in a surround of snow. It wasn't far, but its location and the weather rendered it inaccessible for me. For now.

I had left the door ajar. Snow would drift it, and it would be as cold in the house as it was outside. A house needs its people to survive. It needs warmth and light and noise. In other words, life.

The deteriorating French chateaux of the abandoned development had all but given up the struggle, but the Valentine House still stood. There must be a reason.

At times, when I woke at night after an unremembered dream, I wondered if it were a figment of my imagination. Then I remembered that Annica had seen the house, too. I promised myself that as soon as I could safely do so, I would return.

Never let it be said that I ignored a possible mystery.

Ten

The next time Brent Fowler visited us, he left his innate bonhomie behind. To be sure, he brought treats for the collies and a red tulip plant for the house—translation, for me—but his heart wasn't in socializing. He didn't even comment about the aroma of baked ham wafting from the kitchen or ask if I'd baked a pie for dessert.

Strange.

He stamped snow from his boots with excessive force and didn't appear to notice Misty who waited patiently for him to pet her or at least speak to her.

Very strange.

I hung his jacket, and he placed the plant and the shopping bag from Pluto's on the coffee table. Quickly, I moved the treats to a safer location.

"Did something happen?" I asked, fearing that Blackwell had somehow come up with an excuse that left him exonerated.

He dropped into the rocker. "Not if I have anything to say about it."

Misty eyed Brent uncertainly, her tail wagging. Finally aware of the world around him, he patted his knee and she leaped into his lap.

This sounded interesting, and I didn't think it concerned the puppies.

"Tell me about it," I said.

"There's this jerk who comes to Clovers to see Annica. He gave her a dozen red roses today. I was there. I saw it."

Annica's Texan, Colton Reeves. A jerk? I repressed a smile. "Well, Valentine's Day is coming up. Annica is a popular waitress. You know that."

"You give a good waitress a nice tip, not flowers."

He had a point.

"She didn't have to accept them," he added.

Red roses? The color and flower of love?

"What was she supposed to do? Drop them in the trash?"

"You're missing the point, Jennet. Annica is *my* girl."

"Does she know that?"

"Everybody knows that," he countered. "She gave me a beer stein for Christmas. It said, 'I lost my heart in Heidelberg.' What does that tell you?"

"That she likes Germany?"

"Very funny. We had dinner at the Heidelberg Inn over the holidays. It turned out to be a special occasion."

Mmm. In what way? Well, I couldn't ask.

I knew Annica had searched far and wide for the perfect gift for Brent. Perhaps she'd chosen the beer stein for its sentiment.

"How did Annica react when she saw the flowers?" I asked.

"Pleased. Sort of surprised. She put them in water."

"Did she leave them at Clovers or take them home?"

"That I don't know. I paid my bill and got out of there."

"I wouldn't worry," I said. "They're only flowers."

My advice sounded hollow, even to me. Brent was right to be concerned. What he didn't know was that Annica wasn't interested in Colton. Or so she said. I didn't repeat this intelligence to Brent, although it would have cheered him. I didn't intend to get involved in my friends' relationship. And Annica might change her mind about dating Colton.

Good grief! I'd encouraged her to go out with him. Brent didn't have to know that, either. All I could do was point out something he might have overlooked.

"Annica has a busy schedule with her English classes and her job at Clovers. She's focused on her degree."

"No argument there. What do you think this Reeves character will do next?"

"Give her a Valentine heart of chocolates?"

"You're not helping, Jennet," he said.

"Well, what are *you* going to do?"

"I got her something better than candy or flowers," he said. "Rubies."

"Lucky Annica."

"I don't trust that guy," he added. "He looks suspicious to me. How can I find out what he's really up to?"

"Crane will be home soon," I said. "Let's see what he says."

~ * ~

Brent lost no time in bringing his problem to Crane's attention. Crane had scarcely locked his gun away when Brent relayed the scene at Clovers.

Crane's advice was more proactive than my wishy-washy injunction not to worry.

"If you see something—er, someone—you want, Fowler, grab her before somebody beats you to it."

I refrained from commenting, but I recalled Crane's demeanor before his surprise proposal at the conclusion of a harrowing dilemma in which I'd nearly lost my life. I had known what I wanted for months, but had no idea if Crane wanted me. Until he asked me to marry him. In truth, I had no Colton Reeves waiting in the wings with red roses.

"Annica's busy with college," Brent said.

"I didn't mean that literally."

I couldn't help breaking in. "Let Annica know how you feel about her, Brent. I'll bet you never did that."

He frowned and took a minute to think. "Sure I did."

"But did she get the message?"

Leave it, Jennet, I told myself. *You're meddling.*

Ah, well. The course of true love never did run smooth.

"I'll have a talk with Annica," Brent said. "She needs to know her new boyfriend may be dangerous. Now, what's for dinner?"

~ * ~

Every now and then, when I had a little free time but didn't want to get engrossed in one of my series books or a Gothic novel, I turned to Evanora's diary. She could write volumes about what I considered pure trivia. But that was a diarist's purpose, I suppose.

The weather. Gloomy with frequent rain and wind. She hated the wind. Yellow flowers that resembled daffodils but were probably their wild cousins. A new wardrobe for school, skirts and sweaters mostly, and frequent trips to the corner store with her sister, Sara.

They learned that the witch-like clerk's name was Maybelle.

At some point, Evanora must have conquered her fear of snakes. Her fascination with the woods—in her words, mysterious and enchanting—prevailed. She wandered into the forest as often as the weather allowed, staying close to the edge at first but gradually going further. She entered them through a broken panel in the fence.

She took her diary and pen with her and recorded descriptions of the birds she sighted and the changes she observed as spring turned into summer. One entry was three times as long as the others.

EVANORA'S DIARY

THE HOUSE IN THE WOODS—I made the most amazing discovery today. I found a little house in the woods. It's all deep pink with white trim, and there's a red heart painted above the door. It looks like a birthday cake. I always suspected the woods were magical.

There is no driveway and no path to the front door. Just the clearing and a little stream running alongside it and woods all around. Wildflowers and weeds grow right up to the foundation. My foot got caught in a vine. I almost fell.

The door was open. As soon as I stepped inside, a huge black bird flew out. My heart almost stopped beating. Was it a bat? Would I find a nest of snakes inside?

I almost didn't go any further. Then I saw that the little house was empty. It consisted of one room with a staircase to the second floor. It looked like an oversized dollhouse without the dolls or any doll furniture.

What purpose could it possibly serve?

The upstairs was also empty, one room with a window that looked out on the stream and the woods beyond.

I went back downstairs and took one last look around.

The feeling came over me without warning. This was a lonely, haunted place. It was only a house made of wood, but it seemed alive with memories, and the memories were reaching out to me, trying to trap me as the vine outside had done.

I had to get away. I was feeling a little dizzy. I'd skipped breakfast. But I plan to come back.

Eleven

Like me, Evanora intended to return to the house in the woods. Had she done so? By reinforcements, I assumed she meant her sister, Sara, and her father.

I turned the page and found a long entry about baking a pound cake. How could anyone write more than a paragraph about that subject? Evanora had written a page and a half. I skimmed it and read on. Next she wrote about the weather. It was raining again, making a walk in the woods impossible. Unless you were running for your life.

From what dim corner of my mind did that image come?

Evanora didn't write in her diary for a week. She had a cold, and it made her feel sluggish. Her word. During this time, she read one book after another. Curiously, one of them was *Beverly Gray at the World's Fair*. She was bored, and her entries reflected her state of mind. *I'm so tired of this miserable cold spring*, she wrote. *Will summer ever come?*

I set the diary aside and thought about what I'd read and its implications for me.

I believe in coincidences, which is fortunate as I appeared to be living one at the moment. Because of a casual shopping trip to the Green House of Antiques, I had in my possession the diary of a girl who had found a little pink house in the woods.

As I had.

She'd been looking at wildflowers and birds, not searching for an abandoned puppy. All right. I'd allow one deviation.

When had this happened? I couldn't know as she hadn't indicated the year, but she described the house as deep pink. In my day, the paint was faded. So, maybe twenty years ago? Maybe thirty?

How long does it take exterior paint to fade? Probably not long if it's exposed to the elements. How long had the house been abandoned?

The rest of Evanora's description was similar to my own. The red heart on the front between two gables. The empty rooms upstairs and downstairs. The impression that it had functioned as a playhouse for a child at one time. The feeling of encroaching sadness.

What had I felt?

Now, some distance from the event, I wondered if my feeling was mostly my imagination, which tended to gallop away to unknown realms at will. But at the time I, too, was affected by my first sight of the unoccupied house. I sensed that it retained memories. Suddenly I remember the words I thought I'd heard: *Don't go.*

Also, Evanora had been dizzy, blaming it on a missed breakfast. In retrospect, she had probably been coming down with a cold. But what if the house itself somehow caused her dizzy spell?

Was that possible?

What had once transpired in the Valentine House? More to the point, how could I find out?

Brent was right. I had probably found another haunted house. He might have added, 'The rest is history.'

Three impervious chimes reminded me that I'd better start thinking about dinner. Always dinner. Cooking was an inevitable part of being a homemaker and the wife of a deputy sheriff who was always hungry. At present, the part of my mind that came up with tempting dinners was a blank.

In that case, why not go to Clovers for a take-out meal? In spite of my resolve not to meddle in my friends' relationship, I was curious about Colton Reeves and the roses, and the green-eyed monster that had taken Brent captive.

Bringing home dinner would be a convenient excuse, and, for once, it wasn't snowing.

~ * ~

When I arrived at Clovers, Annica's shift was ending. She delayed her departure to share tea and strawberry cake with me while Marcy readied two orders of stuffed cabbages for Crane's and my dinner.

Annica was wearing her red midi-dress again and the whimsical Valentine card earrings she'd bought at the Green House. I noticed the dozen red roses on the counter right away. They looked as fresh as if they had just been delivered.

I breathed in their heady fragrance. "How beautiful!"

"They're from Colton, my not-so-secret admirer."

"What a generous gift. Roses are so expensive in the winter."

"I wish he hadn't given them to me, though. He asked me to go out with him, again."

"What did you say?"

"Same as before. That I'm too busy to date. That's a white lie," she added, "but Colton doesn't have to know it. I'm going out with Brent for Valentine's Day. He won't tell me where he's taking me. It's to be a surprise."

Colton, I figured, didn't have a chance.

"Does Brent know about Colton?" I asked. "About his interest in you, I mean?"

She shrugged. "I didn't tell him, but he was here when Colton gave me the roses. So, yes, he must know."

Apparently, Brent hadn't warned Annica away from his competition as planned. A smart move. Who knew how Annica would react? She had a strong independent streak. She might leap to Colton's defense. Still, I suspected Colton's campaign to attract Annica's attention was only beginning.

Roses and rubies. Annica was lucky indeed. Being a single girl had its advantages. But so did being Crane's wife. He would remember Valentine's Day with a gift I'd love, and I'd bake my heart cake. We'd be in our own home and wouldn't have to part at the end of the evening.

As Annica wasn't inclined to discuss Colton further, I told her about Evanora's diary.

"That's amazing," she said. "But couldn't you tell that one book was different from the others in the shop?"

"I didn't notice until I unpacked the box."

"Someone will be wanting it back."

"I don't think so. After all, it ended up in an estate sale."

I didn't know this for certain, but that was the source of many of the unique treasures at the Green House.

"And this girl, Evanora, found the Valentine House, too? She must have lived near the woods."

"She did. She wrote about moving to Foxglove Corners. She called it the middle of nowhere."

Annica smiled. "It is, sort of. But I love living here. It isn't for everybody."

"She said something in the house made her feel sad, and she felt dizzy," I said.

"It made *me* curious. May I read the diary sometime?" she asked.

I nodded. "As soon as I finish it."

"And can we go back to the house? Maybe Evanora left something there."

"We didn't see anything."

"We didn't really look." She took a sip of tea. "Or did you?"

"No, not thoroughly."

I almost mentioned the rainbow-colored scarf and the glove but remembered, just in time, that they'd existed in my dream. How strange that I'd remembered that detail. Strange, too, to remember objects in a days-old dream.

"We can't go tramping through the woods until the snow melts," I said.

"That could take months."

"Not quite. We may have an early spring. But yes, we'll go when we can. I still have one collie puppy to find."

Which was the reason I'd ventured into the abandoned development in the first place. At times, I feared I'd never find the fourth littermate. He might well have become a coyote's dinner.

Twelve

I woke to a sound of music. The notes were delicate and poignant, all in a minor key. The melody seemed familiar, but I couldn't identify it. It conjured images of falling water and tears.

The music came from downstairs. Had Candy turned the television on with her teeth again, her latest trick?

Giving in to a yawn, I swung out of bed and pulled my cell phone out of its charger. It was a few minutes after midnight. Crane slept on, and Halley and Misty, our nighttime guardians, kept their vigil in the doorway. Misty was awake, her head tilted. She heard the music, too.

"Let's investigate," I said, putting on my slippers. She followed me downstairs, and I followed the melody—all the way to the credenza in the dining room. Somehow the music box had come alive. It was playing in the dark. The other collies stayed in their chosen sleeping places. Didn't they hear the music?

All right. This was weird. The music box was supposed to be broken.

I turned on the lamp. The winsome little Cupid on the lid smiled up at me from his nest of blue forget-me-nots, and the sentiment

'Truly Thine' seemed to glow in the dark. Presently the tune ended. I turned the key, and the notes began again, tantalizing me with their familiarity.

I knew that melody. What was its name? The answer lay just beyond my reach.

Misty whimpered. Placing her paws on the credenza, she sniffed at the music box.

"Yes, it's odd," I said, even as a ready explanation occurred to me. Maybe the last owner had wound the key too tight, and it had stuck or frozen.

Really, Jennet? Then what freed it?

Lola at the Green House said the music box was broken. That was why they had practically given it away.

Well, I wouldn't solve this strange new mystery tonight. It appeared I'd purchased an antique with unusual properties at a bargain price.

I let the melody reach its end once again, then, turning out the light, went back upstairs. I was in bed, pulling the covers up to my chin, when I realized Misty hadn't followed me.

~ * ~

In the morning, I wound the music box again, wondering if last night's performance was a fluke. Hearing music in the night, coming downstairs to discover a broken music box suddenly playing was the stuff of dreams. Or, rather, of nightmares, especially as apparently Misty and I were the only ones who had heard it.

Was the Green House of Antiques a storehouse for anomalies then?

"What are you doing, honey?"

Crane stood beside me, ready for the day in his uniform with his gun belt strapped on. The silver strands in his blond hair sparkled in the lamplight.

"This music box was supposed to be broken, but it isn't," I said.

"Isn't that good?"

"To a point. Last night it started playing by itself."

"How can that be?"

I shrugged. "With my luck, it's haunted. *I'm* haunted. By accident, I bought the diary of a girl who stumbled across that house in the woods. Now I have a jewelry box that turns itself on. That isn't good."

"I think it's that antique shop you like so much," he said. "It should be called the shop of rare and impossible things. Remember that TV?"

I nodded. "I had the same thought. I think I'll see if the owner can tell me anything about the music box, at least where it came from. Now, let's have breakfast."

I had already brewed coffee and mixed pancake batter. Crane poured the coffee in two large mugs, then sat at the table while the collies gobbled up their morning biscuits. Except for Misty, who loved to eat. A quick glance told me she was in the dining room staring at the music box as if willing it to play again. She must think it was a new toy.

That was the easy solution. Misty knew most dog toys were soft and fluffy. She had a remarkable extra sense. A seventh sense? She knew weird when she saw it.

My pancakes were ready for turning. Obligingly the intricacies of the music box retreated to the back of my mind. Another day of winter break was beginning. They were going by too fast.

~ * ~

The overnight snow had stopped, but more was on the way. I stayed home, brushed eight collies, baked two peach pies, and cleaned house, all of which exhausted me. Seeing Evanora's diary lying on the coffee table, I sank into the rocker and opened it.

Someday soon I would be able to return safely to the Valentine House at which time I wanted to know as much as possible about it. Apparently Evanora had also been curious. Fortunately she discovered a source of information close to her home.

EVANORA"S DIARY

A STORY—Our neighbor, Mrs. Henrietta Baker, had an operation. Every day Mom fixes her a dinner tray, and Sara and I take turns delivering it to her. Today I asked her if she knew about the little house in the woods. She was surprised to learn it was still there.

"I thought they tore it down ages ago," she said.

"Do you know who lived there?"

"No one. Lucas Kimbrough had it built for his little girl. That's a sad story."

At this point, she looked down at her dinner with no enthusiasm. Roast beef and mashed potatoes, the same meal we'd had, with milk and custard. She claimed nothing tasted the way it should since her surgery.

"Can you tell me about it?" I asked.

"There isn't much to tell. Little Cecily Kimbrough was never strong. Whatever ailed her was a well-kept secret. She was an only child, and her father spared no expense to give her whatever she wanted. She loved the woods, and he wanted her to have a safe place to play. She had a couple of friends her own age. All grown up now and gone away."

"Where is Cecily now?"

"She died young. Lucas is long gone."

Mrs. Baker ate slowly and left half of her dinner on the plate. She didn't touch the custard, which was my favorite dessert, and she didn't say anything else about the house.

I think the house was sad because Cecily had stopped going there to play.

HONEY—We have a dog! I was carrying the tray back home yesterday when I saw her. Mrs. Baker had left most of her roast beef and all of the custard. She ran up to me (the dog, not Mrs. Baker), and I fed her the leftovers. She's so pretty. She has light brown fur with white markings, a long, pointed nose, and the softest head. I named her Honey.

Dad said he was going to buy us a dog now that we lived in the country, so Honey can stay as long as nobody claims her. I hope no one ever does. She is already part of the family.

~ * ~

Evanora devoted the next several pages to the new dog, Honey. She seemed happier now. One day, she and Sara took a picnic lunch to the woods, planning to eat in the house, but the day was so beautiful they set up their picnic outside, by the stream. Honey went with them.

Evanora didn't write anything else about the Valentine House. There was only that one comment about the house feeling sad because of Cecily's absence.

I could understand that. As for Mrs. Baker, she had been maddeningly vague. A wealthy man, as I'd assumed, with an ailing child who had died young. He could have given her anything she desired...except time.

Now, everyone connected with the house was gone, presumed dead. With every passing year, every rainstorm, every rough, unforgiving winter, the house lost more of its rosy color. Ownership of the land passed to others, finally to the developer who had abandoned his French style chateaux and departed for lands unknown.

The house remained. The woods remained. Nature always remains, uncaring of what happens to the human race.

The entries in Evanora's diary didn't satisfy me. I sensed there was more to the story, more to discover. I longed to return to the Valentine House. And I would, if only this infernal winter weather would loosen its hold on Foxglove Corners.

Thirteen

The next day winter relented slightly. No snow fell, and the temperature soared to a balmy thirty-five degrees. One could almost believe spring was on its way, albeit moving slowly.

The abandoned development would still be treacherous to navigate, but the roads were clear. As soon as I ensured that the dogs had enough food and exercise to hold them until afternoon, I set out for Blackbourne's Grocers. It was past time to restock the larder.

I wasn't the only one to take advantage of the warm-up. Finding a parking place as close to the door as possible, I hurried inside and began to fill a cart with essentials.

In the canned goods aisle, I came face to face with a surprising sight. A collie puppy sat proudly in a shopping cart, watching everything and everyone with bright eyes. She had a golden coat with a white blaze and appeared freshly bathed and brushed. She was wearing one of those coats to keep dogs warm, something she didn't need with her thick fur.

She had the look of the abandoned puppies. Could she be the last of the missing littermates, safe in a grocery cart?

But for goodness sake. Dogs weren't allowed in supermarkets. Apparently, the little pup hadn't received the message. Why would she, judging from the smiles on the faces of the shoppers who passed her and their kind words?

The woman who pushed the cart had a knitted blue hat that covered most of her graying auburn hair. The color matched the puppy's collar. She eyed me with trepidation.

"Excuse me," she said and attempted to wheel her cart past me.

I couldn't let her get away. "Wait," I said. "Wait a minute. Don't you know you can't bring your dog in here?"

I shouldn't have led with that question.

She glanced around. "No one stopped me, and I'm not leaving her in the car. It's too cold. Anyway, I only came in for a few things."

She had a head of lettuce in her cart, along with three tomatoes, eggs and orange juice.

"Your puppy is a darling." I longed to pet her, even though I knew better. Puppy teeth are still sharp. "What's her name?"

"I haven't named her yet. It'll probably be Cookie."

She gave the cart a shove.

"I think I know where she came from, and you should know she may be sick..."

The woman ignored me and wheeled the cart quickly away and around the next aisle.

I could hardly pursue her, demanding answers.

Why not?

Leaving my cart unattended, I rounded the corner just in time to see Harold, the burly store manager, bearing down on her. "You can't have that dog in the store, ma'am. Take it outside."

She had a ready reply. "Yes, I can. This is my service dog."

"I don't think so. Take the puppy outside and come back. I'll leave your cart in front at check-out."

"Okay, I'll go but I won't come back," she snapped.

She scooped the puppy out of the cart and moved quickly into the crowd. I soon lost sight of her.

"Some people," Harold grumbled. "Think they're too good to follow the rules."

I could continue my pursuit and possibly overtake her but decided not to. I was reasonably certain the last puppy had resurfaced and apparently had a home. Now I could consider my search ended and say goodbye to those ghastly visions of a coyote licking its chops over its dinner.

Still, this wasn't the end of the story. The puppies' sisters were being treated for parvovirus. Was this little one also sick? She had looked pretty lively to me, lording it over the store from her seat in the cart, but I'd only seen her for a few minutes.

The woman must have found her wandering in the woods and—I could only hope—taken her to a vet, which explained why I hadn't found her myself. But suppositions weren't enough. I wanted to know.

It troubled me that the woman in the blue hat had so little regard for rules and the well-being of the puppy as well as the other shoppers. But how could I solve a mystery when the key players kept dancing off the stage? First the man who dumped the litter. Now this rule-flaunting woman.

I reminded myself the story wouldn't be over until the man who had abandoned the puppies was caught and punished. If I could make that happen.

~ * ~

At home I stopped at the mailbox and pulled out a handful of catalogs and bills. A white envelope fell out of the stack into the snow. Stopping to retrieve it, I saw that it was addressed to Crane. The return address had no name, only 12 Juniper Circle, Foxglove Corners, Michigan, and the zip code, all written in red ink.

I didn't know anyone who lived on Juniper Circle, didn't even know where it was.

I brushed snow from the envelope, telling myself it was probably an invitation to a fundraiser or a cleverly disguised request for donations. Something innocuous. But my inner voice whispered, *It's bad news*. That voice was seldom wrong.

Well, I couldn't open it, couldn't know what it was until Crane came home, so I'd better forget about it and think about something else. The diary? I wasn't in the mood to read anything. The house was clean, dinner was planned, I'd already walked the dogs.

What was in the envelope?

After a dry morning that had awakened thoughts of an early spring, it started snowing again.

You'll be sorry you wasted a moment worrying about this, I told myself. *It's nothing. Nothing.*

I set aside the bills to attend to later. The rest of the mail was throwaway junk. I discarded it and placed Crane's envelope on the kitchen table, where he usually sat, and the hands on the clock began their slow movement to the time of his homecoming.

I sat at the window and watched large flakes fall and wondered.

~ * ~

A few minutes after his usual arrival time, Crane opened the door. Waves of snow blew inside while eight collies gathered around him, hindering his progress. He gave them a blanket greeting and gave me a kiss I didn't have to share.

"Winter's back," he said.

"It never went away. Here, give me your jacket. You're all over snow."

As he pulled off his heavy gloves, also covered with snow, his gaze fell on the envelope, the only item on the oak table.

"What's that?" he asked.

"It came for you today," I said.

He locked his gun in the cabinet. I took a sip of my ginger ale. I needed fortification.

"Open it," I said.

"Now?"

"I'm curious."

"All right. Here goes." He pulled a card out of the envelope, a confection in red and pink with lacy white edges and the cut-out figure of an angel or a fairy, a being with wings. A Valentine!

"It's a Valentine card from Veronica," he said. "Why would she send me a card?"

He handed it to me, a good sign. The inscription was simple:

A Valentine to keep in touch. She'd signed it, *Love, Veronica.*

I saw red. Well, figurative red. The nerve of that hussy. *To keep? Touch? Love?*

Some time ago, Veronica, a deputy sheriff in Crane's department, had set her sights on him...after he and I were married. She had lied about spending time with him and, once, had the audacity to bake him a cake. Those were my rights as his wife.

"Why would she send you a card?" I asked. "You tell me."

"She's sentimental. I'll bet she sent one to all the guys in the department."

"Since when do deputies send each other Valentine cards?" I asked, even as I told myself that I sounded jealous. And that wasn't my intention. My goal was to appear cool and collected.

"Since..." He trailed off. "Since never. They don't." He dropped the card in the wastepaper basket. Another good sign.

"Just ignore it, Jennet," he said. "That's what I'm going to do."

I trusted Crane implicitly; Veronica the Viper, not at all. After all, you can't trust a snake not to strike. It's what they're born to do.

Crane was in the living room at the gun cabinet, carrying on a one-sided conversation with Candy that seemed to be about the snow and her walk. On an impulse, I retrieved the card from the basket. For evidence.

Keep in touch, indeed.

Fourteen

I couldn't do anything about Veronica at present. Crane had thrown her card away. But—and here is what worried me—what would she do next? Bake him another cake? Give him a gift?

She wouldn't dare.

How nervy of her to send the card to our house.

She had been lying low for months, although, when Lucy read my tea leaves, Veronica frequently appeared in my teacup as an initial 'V.' I'd assumed she had found another man to chase.

Apparently not.

'Ignore it,' Crane had said.

That, of course, was easier said than done.

"Ignore her," Annica said the next day when I stopped at Clovers for lunch. Tomorrow was Valentine's Day, and the dessert carousel was crammed with cupcakes topped with red and white frosting.

Annica's pink dress had a charming square neckline, and she'd found another pair of seasonal earrings, pearl hearts edged with red stones.

The roses were gone, replaced by pink and white carnations.

Annica noticed the direction of my gaze. "They started to drop their petals. Mary Jeanne took them home. She has a recipe for rose potpourri."

"Has Colton Reeves been in for dinner lately?" I asked.

"Every day, and he keeps asking me to go out with him."

"But you're still busy?"

"I have a long dull novel to read and a paper to write. You remember how it is. You're always busy in college."

"But you're going out with Brent tomorrow," I said.

"Sure. It's Valentine's Day. And it's Brent."

She scooped the little chocolate heart off the top of her cupcake and ate it. "Don't pay any attention to that witch. She's so childish. It's like sending a card to a boy you like and signing it *Guess Who*?"

I had to smile. "Who does that?"

"I did once in high school. Didn't you?"

"No. What would be the point? I'd want him—whoever—to know who sent it."

"Crane loves you," Annica said. "He can't help it if some woman has a crush on him."

"She has no regard for my feelings." I hated the whiney tone that had crept into my voice. "She pretends I don't exist."

"You're wrong, Jennet. She's very much aware of you. She's hoping to rattle you. Don't let her."

It was too late. I had already given too much thought to that wretched card. As soon as I got home, I was going to throw it away. Again. Would that I could get rid of Veronica, too.

Ah, love. One can never be too complacent.

~ * ~

A severe weather advisory is in effect for the following counties... I listened, hoping to hear that the unfortunate counties were all north of Foxglove Corners, but, of course, we were included. Five to six more inches of new snow was expected to start falling by two o'clock this afternoon.

I turned off the television and looked out the window. Nothing yet, but we already had a winter's worth of snow on the ground.

The first snowfall of the season is magical. Christmas snow is traditional. But by February, snow has worn out its welcome. I was glad I was in my safe warm house instead of my classroom at Marston High School hoping to be home before the first flakes fell. There's always a silver lining.

I decided to read more of Evanora's diary. Evanora was a talented young writer. Her sentences flowed with ease and flair across the pages, and her emotions leaped out to ensnare the reader.

Reader? I erased that thought. Evanora was writing for herself, not for some unknown third party.

Well, then, she should have kept her diary locked up or destroyed it. I found my place and began to read.

EVANORA'S DIARY

NIGHT OF THE BAT—Finally something happened in this dismal backwater. It's good. I met someone interesting and very, very cute. How it happened makes a good story.

Sara and I were storing boxes in the attic. In this house, there's a hole in one of the closets. You climb up a ladder, step on a shelf, and lift yourself up to the attic. The floor is unfinished and dangerous to walk on. Dad told us to leave the boxes by the opening, just to get them out of the way. We did. Neither of us wanted to go any further in that scary place. There's nothing in there, anyway.

As we later learned, Sara forgot to close the opening.

That evening, I was reading when I heard Mom scream. It turned out she'd been lying on the davenport half asleep when she saw something black flit by. She thought she imagined it until it flew by again.

"It's a bat!" Sara cried. "Cover your hair. It'll get tangled up in your hair."

"Call... Call..." I've never seen Mom look so helpless. Mrs. Baker was the only neighbor we knew well enough to call, and what could she do?

All this time, Honey ran back and forth, barking, leaping up when she thought she saw the bat.

"Call the police," Sara said.

Mother said, "Open the door. Maybe it'll fly out."

Wishful thinking. What if something else flew in?

I looked up the number for the police and made the call. Meanwhile, we sat close together, the three of us. I kept thinking about Dracula. The bat, probably as frightened of us as we were of it, had flown off somewhere in the house. I didn't know how I'd sleep tonight or ever again, come to think of it. Maybe it was hiding in my bedroom!

"That's what happens when you move to the country," Mom said.

Then _he_ came. Honestly, he's the most handsome man I ever saw. You'd swear he came straight from Hollywood. He's tall, and he has black hair and the nicest smile.

"Do you have bats in your belfry?" he asked.

"One bat," Sara said. She looked ridiculous with a babushka tied around her head. "It may have rabies. Kill it."

He carried a dangerous looking nightstick and a gun.

"I'll take care of it," he promised.

And he did. Afterwards, he went up into the attic. There were no more bats, but he found a hole under the roof that needed to be repaired or some other hideous thing might find its way inside.

His name is Edward Douglas, Ned, and he's an officer in the Foxglove Corners Police Department. He took the bat away. He closed the opening to the attic and checked the rest of the house. We were pronounced bat-free, but it would be a long time before life went back to normal.

And that's the story of the night of the bat, and how I met Ned.

Fifteen

EVANORA'S DIARY continued

WONDERING—Will I ever see Ned again?

Only if we have another bat. That won't happen unless one flies in through an open window. Is there any other way? I can't think of any.

"What a nice young man," Mom said after Ned left. Sara said, "He isn't young. He must be in his thirties."

Ned is more than ten years older than me. Maybe he has a family, a wife and kids. But maybe, he's single. He might have a girlfriend, though. He probably does.

He didn't say anything about seeing me again. Why would he? He was a policeman responding to a call for help. We'd have to have another emergency. Not a bat. Maybe a robbery? Hope springs eternal. I'm so glad we moved to Foxglove Corners. Something wonderful is going to happen here! I know it.

~ * ~

In the next entries, Evanora wrote exclusively about Ned. She didn't see him again, but she learned that Maybelle at the corner store was his aunt. The days passed, and time and time again, Evanora relived 'the night of the bat' and her impressions of Ned. Their paths *would* cross again. She had made a wish on a star.

I closed the diary, making my own wish that Evanora would meet Ned again before I realized how idiotic that was. This encounter had happened years ago. It was only through Evanora's writing that Ned seem so alive to me and so desirable.

He reminded me a little of Crane.

They had either met again, or they hadn't. The past was over.

~ * ~

Valentine's Day dawned with a cold blue sky and, miraculously, no snow falling and none predicted for the near future. After Crane left for his patrol, I baked a cake.

Mixing ingredients, spilling the batter into my rarely used heart-shaped tin, I found myself thinking about Veronica the Viper and the cake she had made for Crane. (Curse her.). We hadn't eaten it, and eventually, I had thrown it away with the garbage. A waste of food, but no one had told her to do it.

I couldn't throw away the thought that Veronica had made it for Crane.

My cake was chocolate, and I planned to write 'Be My Valentine' in strawberry frosting. As for the rest of the dinner… I turned to the Internet in search of romantic Valentine meals, but in the end decided on roasted chicken with stuffing and rice, two of Crane's favorite foods.

After today, I had only one more day of winter break. February had been a see-saw month with snow one day and a faint hint of spring in the air the next.

I took my cake out of the oven to cool, placing it far back on the counter out of Candy's reach, and walked three of the dogs on the lane.

As we passed the abandoned construction, my thoughts drifted to the Valentine House. Evanora hadn't written anymore about it, preferring to fill her diary with memories and fantasies of Ned. It was amazing how she could write so extensively about such a brief one-time event.

She considered asking Maybelle about him, questions like where he lived, if he had a girlfriend, and what his interests were. But she was too shy to do so, and Maybelle wasn't particularly friendly, even though she and Sara shopped at the corner store frequently.

A crush needs material to feed on. Evanora never saw the object of her affection. But then, crushes are part of growing up, I supposed, and unrequited love leads nowhere. Those are the grim facts of life.

Velvet came to a stop in the lane to sniff at a bit of purple debris trapped in a dead vine. It was paper, undoubtedly still carrying a trace of some tantalizing scent.

"Leave it," I said and gave her lead a tug, as my thoughts turned to the Valentine House. The diary had whetted my interested in it. When would it be safe to walk in the woods again?

Not yet, I decided, but soon. When the snow began to melt. Annica planned to go with me, and by then, I should have finished reading Evanora's diary.

~ * ~

Valentine's Day isn't an actual holiday. As a rule, people don't decorate their houses, and schools don't close. Those so inclined present their loved one with flowers, candy, and cards or, like me, they bake a heart-shaped cake.

It's safe to say that most people let the day pass unmarked. Not my friends.

Camille crossed the lane in mid-morning carrying a basket filled with heart-shaped bones for the dogs and chocolate chip muffins for their humans. She glowed with good health and zest for life.

"I'm glad you're feeling better," I said.

"So am I. It's dreadful to feel sick and weak day after day." She paused, eyeing the teakettle I'd just filled. "I saw a coyote near the woods just now. Only one."

"I wonder if it's the coyote that ate my stew," I said.

"That was my thought. And here I was, with food. I don't think we should go back and forth with food until he moves on."

"I agree, but you don't go out that often."

"In the winter, no, but in spring and summer I'm always outside gardening."

"Food should be more plentiful then," I said, keeping to myself my thoughts of the coyote roaming up and down the lane, selecting the best carrots and tomatoes in my neighbors' vegetable gardens for himself. "And I can't see a coyote sidling up to a human like a dog wanting to be petted."

I took two muffins out of the basket and gave each of the dogs a bone. If I spread them on the floor Candy would eat more than her share.

"I don't think our bold coyote is going anywhere," I said. "He's found a home in the woods. Maybe he has a mate and a family."

That didn't cheer either of us.

"I used to leave out food for the birds and wild creatures. I don't think I'll do that anymore."

"Fill a jar with coins and shake it the next time you see him. And yell. That should scare him off."

"What a bother. But I'll admit I'm afraid. He just stood there and looked at me. I hear them howling at night. That's bad enough. I don't like them to come so near."

The teakettle was whistling. While we had our tea and muffins, I told Camille about Evanora's diary, then brought the music box into the kitchen. She exclaimed over the Cupid and the sentiment 'Truly Thine.'

It was working. "Do you recognize the melody?" I asked.

"No, but it's familiar. I should. Wind it up again."

I did. Three times. Neither Camille nor I could identify it, although Camille said it sounded a little like *Greensleeves*.

"You discover the most unusual things, Jennet," she said. "What's your secret?"

I often wondered that myself. I poured the tea and said, "I lead a charmed life."

~ * ~

My next guest was Brent. It wasn't even noon, so I knew he hadn't come for dinner. Also, he had plans with Annica.

He opened a jumbo bag from Pluto's Gourmet Pet Shop and drew out a giant-sized heart tied with a lacy red bow. The collies circled him, yipping frantically.

"A Valentine for dogs?" I asked.

"They look like people candy, but they're filled with beef and chicken and liver. All the things dogs love."

"Well, thank you. For them. You know, they have no idea it's Valentine's Day."

"Sure, but they know all about love."

Looking at my wonderful collies, I couldn't deny it.

He pulled out another large heart. "This one is for you and Crane. I didn't get it at Pluto's."

"I hope not. Thanks." I set it next to the cake.

"I want you to see what I'm giving Annica for Valentine's Day." He took another smaller box out of the Pluto's bag. Inside was a brooch shaped like a flower basket filled with precious stones.

They reminded me of the red and white carnations with which Annica had decorated Clovers. Rubies and diamonds.

"Do you think she'll like it?" he asked.

"She'll love it."

"That Texan can't afford anything like this," he said.

"Love isn't about expensive presents," I pointed out.

"That jerk just likes to show off. He doesn't love Annica."

He stopped short of saying, "Like I do."

Sixteen

Crane said, "Close your eyes."

I did, shutting out the flicker of flames from the tapers in the candlesticks and my festive dinner. I felt his hands on my neck... warm...and something cold against my skin. A chain.

"Okay, open them. Happy Valentine's Day, honey."

The chain was long and silver, dipping just below my breasts. It held twin heart lockets, both embossed with scrolls around a floral pattern. One for each of us, with room for four small pictures. The silver had an unearthly shine in the candlelight.

Who needed rubies and diamonds?

Well, Crane had already given me diamonds—my engagement and wedding rings.

I turned to kiss him. "It's so beautiful. I just baked you a cake... with my love eternal. If that's all right."

"It's just what I wanted," he said, meaning love eternal, I hoped, and not the cake.

"Let's eat dinner so we can cut into it," he said.

An assenting woof from the kitchen broke into the moment's silence. It was Candy, of course, 'dinner' being one of her favorite words.

"The dogs already ate," I said, "but they can have dessert later. Brent brought them a Valentine heart of dog treats this morning."

"I saw it on the table. It's a good thing I didn't sample them."

"Did you see Veronica today?" I asked.

Drat! I hadn't meant to mention her name. By mutual agreement, we banned serious and distressful talk during dinner. Veronica qualified as both. But I'd spoken without thinking and all but invited her to our private celebration.

Why? Probably because she was still on the edge of my mind, hovering there like a rattlesnake ready to strike.

Oh, well, the damage was done, and I *did* want to know if he had spoken to her about the card. In other words, I couldn't leave well enough alone.

"Not today," Crane said and passed me the chicken. And that was that.

Quickly I changed the subject. "Brent showed me the brooch he bought for Annica. He's still concerned about that man from Texas who gave Annica the roses."

"So he told me. Fowler doesn't like competition."

"Annica says she isn't interested in Colton, and it's no secret how she feels about Brent."

"Tell that to Fowler."

"I'm strictly staying out of their business," I said.

"That's best."

It was safer to think about the one-sided romance unfolding in Evanora's diary. In truth, reading about the all-wonderful officer, Ned Douglas, was like breezing through a romance novel. In fiction, Evanora would meet her policeman again and, after a setback or two, which was necessary for conflict, would live with him happily ever after.

This, however, was someone's real life. I wondered if Evanora would have her happily ever after. After all, life seldom imitated romance novels.

I touched my double heart lockets, reminding myself how lucky I was to have met Crane.

If it hadn't been for the tornado and my buying the green Victorian farmhouse in Foxglove Corners, it wouldn't have happened. Coincidentally, Evanora had met Ned because of her family's move to the same little town…and a bat in the house. I was eager to see how Evanora's story turned out, but first I had my own evening to enjoy.

We were almost through with dinner, almost ready for coffee and cake in front of the fireplace. For my own romantic interlude. I couldn't possibly love Crane more and wanted everyone to be as happy as I was.

~ * ~

That night, music pulled me out of a pleasant dream of walking in the woods. There was nothing sinister about the abandoned construction on this day. On the contrary, it was very much like strolling through the enchanted forest of fairy tales.

The snow had melted, and the leaves were all shades of green. The air was sweet, scented with a thousand flowers, and filled with birdsong. A melody lured me to an unknown destination.

No, not unknown. I was looking for a little house in the woods with a Valentine heart painted between its twin gables.

The music will take you there, came a whisper. *The music knows the secret.*

Then suddenly I was awake, memories of the dream already fading, every beautiful thing leaving except for the music.

Abruptly, realization struck. I was listening to the music box. It must have turned itself on again, playing the haunting air that neither Camille nor I could identify.

Why didn't it wake Crane? But then, he could sleep through the howling of coyotes.

I wasn't surprised Misty heard the music. In the light of a stray moonbeam, I could see her pretty tilted head. She was on the verge of barking. Even Halley was awake, but that might be because Misty had moved.

"Come," I whispered. "Downstairs."

I reached for the miniature flashlight I kept in my nightstand drawer. In the hall, I turned on the light and, with my guardian collies in my wake, walked toward the music.

Like I'd followed the music in my dream. The melody was the same.

How strange that none of the other collies had joined us.

The music box sat between the candlesticks on the credenza where I'd left it.

Did you expect it to move?

It played its melody to a dark, silent room. I aimed the flashlight on it. The colors on the lid seemed more vivid to me. The forget-me-nots were a deeper shade of blue, almost cobalt, the Cupid's cheeks rosier, and its eyes were as blue as the flowers. They seemed to glitter.

But that was nonsense.

I half expected it to feel warm. I even touched it. Of course it felt the same. Cool but pulsating with life.

What would happen when it reached the end of the melody? Surely it wouldn't keep playing. I couldn't know how long it had played already before waking me.

I sighed. A rogue music box playing through all hours of the night. Just what I didn't need.

I thought briefly of destroying it. Dropping it on the floor, throwing it against the wall. Killing it once and for all.

This lovely little antique?

Really, Jennet, it hasn't harmed you in any way. It's just a little strange. More than a little. Besides, would such an assault affect the power that allowed it to activate itself?

I waited.

One of the candlesticks fell over, bringing me out of my dark fantasy. There was nothing supernatural going on here. Misty had given the music box a mighty swipe with her paw. She'd knocked the candlestick off the credenza instead.

That was no way to treat a beloved heirloom.

As I replaced the candlestick, the music stopped in mid-refrain and didn't start again. The only sounds on the entire first floor were breathing. Misty and Halley and me. Halley brushed against my leg, her soulful dark eyes filled with dismay.

Remember when it was just you and I? she might have said. *Now you're having adventures with Misty.*

I laughed aloud at the ludicrous thought.

"I love you both equally," I said, giving each one her own pat on the head. "Always. It's back to bed we go."

With the contact of warm fur came decision. Tomorrow was the last day of my winter break. If it didn't snow, I'd visit the Green House of Antiques. When I'd found myself in the possession of a haunted television set, I'd traced it to the source. With luck, history would repeat itself.

Haunted the music box might be, but its days were numbered.

Or so I told myself.

Seventeen

All good things must come to an end. The calendar told the sad story. Today, then the weekend, then back to school on Monday. Back to dangerous commutes on the freeway and less time with Crane and the collies.

I had high hopes for my last vacation day. I didn't think I'd solve my new mystery but hoped to make a sizeable dent in it. Specifically, I wanted to know where the Green House of Antiques had obtained the music box. That was the natural starting place.

Before leaving the house, I wound the music box again. Music wrapped around me, smooth poignant notes that seemed to reach into my heart.

What on earth?

Was it playing a different tune? How could that be?

When the notes stopped, I turned the key again and listened intently. I wasn't mistaken. The song *was* different. The music box had two melodies, and no discernible way of selecting one or the other. If there had been a tag near the key, it had long since vanished.

You're playing with fire, my inner voice warned. Unfortunately, it refused to supply an explanation, so I didn't take it seriously.

I bundled up and headed for Lakeville, trying to forget that Misty had wanted desperately to go with me. I couldn't take her into an antique shop with her wagging tail in close proximity to all those fragile and expensive collectibles. So I had to disappoint her.

~ * ~

The Valentine decorations were still in the window, although many of the items had been sold. Myriads of shades of red and pink sent their warm glow out into the frosty air. A set of heart chimes announced my arrival to an empty store.

The Green House wore a 'just awakened' face. Lola, the clerk whom I recognized from an earlier visit, emerged from a back room drinking from a tall steaming mug. Her red skirt and turtleneck sweater blended nicely with the decor, and she wore a pair of the shop's vintage earrings, dangling garnet teardrops.

"Good morning," she said. "You're up early. What can I help you with?"

I'd decided on a pretext that was ninety-five percent truth. "I'm looking for old-time books in a series."

"As in Nancy Drew? Penny Parker? Judy Bolton?"

I nodded. "And others."

"We have a good selection, but they're scattered throughout the shop. We find that we sell more that way."

I knew that from past visits. "Is the owner in?" I asked.

"One of them will be, a little later. Ms. Zara is a new partner."

That was news to me, but good news. The owner, the woman I knew, rarely came to the shop, relying on her staff to keep it solvent. If Lola couldn't tell me about the music box's history, maybe Ms. Zara could. In any event, Lola was standing in front of me; Ms. Zara wasn't.

I asked my question. "The last time I was here, I bought an antique music box. It has 'Truly Thine' written on the lid."

"The Valentine box! What a little treasure! I almost bought it myself. I just love those vintage Valentine pictures."

"Do you know where it came from?" I asked.

"I do. An estate sale. We get advance notices of them, so we can be on hand to scoop up the best antiques."

"Do you remember which sale it was?"

"The Sherbourne sale in Maple Creek. We hardly have anything left from that haul. Just a few bracelets and pins."

Sherbourne. Maple Creek. I'd remember that. What I'd do with the information was another matter.

"I'll see if I can find a good book now," I said and wandered through the store, if 'wander' could describe my hasty perusal of the items on offer. Now that I had a clue of sorts, I was eager to pursue it.

In a dim corner on a roll top desk, I found *The Ghost Parade*, an early Judy Bolton. Leafing through the yellowing pages, I saw a spooky illustration I'd never seen in other editions. The book was in mint condition, complete with a dust jacket, priced at thirty dollars. Didn't these people ever read their books or were they just extra careful with them?

Deciding not to wait for Ms. Zara, I paid for my find and left the shop, setting the heart chimes in motion. I could always return some day after school.

I breathed in the frigid air, which wasn't so frigid as it had been only a half hour ago. The sun was high in the sky, its rays practically golden. The snow had been cleared from the street and sidewalk and was on its way to a welcome meltdown.

Standing still for a moment, I took several deep breaths. Could that be the glorious scent of spring in the air?

~ * ~

"I have something new." Miss Eidt handed me a tattered paperback with a yellow-haired Victorian lady in white ascending a winding staircase. Standard Gothic fare; an unfamiliar author and title. The light fell gently on Miss Eidt's hand, on her mauve nail polish and a diamond solitaire ring in a gold setting.

She wasn't referring to the book.

I took her hand in mine. "Oh, it's exquisite! When did this happen?"

"Last night," she said. "Over dessert at our Valentine's Day dinner. It was strawberry shortcake."

"'Our' meaning you and Chester Maywood?"

"Yes. Chester and I."

I had known Miss Eidt for a long time, ever since my move to Foxglove Corners, and had never seen her so happy. Her glow owed nothing to the morning sunshine pouring through the window.

What to say? Not one of the responses clamoring in my mind. Not, "This is so sudden!" Not, "Are you sure?" Not, "What do you really know about him?" Not...

"I am so, so happy for you," I said. I would have hugged her, but the desk stood between us; and the library, unlike the Green House, was fairly busy. "I should have brought doughnuts so we could celebrate in style."

But I hadn't known. I couldn't have dreamed...

Miss Eidt was the town's beloved librarian. A fixture. She was always there, always recommending books and helping people with their research, taking pride in her summer reading club for teenagers and the Gothic Nook she had recently created.

Always alone, dressed in neat pastel suits and dresses with her trademark pearl necklaces. Alone. Until Chester Maywood had walked into the library looking for books on building a house.

I could tell immediately that he was a gentleman: attractive, distinguished with his cane, and best of all, in Miss Eidt's age group. I knew they'd been seeing each other and had noticed that Miss Eidt seemed younger these days and more vibrant. Her hair, for instance. It was shorter and cut in a more fashionable style.

What woman, no matter what her age, wants to be a fixture?

Ah love! It was in the very air as if Cupid had flown through Foxglove Corners aiming his arrows indiscriminately—at Colton Reeves, at Veronica, at Chester Maywood.

Did Cupid know what he was doing?

In Miss Eidt's case, I was certain he did.

"Don't look so shell-shocked, Jennet," she said. "It isn't happening tomorrow. We'll have a long engagement."

"A long engagement is good. It'll give us time to plan."

Showers and flowers, a get-together for Miss Eidt's many friends. We wouldn't call it a shower. She wouldn't want one. Helping her find the perfect wedding dress, the cake... The list went on and on.

"Will you still be our librarian?" I asked.

"Certainly. The library is mine. It's my soul. Chester is my heart."

"Nicely said." I breathed more easily. To lose Miss Eidt would be tantamount to losing a Foxglove Corners landmark.

"I'd like a spring wedding," Miss Eidt said. "Next spring, that is. We'll need time, for Chet to build his house, for me to sell mine. For me just to enjoy being an engaged woman. It'll take some getting used to. Now enough wedding talk. Are you interested in this book or shall I shelve it in the Gothic Nook?"

I didn't have to think about that. The cover alone drew me in. "I'll take it. While I'm here, did you ever hear of the Sherbourne family in Maple Creek?"

"I don't think so. Why?"

"They had an estate sale recently. I bought one of their antiques and I need to find out all I can about it."

"Again, why?"

I described the music box, ending with its newly discovered talent. "It turns itself on, and the melody just changed this morning."

I watched her eyes light up. "A Valentine mystery, Jennet. How perfect! How can I help?"

Eighteen

"I'm not sure anyone can," I said. "All I have is the name Sherbourne and the town, Maple Creek. It'll be like looking for a needle in a haystack."

"You've found needles before in unlikely places."

"I'll see if I can find the family name online," I said. "Then I'll look in the vertical file."

Although Miss Eidt had stepped with some reluctance into the modern age, she held on to a genuine artifact, her collection of newspaper clippings about various subjects that interested her, all in neatly labeled manila folders.

I was probably the only one who referred to it, a google search being more efficient, but I had found a wealth of information in those files on previous occasions.

Not today, though, and not with Miss Eidt's help. Before she could join me in her office, she was beset with requests for help and friends congratulating her on her engagement.

Well, I worked best alone. But even though I found an illustrated article about the music box collection of Miss Katherine Marsh of

Maple Creek, apparently I had the only music box in existence that was capable of turning itself on.

I learned, however, of the existence of Sherbourne Bakery in Maple Creek. It was a lead, more or less, and Maple Creek was close enough to visit on another day. Today I only had time for a quick stop at Clovers where Annica would soon begin her shift. I made a copy of the Marsh article and slipped it into my purse.

When I left the library Miss Eidt was deep in a conversation with two ladies of her own age. I couldn't remember seeing her so happy and animated. She'd apparently abandoned her policy of talking quietly in the library.

~ * ~

The air was definitely warmer as I dodged little islands of melting snow in the parking lot on the way to the restaurant. The painted clovers in the border had a newly blossomed look. Ah spring!

Like the Green House of Antiques, Clovers held on to its Valentine Day decor, and the tall vase of yellow roses contrasted brightly with the pink and red color scheme. Annica, like Lola, still wore red, a floaty polka dot shirtwaist with the brooch Brent had bought for her. I could guess who had given her the roses.

Marcy looked up from the table she'd been serving. "Visit with your friend, Annica," she said. "I have it covered."

The restaurant wasn't busy. I settled myself at my favorite booth and Annica brought us a pot of tea and coffeecake decorated with red sugar. Valentine Day surplus, I imagined.

"I love your new brooch," I said.

Annica touched it lightly. "Brent is so romantic—and generous."

"Did you have a pleasant dinner?"

"Very. And you?"

"It was everything I hoped for."

"Well." She cut into her coffeecake with a fork.

"Are the roses from Brent?" I asked.

"Uh, no. Colton Reeves strikes again. I may have to go out with him to stop this floral avalanche."

"That's crazy," I said. "You'll only encourage him."

"I guess you're right." She glanced toward the door, her expression apprehensive, but no one was coming in or leaving at the moment. Her demeanor boded ill for Colton.

"I have the best news," I said. "Miss Eidt is engaged."

"Why, that's wonderful. To that gentleman she was seeing?"

"To Chester Maywood, yes."

"Valentine's Day was good to us this year." She touched her brooch again as if to make certain it was securely fastened to her dress.

I smiled. It certainly had been good to me, but on to other matters. "As soon as the snow is gone, I'd like to visit the Valentine House again."

"Me, too." She paused. "For any particular reason?"

"I've been thinking about it lately and reading the diary. And last night the music box turned itself on again. It had a different tune this time around."

"Do you think all three are connected?" she asked.

I hadn't thought about that. Evanora had mentioned the house in her diary but not the music box. Still, I'd only read about a quarter of the entries. In my opinion, coincidence was alive and well in this case. I had acquired the diary and the music box on the same day in the same place shortly after discovering the house in the woods.

"The Mystery of the Old Music Box," Annia murmured. "Or The Mysterious Music Box or..."

"Featuring Jennet and Annica," I added.

"Or how about Jennica?"

"Yes! Seriously, I'm going to finish reading the diary this weekend. Then, we'll know what happened at the Valentine House."

If indeed anything had happened.

"And I'll tag along," Annica said.

~ * ~

EVANORA'S DIARY

I saw Ned again!! He came into the country store while I was buying milk and bread. He bought chips and a Coke. He looked so handsome in his uniform, and he's so nice. He asked me if we'd been troubled by bats again. I told him my father had sealed up the attic opening.

He said, "You want to be careful around wild creatures. A woman I know was feeding nuts to the squirrels, and one of them bit her. She ended up in the hospital with an infection."

"I wouldn't do that," I said. "Are squirrels rabid, too?"

"They can be."

"I'll remember," I said. "I like to go walking in the woods. If my dog sees a squirrel, she tries to catch it, but usually I don't come in contact with wildlife."

I wished I could think of something clever to say to him. Something witty to make him notice me. Maybelle asked how Delilah was. Who could she be? His girlfriend or wife?

He gave her a short answer. "Good."

Maybelle is Ned's aunt. She would know. But how could I ask her? I wasn't supposed to be listening to their conversation. Anyway, it was none of my business.

He paid for his snack and left the store. I wish he could have stayed longer, but he was working. Somewhere, someone needed him. I wished I could have taken his picture, but I know I'll remember his features. There's a tiny vertical line above his nose. He must frown a lot, but there are lines around his eyes, too. So he also smiles a lot. His eyes are a lovely shade of light blue, set off by a tan. He's just handsome. What more can I say?

~ * ~

She could say a lot more about very little. The next three pages were filled with variations on the same theme: the absolute perfection of Officer Ned Douglas. I skimmed the paragraphs. The sentences were long and heavy with adjectives and superlatives. I, too, wished I'd had a picture of this paragon.

She ended an entry with speculation. *Who is Delilah? Maybelle would know, but she'd never tell me. She was never friendly with me and Sara, not from the first. I have no idea why.*

Nor did I, but duty called in a voice that couldn't be ignored. I set Evanora's diary aside and started dinner. Like Evanora, I found myself wishing something would happen. In her life, that is.

Nineteen

You know you're dreaming when reality is distorted, and you move from one scene to another without a proper transition. I dreamed about the music box that night. Perhaps it had turned itself on again and was playing one of its melodies in the dark. I didn't know; it didn't wake me this time.

I was walking in woods lush with the verdant greens of midsummer. And there was the house with the red heart between twin gables, a glowing beacon.

A voice whispered, 'Come closer, and I'll tell you the secret.'

I took a step forward and found myself in an aisle at the Green House of Antiques, looking at a display of tintypes, searching for a familiar face. I saw the music box on the table, surrounded by vintage greeting cards. How could that be? It was on the credenza in my dining room.

Lola materialized and grabbed it, causing several cards to fall to the floor. "This isn't supposed to be out here," *she said.* "It isn't for sale."

"Why is it on the table, then?" I asked. *"And there's a price tag on it."*

"I made a mistake," she said. *"You don't want it."*

"Because it's broken?" I asked.

"Because it's evil," she said.

I woke to hear the coyotes howling in the woods. The greenwood and the Green House were gone, as was to be expected of images in a dream. The entire household slept. Crane lay beside me, Halley and Misty guarded the door, and the other dogs slumbered silently in their chosen sleeping places. Only the coyotes were awake, howling, telling secrets to one another. The coyotes and me.

'I'll tell you the secret,' the voice had said.

What secret?

~ * ~

During the weekend, whenever I had free time, I read a few pages of Evanora's diary. Evanora learned that Delilah was Ned's former girlfriend who, along with Maybelle, who thought Delilah would make Ned the perfect wife, refused to accept the end of the relationship. So Ned was free, more or less, and Evanora lived in the hope they would meet again and he would see her as more than the girl whose house had been invaded by a bat.

EVANORA'S DIARY

I can't help comparing myself to Sara. Her hair is longer and brighter, and she has a way of drawing people's attention to herself. She resembles our mother. Sara is never at a loss for brilliant things to say. I've never been jealous of her because I'm smarter than she is, and once, I overheard Aunt Nora say that I'm prettier than Sara. Sara is more outgoing. Aunt Nora was just being kind, but it was a nice compliment.

Today, something wonderful happened. I was leaving the woods with a basket of berries. They grow wild, and Mrs. Baker told me they're called dewberries and they're edible. I've tasted them. They're okay, but I like blueberries better.

Ned happened to be driving by, and he stopped his patrol car right in front of the house and got out. I was afraid I was doing something wrong. Like maybe there's a law against picking berries in the woods. But I wasn't in trouble. He was smiling.

Honey started barking and racing around him.

"I like your dog," he said. "What's her name?"

"Honey," I said. "We found her running in the woods and adopted her."

He asked if I'd seen any bats lately. Was I never going to live that down? I couldn't think of anything to say except 'no.' Then he asked if the woods belonged to my family.

"I don't know who owns them," I said. "There aren't any 'No Trespassing' signs around. I like to look at birds and flowers."

Did I really say that? How inane it sounds now.

He didn't notice. "I like to hunt and fish when I have time off," he said. "Do you ever go fishing?"

"I don't like to kill things," I said.

"Not even a bat?" he asked.

Would he never forget about that blasted bat?

"I'd be afraid to go near a bat," I told him. "They get all tangled up in your hair."

He looked at my basket. "What are you going to do with all those berries?"

"Have them for breakfast in cereal or maybe bake a pie. They're called dewberries."

He reached for a handful of berries and ate them, frowning a little.

"They're not very sweet," he said.

I'd tasted them myself, so I knew that. "They'll need a lot of sugar."

"If you bake them in a pie, save a piece for me," he said. "Now, I'd better move on."

That was all. He drove away. I took my berries inside and washed them. Did he mean it about the pie?

~ * ~

Unmindful of time passing, I read on. Evanora's diary was indeed like a romance novel. Did Ned's duty take him to Evanora's isolated road or was he hoping to find her outside one day? Impossible to tell.

She made a dewberry pie, but she didn't see him. It didn't bother her. She was certain they would meet again. In her diary, she wrote exclusively about Ned, weaving marvelous fantasies with golden thread and dream dust.

His hair was black with blue lights when he walked in the sunshine, and his eyes were blue. Like cornflowers. She wrote, *Black, black, black is the color of my true love's hair, his lips are something wondrous fair…*

She was on the threshold of a wondrous new experience and was well aware of it.

I'm falling in love with him, she wrote. *My love… My true love…*

A dog was barking. One of my dogs.

I glanced out the window. A deer had ventured across the lane and stood in front of the house grazing in the flower bed. Candy took exception to its presence. She placed her paws on the windowsill which made her look taller than she was. The deer appeared to be unimpressed.

"Calm down," I ordered her as the clock chimed.

It was late, time to set Evanora's story aside and make dinner for my own true love.

~ * ~

Every time I turned around it seemed the clock was chiming. Hours passed with the blink of an eye. Two nights came and went and, suddenly, it was Monday morning.

Back to school and farewell to leisure time. I cooked Crane his usual hearty breakfast, packed a lunch for myself, and gathered my books. It was my week to drive to Marston, and I was happy to see sunshine and melting snow.

"Smooth sailing all the way," as Leonora said when I picked her up. "Now we can look forward to Easter."

"Not for a while, though."

But the landscape had an 'end of winter' look and, once we were on the freeway, the snow cover was less evident. Foxglove Corners was always snowier and windier than Oakpoint, which lay thirty miles to the south.

On the way, I brought Leonora up to date on the mysteries, ending with the description of the music box. By now, my dream was a hazy memory.

"By some dark magic, it turns itself on," she said. "Does it play when you wind it up, too?"

"Yes, and whenever it feels like singing."

"Singing?"

"I meant playing."

Then why had I said singing?

"I'd like to see it," she said. "Maybe I can recognize the songs."

"I wonder which one it'll play when I wind it."

I would have to wait and see. It hardly mattered, as I couldn't identify either melody. But the music box was a curiosity.

It's evil.

The voice from my dream slipped in and out of my mind.

"I'd like to see the Valentine House, too," Leonora added. "Whenever you find a house that intrigues you, it's always vacant, and it always comes with a mystery."

That wasn't true of every evocative house I'd encountered, but it certainly seemed to be a pattern.

"We'll all go," I said. "It'll be soon, now that spring is on the way."

~ * ~

It wasn't anywhere near Foxglove Corners. The forecast on the radio was disheartening. Rain and snow were even now making their way toward Foxglove Corners and should arrive on Wednesday evening. I turned the radio off and found a parking place close to the door. Today, the sun was shining, and the high school appeared to exist in a bubble of energy with everyone finding their way back to the fold.

Well, almost everyone.

A dozen students in my first hour World Literature class were absent, and even more in the second period. I'd planned well, creating a lesson for each class that could easily be made up. In a few days, attendance would be normal.

Principal Grimsley prowled the halls, his signature smile pasted on his face. Bells rang, groups paraded in and out of my classroom, and by the end of the school day, routine had reestablished itself.

The woods of Foxglove Corners and their mysteries seemed so far away they might have existed on another plane. It was an illusion, of course. I knew they were waiting for me, and suspected that in my living room the music box had turned itself on and was playing its melody to a family of confused collies.

Twenty

By the weekend, enough snow had melted to make a hike in the woods possible, if not advisable. Annica appeared for our excursion in tall boots, khaki pants, and emerald earrings. She also brought the camera she'd received for Christmas.

The snowmelt was slowly turning to mud. I was glad I'd worn my old boots, and that I hadn't taken Misty, as she'd be sure to step in every puddle along the way.

As we approached the abandoned construction site, Annica echoed Leonora's observation. "All our mysteries are centered around old houses," she said. "I'm not complaining, but why is that?"

I thought about it, thought about my most recent adventure with the haunted sleigh. "Not all of them."

"Okay. Most of them, then."

"I suppose because people live in houses. When they die, something of them may stay behind. Their spirits long to go back home."

I remembered information I'd read in Evanora's diary, a solitary fact about the child, Cecily, who used to play in the Valentine House.

She had died young. It was easy to imagine a ghost-girl haunting the place where she'd spent many happy hours. Her playhouse in the woods.

I had a sudden clear picture of a little girl with long blonde hair whose dress blended with the greens of the encroaching vegetation. She was strolling toward the beckoning red heart between the twin gables; now she was skipping. Here, within the walls of the house in the woods, she would dream the long summer hours away with her dolls and the miniature tea set spread out on a scaled-down table. It was painted blue, her favorite color.

Maybe she was alone. More likely, her friends were with her.

In my mind, I heard again a whispered plea, *'Don't go.'*

Was it her spirit who wanted company?

We couldn't stay on that day, but we were retracing our steps. Maybe the house in the woods was haunted by a child who reminded me of Alice in Wonderland in the original illustration.

"How long has the Valentine House stood empty?" Annica asked.

"A long time. There's no way to tell. Evanora wrote about it, but she didn't date her entries."

She had given the reader no clue. Not a single passing reference to what was happening in the world or even a stray mention of a current fashion like crinolines worn under a skirt to make it fuller, which would suggest the late nineteen-fifties. Nothing that would help me establish the timeline.

Of course, who wrote diary entries for a future reader?

"A long time," I repeated.

"Do you think this Evanora is still living?" Annica asked.

"My guess would be no. Otherwise, her diary wouldn't have ended up in an estate sale."

More accurately, it had been mixed in with a collection of girls' series books, indicating that whoever had filled the box had been careless, or at least unobservant.

"I started to keep a diary," Annica said. "I sure don't want anyone to read it—ever."

"Then don't lose track of it."

"I'll leave instructions to have it burned before I die," she said.

I smiled. "You do that."

We passed the last house in the abandoned construction site, the one that had a few walls still standing and offered makeshift shelter to the occasional vagrant. I gave it a wary glance. It didn't appear anyone was inside today.

Belatedly, it occurred to me that we were taking a chance whenever we walked in these woods.

We stepped over a large fallen branch and walked on in a northerly direction. There seemed to be an existing path, one made long ago by others heading toward the house. For a moment, it seemed as if I could see the red heart shining through a tangle of bare trees. A second look told me it was a trick of the light. Or my imagination.

At last the house came into view, looking a little shabbier than it had the last time we'd come this way.

"I'm glad it's still here," I said.

"Did you think it would fall apart in a matter of days?" Annica asked.

"No, it's just…" I didn't finish my sentence, having lost my train of thought. "The heart seems washed out," I said. "Like it faded."

The door was as I had left it—ajar, inviting. We entered and stood in the middle of the room. The cold of an unheated structure wound itself around me in layers, tightening around my heart. A vague uneasiness nudged at me along with a strange thought.

I've been here before.

Yes, of course. Days ago, with Annica.

No. Another time. Later?

In a dream.

On that occasion, if you could call a dream an occasion, a silky scarf lay on the table, along with a single glove, and there was a picnic basket on the floor. Thus encouraged, images sprang to vivid life, along with a murmur of half-heard voices. Where had they come from? I was alone. The whispered words remained just beyond the edge of my consciousness. A conversation I couldn't properly hear.

Voices in the dream, I reminded myself. No one whispered; no one tread on the floorboards of this real-world little house.

I had no idea why my dreams were so strange. And how odd was it to remember a dream after several nights had passed?

I resolved to visit Lucy Hazen at Dark Gables one day after school or one weekend. Soon. Lucy had the ability to foretell future events—sometimes, or to warn me of impending danger—usually without being specific.

But what danger could a vacant house pose?

Annica walked to the window. "I was hoping to find a clue, but I don't see anything."

"What kind of clue?" I asked.

"A toy. Maybe a doll or a storybook. It's pointless to take a picture of an empty room."

"Whoever cleaned out the house did a thorough job."

Everything must go. Cart it away. Send the furniture to some charity. Burn the rest. Let the house fall down. There's no one left to care.

That voice, of course, was pure imagination, but I thought it could have reflected reality.

"Let's see if there's anything upstairs," Annica said.

"Okay, but be careful. Remember, those stairs aren't in the best of shape."

Neither was the railing.

We hadn't found anything left behind on our last visit, and there was nothing to find today. Up here, it was colder and more desolate, if possible, than it was on the first floor.

Again, Annica walked over to the window. "I wonder why they built a second story."

"To make it seem like a real. house, I imagine."

"It *is* a real house."

"Well, no. You can't cook here. There's no bathroom. No running water, no heat."

"At one time, there might have been an outhouse."

"Let's not get carried away," I said. "Children came here to play. When they were tired, they went home."

Annica turned away from the window, a half smile on her face. "When I was a little girl, we used to make tents with an old blanket and go inside. I wonder if kids still do that?"

"Maybe. Those whose parents can't afford a playhouse. But kids today have other ways to amuse themselves."

"Yeah. Video games." She swept the room with her eyes. "I wish they'd left one little thing behind."

"They did," I said. "Their emotions."

"All I feel is hollowness. Like we walked into a mausoleum. Or an Egyptian tomb. How about you?"

"Hollowness is an emotion. This was once a happy place. Not anymore. Now it's barren. Lost and lonely…"

I imagined a strong wind tearing through the door, sweeping all the joy out of the house, leaving behind a desolate shell.

But no wind could eradicate memories or the emotions which Lucy believed were absorbed into the walls of a house.

'Don't go,' the voice had said. I didn't hear it today. Maybe I'd never heard it.

"The next step is to try to find out more about the builder and his little daughter," I said.

"How will we do that?"

"I have a name. Sherbourne. And the library."

"Good," Annica said. "We're going to go ahead try to solve the mystery even without a clue."

"We have a clue. The diary. Evanora might have mentioned the house again. From what I've been reading, all that interests her is the man she met. But I have a lot more to read."

"Hurry up and finish reading it. Then lend it to me."

"I'll try," I said.

Twenty-one

EVANORA'S DIARY

ONE MAGICAL DAY—Oh, what a beautiful morning! The sun was shining, and the air smelled of flowers. I was wearing the new dress I made. It's mint green. That color always makes me feel pretty.

I think these woods are enchanted. They're filled with strange, beautiful flowers and butterflies I never see in any other place. The morning dew lasts longer, and the air smells sweeter. I saw a bird that was so small I wondered if it was a butterfly. I wouldn't be surprised if the fairy folk live here, hiding behind their mushrooms.

I have something wonderful to write about. I saw Ned's patrol car on our lane parked in front of Mrs. Baker's house. I could hardly believe my good luck. There isn't any crime in our neighborhood. He has to be here for me.

Honey greeted him like an old friend. He made a fuss over her. He likes dogs. Dad says you can always trust a person who likes dogs.

He said, "I was hoping to take you up on that offer for a piece of pie."

That wasn't how I remembered the conversation. I felt myself blushing. "Oh, I'm sorry. It's long gone."

"Can't you bake another one?"

"I'll have to pick the berries."

"We can do that," he said.

I don't think he's really interested in pie. Just then, Honey took off into the woods. She loves to chase squirrels and rabbits. One time she caught a wild creature, a groundhog I think, but she opened her mouth and it got away. I didn't want that to happen again. I called to her to come back, but she didn't.

Ned said, "Let's go after her."

We went into the woods together.

"Should you do this?" I asked. "Aren't you on duty?"

"Finding runaway dogs is part of my job," he said.

Along with keeping company with girls? I thought.

We found Honey at the little house in the woods. She'd given up the chase and lay panting in front of the door.

"You didn't hear me calling you?" I demanded.

She wagged her tail.

"What an odd little house," Ned said. "Who lives there?"

"No one," I said. "Our neighbor says it used to be a playhouse for a rich little girl. When she died, her family just left it here."

"Why is there a heart up there?" He pointed to it.

"It's just a decoration on a child's playhouse."

He asked if the house was locked.

I knew it wasn't. I told Honey to move. The door opened easily enough. I knew what we would find. Nothing.

Suddenly, the strangest feeling came over me. For the little lost girl, this must have been the happiest place on earth. Imagine being rich enough to have a house of your own filled with your favorite toys and books. You could play at being a grown-up and entertain your friends with a picnic lunch or read quietly with no one to disturb you.

Now all that was gone.

Nothing good or beautiful lasts forever. In the end, all that's left are empty rooms. I was cold even though the sun was hot outside. Emptiness and cold. I shivered.

"See," I said. "It's vacant. Unless a robber hid his stash upstairs. Is that what you were thinking?"

"No," he said, and I found myself turned around and captured in his arms.

He kissed me. I've been kissed before but never like that. Never, ever.

ANOTHER DAY—That was how it began, that glorious summer day in the woods. Someday I will write a novel and call it <u>The Dewberry</u> <u>Summer</u>. That's how I'll always think of this secret time with Ned.

Picking dewberries, sitting beside the stream while Honey explores the woods, always finding something different to sniff. I found something different, too. My dreams of Ned have come true. Our time together is short but so very precious. Better than any dream.

The purest eyes and the strongest hands.

I love the ground on where he stands...

FOUND OUT—I couldn't keep my secret long. Sara noticed Ned's patrol car parked on the lane. She asked if Mrs. Baker was having a problem. I told her I didn't know. Maybe she was robbed. "Every day?" Then she said she saw me go into the woods with "that cop."

"What do you do there—in the woods?" she asked.

I told her we pick berries and eat them. She laughed. "Do you think I was born yesterday, Eva? You'd better stop whatever you're doing. Mom won't like it one bit."

That was true enough.

Sara had an infuriating smile on her face. I couldn't let her see that she'd frightened me. Our mother is always busy in the house. She doesn't like to be outside except when she can't avoid it. She fitted out a special little room upstairs for her sewing machine and materials. I guess she doesn't think she has to watch her grown daughters' activities. That's good for me.

"I won't tell anyone," Sara promised.

I don't really trust her. She would tell herself she was only protecting me. From what? I think Sara is jealous of me. She's always been the one who had boyfriends. Ned is mine.

I refuse to worry about what Sara will do. Soon I'll see Ned again. Just the thought of being with him makes the long dull days in the country bearable.

THE DAY OF THE WITCH—Maybelle at the store was never friendly to me, but today she acted like she hates me. That must be my imagination. Maybelle has no reason to feel anything about me. I'm just a customer. I tell her what I want and pay her. She bags up the milk or bread or whatever. I say 'Goodbye.' She doesn't answer.

I'm not used to people being rude to me. I get along with everybody. It may not be me she objects to but something personal. Maybe she isn't feeling well. She doesn't look good to me and uses too much rouge and lipstick trying to make herself look better. (It doesn't work.) I mentioned her attitude to Sara yesterday. "That's funny," Sara said. "She's always nice to me. Maybe you remind her of someone she doesn't like."

That could be.

WEDNESDAY RAMBLINGS--I asked Ned if he wasn't afraid of getting in trouble with his superiors by meeting me in the woods. "I'm entitled to a break," he said. "I choose to spend it with you." The playhouse has become our secret place. Sometimes I pack a picnic lunch. He brings the pop. From Maybelle's store, I think. We can be alone and it's like having our own house—while it lasts.

He always has to leave. I understand. He has a job to do.

Every now and then, I wonder how long it will last, this wonderful time with Ned. We can't meet here in the wintertime. (Can we?) Maybe by then, we'll come to an understanding. I'll be able to tell Mom and Dad about him. He'll call for me at the house like a regular date. We'll go somewhere. Maybe to the Crystal Theater to see a movie. Maybe one day, we'll have a real house of our own. I can dream. My last dream came true.

But what if one day he loses interest in me? What if I'm just a summer fling to him?

Twenty-two

With a sigh, I set the diary aside. Evanora had become so real to me that I wished I could talk to her, to tell her she was playing with fire, and those who play with fire almost certainly get burned.

But that was impossible. The events recorded on the pages were long in the past. When reading Evanora's impassioned words, it was easy to forget that.

She had mentioned the possibility of seeing a movie at the Crystal Theater. It no longer existed, but if this happened in her future, and I could find out what movies were playing that summer, I'd have a clue to the time. For all the good it would do me.

Once again, I wondered how old Evanora was. Her late teens, I supposed. Probably not twenty-one yet if she planned to go to school—college?—in the fall.

Her woodland trysts with Ned, who was certainly older than she, were ill-advised at best, no matter how exciting they seemed to her. He was years ahead of her in experience. Was he merely amusing himself with a naive young girl who adored him?

I thought of Annica's diary, no doubt filled with pages about her dates with Brent Fowler and of her plan to leave instructions for it to be burned when she died.

The problem was no one could know when that day would arrive. Obviously, Evanora hadn't taken that precaution.

At times, I felt a trifle guilty reading about her romance and wondered anew how her diary had found its way into a box of old series books. She was most certainly gone from this life and probably no longer cared if her secret was revealed.

If, on the other hand, she was still alive, wouldn't she want her diary returned? That would be awkward, as she'd realize I'd read it. Well, that wasn't likely to happen.

Misty was awake, sniffing the diary whose pages had a trace of lavender scent. I had a fleeting image of Evanora sitting alone by the little stream, preserving her memories as the fragrance of the surrounding woods imprinted itself on the pages.

My vision was as real as a lovely old-time print. *Girl Writing in Diary.*

I told myself that I shouldn't read any more, should exercise a little control, a little kindness to a departed soul.

Uh... No.

Noble aspirations aside, I couldn't possibly *not* know how it all turned out. Evanora was heading for a fall. Would her love lose interest in her? It seemed likely. In any event, I had to know what happened next.

~ * ~

EVANORA'S DIARY

BETRAYED—I knew I couldn't trust Sara. She told our mother. Mom surprised me. She wasn't upset or angry. Just disappointed. "You shouldn't be alone with this man, Evanora. In the woods of all places. I thought you had more sense. What will the neighbors think?"

"There's only Mrs. Baker," I said.

The house on the other side of us is for sale, and Mrs. Baker was as fond of staying inside as Mom.

"It isn't seemly," Mom said. "It isn't safe."

Seemly? What kind of old-fashioned word was that?

"What could be safer?" I asked her. "Ned is a policeman."

"That's not the point. He's too old for you."

That was a weak argument as Dad is twelve years older than Mom.

"Ned is absolutely wonderful," I said. "Remember how he took care of the bat?"

To myself, I added, I love him.

"I'd like to see him again," Mom said. "He likes pie. Let's bake a pie and invite him to dinner."

"Could we?" I asked.

"Why not? We'll have a ham and blueberry pie and get to know him."

"I'll ask him," I said.

Sara will be unhappy about this development. She likes to stir up trouble.

Mom said, "We won't tell your father about...the woods. I know how he'd react."

So did I.

"Sara will tell him," I said.

"She won't. I'll make sure of it."

Everything will be all right then. I truly believe it. Mom is on my side.

RAINY DAY—We're in the midst of a storm today. All morning I watched the lane for Ned's patrol car, but he didn't come. Honey is nervous, trying to find a safe place to hide from the thunder. I wish she'd stay with me. Ned is out there somewhere. I hope he stays in his patrol car dry and safe. No one will break the law in this wretched weather.

Will it never stop raining? I can't wait to invite him to dinner. Guess I'll have to, though.

I'll close my eyes and remember the last time. I was so happy. It was so peaceful in the woods in Ned's arms. A flower that smells like lilacs grows near the house. I'll have to find it and bring home a bouquet.

~ * ~

The real world intruded. The collies were barking. The clock was chiming. Crane's voice broke the silence. "Back, girls! Where's Jennet? Jennet!"

Good grief. I'd lost myself in Evanora's world. I had steaks to broil, a salad to make…Too many things to do before Crane and I could sit down to dinner.

I took time to give Crane a long welcome home kiss. I almost searched his clothes for traces of rain.

Get a grip, Jennet. It's raining in Evanora's world, not yours.

"I lost track of time," I said. "I've been reading the diary that came with the books I bought at the Green House. It's fascinating"

That wasn't quite the word I wanted. Crane locked his gun in the cabinet and turned to me. "You're reading somebody's diary?"

"It reads like a romance novel. But it's real. I mean, it was real."

He gave me a meaningful smile. "Romance, huh?" He knew I preferred mysteries and Gothic novels.

I set the steaks in the broiler and spread salad makings on the counter.

"It's about a young girl who meets a charming policeman," I said. "They have an affair of sorts. She isn't specific, but from what she writes, I know that's what's happening."

Crane opened a can of root beer and sat at the table while Candy checked to see if he had a snack.

"I saw a heartbreaking sight today," he said. "Some lowlife abandoned an old dog on Huron Court with his belongings in a box. Just left him there."

"On Huron Court," I echoed.

Huron Court, the road that sensible people avoided as it had a slender hold on time. An isolated country road. The perfect place to dump an unwanted pet far from censoring eyes.

"Was it a collie?" I asked.

"No, a mix. A medium-sized brown dog with floppy ears. Whoever dumped him left his food bowl, a stuffed rabbit toy, and a ball in a box...and his name on a card. Brownie."

"Do you think the man who left the puppies on our lane struck again?" I asked.

"Could be, but lots of people abandon dogs. I hope there's a special place in hell waiting for them. It's especially bad since the Woodville sisters moved to Loosestrife Lane to take care of Brent's geriatric collies."

"Where did you take him?" I asked.

"To the shelter in Lakeville. It's filling up. I felt like bringing him home, but we're not a kennel, even though it looks like it."

Gently, he moved Candy's nose from the table.

"People assume someone will take their unwanted dogs. It makes them sleep easier at night."

I tossed the salad without thinking about what I was doing. A carrot slice here, a cherry tomato there, a spoon of thousand island salad dressing. My thoughts were on the abandoned dog. Brownie. I could almost see him waiting patiently on that infernal road with all his possessions. What could he have been thinking?

More to the point, what could I do?

Twenty-three

Crane's description of Brownie haunted my dreams and my thoughts the next day. I kept seeing a brown dog on a country road surrounded by his belongings as he waited for his human to return. How could Brownie know that would never happen? Could he have suspected he'd been thrown away?

Dogs know when they're not wanted. They panic, they grieve, they forgive.

Then a kind man in a uniform had come along, but he didn't take Brownie home. Now he languished in a shelter with other castaways. Had they let him keep his bowl and ball? Probably not.

Not that I would wish misfortune on another, but how fitting it would be if Brownie's cruel owner fell into another season and time. He had left his dog on Huron Court, after all. Let him know what it was like to be lost, never knowing whether or not he would ever see his home again.

Along with the heartrending pictures came an insistent command. *You have to help Brownie.*

All right. I will. How?

I thought of *Banner* reporter Jill Lodge, cousin of the paper's owner, Cameron. If I could persuade her to write a story about Brownie, people would take his plight to heart and line up to adopt him. Publicity almost always makes the difference in a case like Brownie's. An appearance on the nightly news would be better still.

That would take time, though. An even better option was Brent Fowler, with whom I could share Brownie's story this evening over dinner. Brent was as strong and caring as Crane and had the resources to move mountains. Figuratively, that is...we don't have mountains in Michigan.

Brent had purchased an entire house and hired Lila and Letty Woodville as caretakers so that unwanted geriatric collies would have a peaceful place to live. He had already adopted several dogs in distress, the latest one, Nova, only last Christmas. I left him a voice mail, inviting him to dinner, and sat at the kitchen table to plan my menu. Brent loved whatever I cooked or baked, but I wanted this meal to be special.

I took a roast out of the freezer and baked a chocolate angel food cake. I had a quart of fresh strawberries to make a sauce for it. For a side dish, I assembled the ingredients for ambrosia, a rich concoction I only make on holidays.

We hadn't seen Brent in ages. I'll admit I was curious about how he was dealing with his competition for Annica's attention. I hadn't seen Annica in a while either. This evening should be informative and, I hoped, successful.

With the roast in the oven and the collies cared for, I set aside time for myself to continue reading Evanora's diary.

EVANORA'S DIARY

JOY—Finally the rain stopped. The earth couldn't have looked greener and more beautiful. Everything smelled like perfume. I took Honey and slipped into the woods when Sara was visiting a friend and Mom was shut away from the world in her sewing room. I waited for Ned by the little stream. I knew he was on his way when Honey started barking and ran back toward the road.

He had a pink flower in his hands.

"It reminded me of you," he said.

I took it, avoiding the thorns on the long stem. It was pink, not red, but still a symbol of love.

"Did you find it in the woods?" I asked.

"Nearby. Your neighbor has bushes of them covering her fence."

And she didn't like them disturbed. Obviously, she hadn't seen Ned steal one.

I thanked him, and he smiled.

Ned is all brightness, like sunshine after rain. Even with his black, black hair, he's positively radiant. He has those marvelous cornflower blue eyes. They're as bright as the sky.

He sat beside me on the blanket I'd spread on the ground and said, "I hoped you'd be here today."

"I was so tired of staying inside," I said. "I thought it would never stop raining."

"It did. It always does. Do you have a kiss for me?"

"Many," I said. "I've been saving them."

How lonely these past days have been without Ned. For the next several moments, all was right with my world.

Later, I said, "My mother would like you to come to dinner."

He hesitated. Then he said, "To dinner? At your house?"

"Sunday dinner with us. This Sunday. We're going to bake blueberry pies for dessert."

"Okay," he said.

I must have imagined that hesitation.

"This Sunday at two o'clock sharp," I said. "We eat dinner early on the weekends."

He pulled me into his arms then and time stopped.

How can I wait until Sunday?

GLUMDAY—Two o'clock sharp. Everything was ready for Ned. I had my mint green dress on again and had washed my hair. I thought I looked pretty good.

Two o'clock came and went.

I said, "He's running late."

A half hour passed. Two-thirty.

I ignored Sara, who was pretending that everything was all right when it was all wrong.

"Did you give him the right address?" Dad asked.

He must have forgotten that Ned had been here before to get rid of the bat.

"He knows it," I said.

Two o'clock sharp. This Sunday.

Honey was whining. She had been banished to the kitchen because of the company. Company that didn't come.

"I'm hungry," Sara said, taking a slice of ham from the platter.

"We'll wait a little longer," Mom said. "The pies turned out good, didn't they?"

No one answered her.

Three o'clock.

I kept telling myself that Ned would be here any minute now. He'd knock on the door. I'd let him in. He'd have a legitimate excuse. He was an officer of the law. Maybe someone had been murdered. He'd bring flowers for Mother.

My thoughts were all jumbled together. I was terribly disappointed, but also humiliated. Time marched on. There was no way to stop it.

Evanora's boyfriend can't be bothered to show up for dinner or even call. That's what they were all thinking.

"He's not coming," Dad said. "I say we eat."

So we did. The ham was too salty. I cut it in small pieces and pushed it around on my plate.

"Eat your dinner, Evanora," Mom said.

"I am."

I could have wept when Mom brought in the pie and cut a nice large slice for everybody.

"I don't want any," I said.

If I took another bite of anything, I'd be sick.

Always one to seize an opportunity, Sara said, "Give me her piece." Then she said, "He probably forgot, Eva. Or he misunderstood. Sometimes you're unclear and you speak too softly."

"That may be it," I said.

But I didn't believe her, and I didn't mean what I said.

Twenty-four

After that day, after Ned had humiliated her in front of her family, how would Evanora feel about him? Angry, I supposed. At their next meeting, she would likely confront him, demanding to know why he had failed to honor his commitment. Would he have an excuse? Would she forgive him?

In her place, would I?

It would depend on his reason.

The idea came to me suddenly, unbidden and unsuspected. Could it be Evanora who haunted the Valentine House rather than the child who had died young? Of course, then, Evanora would be a spirit revisiting the place where she was once happy.

'Don't go.'

A lonely spirit.

"That's it," I said.

Misty tilted her head, looking at me with a question in her lovely dark eyes. 'That's what?' she might have asked.

"The answer," I said, and I knew I would return to the house in the woods as soon as I could, with or without Annica.

I glanced at the clock, checked the roast and the dogs and read on:

EVANORA'S DIARY

AFTERWARD—I don't know how I managed to sit through that dinner. Nobody said anything about Ned standing me up. Mother said, "We'll have ham sandwiches all week, and there's half a pie left."

Sara and I washed dishes and dried them. Dad read the Free Press. *Mother went upstairs to her sewing room. It was a typical Sunday afternoon.*

If the day had gone as it should have, Ned would still be here visiting with us after dinner. Mother would have been able to question him discreetly. Dad... He'd have been less discreet. Sara would have flirted with him. She can't help herself. At some point, Ned would ask me if I wanted to go for a walk. We would take Honey walking up or down the lane but not into the woods.

When the kitchen was clean, I went to my room and read more of the book I'd started last night. Eventually the clouds rolled in, and it started to rain again. The thunder was so loud and strong, it made me weep.

~ * ~

Evanora didn't see Ned for some days after that disastrous Sunday dinner. She expected him to get in touch with her on Monday to explain why he had failed to come to dinner.

He didn't. She had never given him her telephone number. Why would she when they met in the woods? By Tuesday, she had to accept that she wouldn't see him, but that didn't stop her from gazing at the lane from her bedroom window watching for a police cruiser to pass by or maybe stop.

She convinced herself there had been a murder in Foxglove Corners that Ned had to deal with.

~ * ~

EVANORA'S DIARY

AFTERWARD, continued—Will I ever see Ned again? Do I want to?

Yes, yes, a resounding yes. It can't end like this—in silence. I have to know why he did this to me.

Let's say that a person was murdered on Sunday afternoon. The case must be taking up all his time. He can't spare a stolen hour in the woods with a girl.

So I keep telling myself. Who knows? I may be right.

Sara is the practical one.

"Quit moping around, Eva. So your boyfriend stood you up. It happens. There are other fish in the sea. Pretend you don't care. Put a smile on your face and do something constructive."

"I <u>don't</u> care," I said.

"I don't believe you." Then she said, "I think there was some mix-up."

"What kind of mix-up could there possibly be?"

I really wanted to know.

She shrugged. "Some kind. You can always invite him to dinner again. Another Sunday."

"No, I can't."

I won't. I won't go through that again. Never. All the anticipation, all the preparation, all the hope. All for nothing. Never again.

But the days are so lonely without Ned's company to look forward to.

Sara said, "Zane and I are going to the beach tomorrow. He has a friend. Let's go on a double date. We never did that. Okay?"

"Not okay," I said. "I'm not in the mood."

To squeeze into a swimsuit and get all wet and full of sand. I don't like lying in the sun. I don't want to meet this friend of Zane's. He won't be Ned. I want to walk in the cool, quiet woods and meet Ned by the stream. That's all I want.

SARA—Today Sara said, "I could kill that man for what he did to you."

Was I that transparent? I thought I was hiding my feelings well.

"He didn't do anything to me," I told her.

"He stole every bit of the joy you used to have. You never go walking in the woods anymore. You don't bring wildflowers home. You don't even pay attention to Honey. You're not you. I miss my sister."

I started crying then. Not for Ned. Not this time. I never heard Sara say anything so heartfelt to me.

She was right. Ned had stolen all my joy. How could I have let a man do this to me?

~ * ~

"Because you loved him," I said. I was close to tears myself. Poor Evanora. With Ned, she had walked on clouds. What a long fall to earth!

The next pages were similar in content and tone. A week passed. Long days without Ned. She wrote, *The only acceptable excuse is that he's dead.*

Evanora resigned herself to the fact that she might never see him again. At the same time, she thought that would be unlikely. Foxglove Corners was a small place. Sooner or later she would run into him. Then, what would she say? What would he say?

Evanora wanted, above all, to go back in time to those happy days when Ned was a part of her life and anything was possible. She wrote a single line on one page: *I know a bank where the wild thyme blows.*

Eventually, I tired of her rambling. One can only take so much drama. I closed the diary, tossed a salad, and set the table for three. Crane came home. I told him we were having company.

By the time Brent arrived, I had left Evanora's world and her lost romance far behind. I was a hostess with an agenda.

Over dinner, I told Brent about Brownie, breaking my rule that banned distressing conversation at the table. It wouldn't be distressful if Brent agreed to help.

He did. I knew I could count on him.

"I think I know who might consider adopting a good dog," he said. "Jeff at my barn just bought a small farm. Jeff is devoted to my dogs, especially Nova."

"Take him to see Brownie," I said. "Now that Brownie's in the shelter's care, Jeff will have to fill out an application and wait."

"That's all right. He hasn't moved yet. Where did you take the dog, Sheriff?"

Crane told him. "I hated to leave him there. They're filled almost to capacity. They put him in a cage..."

"Let's hope it's just temporary," I said.

If Jeff and Brownie were a match, Brownie's future would be ensured. What dog wouldn't thrive on a farm? And I felt Jeff would be an excellent owner.

We ate our cake in the living room where Crane had built a fire. Brent seemed uncharacteristically quiet. I poured steaming hot coffee for us and said, "Is Colton Reeves still in the picture?"

"Reeves. That sneaky Texan. I saw him at Clovers the other day. He asked me if Annica and I were in a relationship. In a relationship," he repeated, affecting a drawl.

"What did you tell him?"

"That yes, we were, so he'd better stop bringing her flowers."

"He brought her flowers?"

"Red roses. He always gives her roses."

I made a mental note to see Annica as soon as I could. Maybe we'd have a Clovers dinner tomorrow.

Seeing that Brent was getting agitated, I asked if he'd like more cake. "How about you, Crane?" I added.

They both did. I cut two more slices, doused them with strawberry sauce, and served them. Brent broke off a piece with his fork and frowned.

"It's my fault," he said.

Twenty-five

"What's your fault?" I asked. "The situation with Annica and Colton Reeves?"

Brent's frown deepened. "There *is* no Annica and Colton. It's Annica and *Brent*. No, I'm talking about all the strays in Foxglove Corners. There are more of them than ever. They used to have a safe place to go when Lila and Letty ran the shelter. Then I hired them away for the caretaker's job at my collie house, and they had to close the shelter."

"Wait," I said. "That was *not* your fault. They would have had to close it when Major March died anyway."

"Foxglove Corners needs a shelter of its own where all breeds are welcome."

"I won't argue with that," Crane said.

I scooped up the last crumbs from my plate with my fork. Brent had fallen silent again, but it was a good thoughtful silence. He needed a project he could undertake with all his heart. I had an idea there would soon be a new animal shelter in Foxglove Corners, maybe even in the old white Victorian on Park Street which was for sale. As for

Brownie, he might well have a new owner and a small farm to call home.

"How can we find out who's dumping these dogs?" he asked.

"Catch him in the act," Crane said.

Which was easier said than done. On the other hand, I had almost done it before, but I'd been seconds too late, and too far to see the man's face clearly. Apparently the only suspect had slipped out of the law's net.

"Going back to Colton," I said, "what did he say when you told him you and Annica were in a relationship?"

"A dumb quotation. All's fair in love and war."

"He's a jerk. But it's up to Annica to put a stop to his overtures."

"No, it's up to me."

That sounded ominous. I hoped Brent would focus on creating a new shelter for the strays of Foxglove Corners. Colton Reeves was a definite problem, but I said a silent prayer he would go back to Texas.

~ * ~

Annica didn't appear to know about the testy exchange between Brent and Colton, and I didn't enlighten her. I *did* notice the fresh roses on the counter, though. A dozen in each of the two vases. They were yellow, a sunny spring color.

The yellow rose of Texas.

Marcy was preparing my dinner order of roasted chicken, mashed potatoes, and apple pie, while Annica and I drank hot chocolate. I kept one eye on the clock. Leonora and I had been delayed at Marston by a short English meeting, but I didn't want to postpone my visit to Clovers.

"Mary Jeanne appreciates the free decor," Annica said. "We're about to turn green for Saint Patrick's Day. I wonder if Colton will send me green carnations."

"Is your Texan still making a nuisance of himself?" I asked.

"I wouldn't go that far. He gives me flowers regularly and invites me to go out with him. I refuse...politely, of course. It's a never-ending cycle. He showed me pictures of his ranch," she added. "It's really quite impressive."

"The C Bar R?"

She laughed. "I thought he'd live in a regular house, maybe one with Spanish styling."

"Are you sure the ranch belongs to him?" I asked.

"That's what he said."

"Because I wonder why he's in Michigan if he owns a ranch in Texas."

"He's doing something with batteries," she said.

I remembered she had told me that before.

"How long is he staying?"

"I don't know. I don't want to seem curious because then he'll think I care." She glanced around as if to make certain Colton Reeves hadn't come through the door. "Let's drop it, Jennet."

"I guess you haven't been tempted to accept one of his offers, then," I said.

"I have not. I *am* busy, you know."

"Too busy to go for a hike in the woods with me?"

"You want to go back to the Valentine House?"

"I'd like to explore it again, from a different perspective," I said. "I think the house may be haunted and not by Cecily, the little girl who used to play there."

I summarized what I'd read of Evanora's diary for her. "Evanora and Ned used to meet at the house. Their relationship hit a snag."

"A woodland tryst," she murmured. "What kind of snag?"

"Evanora invited him to dinner with her family, but he didn't show up. She hasn't seen him since."

Annica stared at me. "You sound like this just happened. How old is the diary?"

"Old enough that the pages are yellowish," I said. "But when I'm reading it, it all seems so immediate."

Annica swirled the mini-marshmallows around her cup. "Something like that happened to me once. I invited a man I liked to dinner. He didn't show up, didn't call. Nothing. The next time I saw him he called me 'Pat.' After that, I forgot about him."

She spoke of the incident lightly. Evanora had been devastated. Well, each relationship is different, and Annica and Evanora lived in different times. Their personalities were quite different.

"Would you like to go with me to the house?" I asked. "It'll have to be after school or on a weekend."

"Sure, but what makes you think the place is haunted? We didn't find anything there."

"I just have a feeling," I said.

I almost mentioned the dream I'd had…days ago now. A scarf on the table. A forgotten glove. A picnic basket on the floor. Voices just beyond my ability to hear them.

And something else that had happened on our last visit. A plea that I might have imagined.

'Don't go!'

Something in the house had called to me. It was time I responded to it.

~ * ~

That evening while Crane leafed through the *Banner*, I bypassed the perfectly good Gothic novel I'd been reading and reached for Evanora's diary. Rosalind would have to stay in the insane asylum to which her evil husband had committed her—for now, anyway. I found my place in the diary and read:

EVANORA'S DIARY

SEQUEL—I met Ned again. Not by accident. He was driving his patrol car on the lane. He stopped in front of Mrs. Baker's house. Honey greeted him as if he were a long-lost friend. I was more circumspect. I think.

He leaned on the fence, an incongruous figure in uniform against a background of pink roses.

"How are you this fine day?" he asked.

Was he talking to Honey or to me? I thought about pretending I was fine, that everything was fine, but I couldn't.

"We missed you on Sunday," I said.

"Sunday?" He looked genuinely confused.

"For Sunday dinner, at my house," I said. "We were expecting you. We even baked fresh blueberry pies."

I told myself to stop babbling and let him explain.

"Was that this past Sunday?" he asked. "I'm sorry, Evanora. They've been keeping me busy. There've been burglaries in town. I have my eye on the ring leaders."

"No one got murdered then?"

"Reine's Jewelers in Lakeville was robbed. They were closed at the time. That was one busy day. How can I make it up to you?" he asked.

You can't, I thought.

"I could take you out to eat. I know a place where they have the best ribs in Lakeville."

"Maybe," I said. "Some time. Won't you still be busy catching burglars?"

"I have days off," he said.

I wasn't ready to forgive him. I certainly wouldn't forget and wouldn't trust him in the future. It should be easy to find out if Reine's Jewelers had suffered a break-in. Then I would know if he was lying, but I wouldn't know why.

He was waiting for my answer. I'd waited for him on Sunday. How could he make it up to Mom who had worked so hard to cook a special dinner for my gentleman caller? How could he erase the humiliation I'd felt?

"I'll see," I said. "Maybe we can do that."

Twenty-six

"Lord, what fools these mortals be," I said.

Evanora's whimsical idea of an enchanted woodland reminded me of that quotation from *A Midsummer Night's Dream*. I could almost see Puck peering out from behind his mushroom at the naive young girl. "Let us their fond pageant see." He would sit back and enjoy the spectacle of the woodland lovers.

Both Crane and Misty looked at me. I didn't realize I'd spoken out loud.

Crane looked up from his paper. "What did you say, Jennet?"

"Evanora," I said. "She's heading for a fall."

Crane smiled. "Don't you mean 'headed'?"

"Her story is gripping. It seems real to me."

I flipped through the pages. They were filled with writing. I had a lot still to read. Good.

EVANORA'S DIARY

THE EXCUSE—I'm giving Ned the benefit of a doubt. I went through back issues of the paper. Reine's Jewelers was robbed on

Sunday. They lost their entire collection of diamond engagement and wedding rings. So Ned <u>was</u> busy, as he said. But why didn't he call to tell me? I asked him. He said he didn't know my phone number.

I gave it to him, but I didn't invite him to another dinner.

A little later, I remembered his initial confusion. 'Was that this past Sunday?' So was he busy or had he forgotten? Maybe he had never planned to show up.

Sara saw us talking together. "I can't believe you forgave him," she said.

I told her about the robbery. "He's a policeman. His duty comes first."

"He isn't a detective, though. Doesn't he just drive around and give tickets?"

"And stops if he comes across a crime in progress," I said.

"Is that what happened last Sunday?"

"He didn't say that. Not exactly."

"What did happen then?" she wanted to know.

"He said he was busy. Please don't worry about me, Sara. I know what I'm doing."

"I hope so," she said. "I don't want to see you hurt again."

~ * ~

The meetings at the Valentine House continued. Evanora chose to leave that ill-fated Sunday dinner in the past. She decided to tread warily but enjoy her time with Ned, every stolen hour. In the meantime, she would guard her heart.

That was her plan. However, wrapped in the spell of the magical woods, safe and warm in Ned's embrace, inevitably she forgot her resolve. She was in love with Ned. Surely he loved her, too, and surely the summer would go on forever.

When you are young and in love, reality melts away.

~ * ~

EVANORA'S DIARY

APRIL—Who would think a humble country store would be the scene of drama? I'm the one who buys milk and coffee and bread for sandwiches. I've grown used to Maybelle's hostility. She doesn't even return my cheerful good mornings. So I just tell her what I need, pay, and leave.

While I was there today, a woman came in. She was tall with long red hair and freckles. She hardly wore any makeup. I smiled at her. She frowned and looked away. Why are people so unfriendly in Foxglove Corners? Sara never complains, and Mom rarely goes out, but I wonder. Maybe it's just me.

Maybelle greeted her warmly, the first time I've seen her in a good mood. She said, "How can I help you today, April?"

"I want something to hold me over till dinnertime."

"Does Ned know you're back in town?"

"Not yet, but he will."

April? Another one of Ned's (former) girlfriends? I thought her name was Delilah.

I wished I had an excuse to stay. I could have said I'd forgotten something essential...like mustard. But I didn't think that fast. Does April know about me and Ned?

THE GIFT—What a wonderful surprise I had today! It's my birthday. I can't imagine how Ned found out. He had a present for me, still in its bag from Reine's Jewelers.

He said, "I saw this and thought you'd like it."

Inside the tissue paper I found a beautiful little music box. It has a Cupid sitting in blue flowers on top. Above his head is an inscription: 'Truly Thine.' For a moment, I couldn't speak. Truly thine. Was that Ned's special message for me?

"Do you like it?" he asked.

"I love it," I said. "It's so beautiful. What does it play?"

"Let's see."

He turned the key, and a sweet melody floated out into the air. I didn't recognize it. That doesn't matter. It can play "Stars and Stripes Forever" for all I care. I'll keep it until I die.

Mom baked a cake and I had presents to open at dinner that night, mostly clothes, but Ned's present was the highlight of my birthday, this wonderful gift from Ned.

He is truly mine. I don't have to doubt his fidelity any longer. Ever again.

THE MELODY—Alone in my room, I listen to the music box's tune over and over again. It's sort of familiar, but I can't identify it. It's Ned's song. Ned's message to me. Truly Thine.

Gradually, though, it comes to me that the delicate fairy notes have a sad sound. Like Greensleeves, but not quite.

Ned must care for me to give me such a special present. And how did he know today was my birthday? He won't say.

~ * ~

On the way home from Marston the next day, Leonora and I stopped at Dark Gables to visit Lucy. I had so much to tell her—about the Valentine House, the old diary, the music box—everything, and a request to make.

When I finished bringing Lucy up to date, I said, "Annica and I are going to hike out to the house in the woods tomorrow. Would you like to come with us?"

Lucy hesitated, her look reinforcing her response. "In the woods? In the mud? Tomorrow?"

"That's what I said. I suspect I've found another haunted house, and I'd like to know if you sense anything out of the ordinary there."

"I'm not exactly an outdoor sort of person," she said.

"You can wear your winter boots, and I'll help you when the walking gets rough."

I had a fleeting image of Lucy in her long black dress, making her way across the debris of the deteriorating structures and fallen branches. Lucy and the woods of the abandoned construction site weren't compatible, even in boots, even with a helping arm.

She waited for a few minutes before answering. "Let's compromise. You and Annica go alone tomorrow. If you still feel the house is haunted, I'll accompany you the next time and give you my input."

I was disappointed but had to accept her decision.

"Now do you ladies have time for a cup of tea?" she added.

I glanced at Leonora, who shook her head.

"Another time, Lucy," I said. "We're running late."

"I wish you'd reconsider involving yourself in this particular matter," she said. "I remember the last time you investigated a haunted house. You fell down the stairs. We thought we'd lost you."

Yes, the stairs at the house on Loosestrife Lane. I'd literally fallen into the life of the spirit who haunted the halls of Brent's collie house. I certainly didn't want to repeat that experience.

"A sadness hangs over the house, but I've never felt threatened."

'Don't go!' the (imagined?) voice had said. Not *'Go away!'*

"I'll be all right."

"Just be careful," she said. "Very, very careful."

"I will. The house consists of two large rooms, one on top of the other. There isn't much room for a misstep."

"It has a staircase, of course," Lucy added.

"Of course."

One with an unstable banister, but she didn't have to know that.

"I'm not even sure Evanora has passed on," I said. "She might well be married to her Ned and a grandmother by now."

With the diary long since forgotten.

Did I believe that?

"Are you going with Jennet and Annica, Leonora?" Lucy asked.

"I wasn't invited."

"You know you're welcome to come," I said quickly.

She smiled. "I'll let you know."

"Just be careful," Lucy repeated.

"I will," I said, "but really, nothing is going to go wrong."

Twenty-seven

The next morning Annica brought a half dozen hot cross buns from Clovers to fortify us for our visit to the Valentine House. We drank our tea and tried to ignore the dogs' pleading stares. They knew our buns were better than their biscuits.

"Have you finished reading Evanora's diary?" she asked.

"Not yet."

"Why not? You're an English teacher. You have to be a fast reader."

"I am, but…"

"How long can it be?"

I should have finished the diary in two or three evenings, but somehow I found myself constantly stopping to think about what I'd read. Then real life cut rudely into my leisure time. Household chores. Collies to take care of. Sleep. School. Reading of any kind fell to the bottom of the list.

It seemed that no matter how many pages I read, there were always ten times as many more. It was as if they replicated themselves. At this rate, I could never reach the end.

What utter nonsense! Did I have an enchanted diary now?

"I keep getting interrupted," I said.

"Can you at least tell me what's happening in Evanora's life?"

I nodded. "Ned is back in her good graces. He gave her a music box for her birthday. It's the very music box I bought at the Green House."

"Shades of the *Twilight Zone*," Annica said. "Now you have Evanora's diary and her birthday present."

"And we're about to visit the house where she and Ned used to meet."

"It's uncanny," she said.

"Yes, and it frightens me—a little."

"We're on the verge of an exciting new mystery." Annica reached for another bun and scraped off the lemon cross with her knife. "I wish Lucy had agreed to go with us."

"She will the next time, if we find evidence of supernatural activity."

"You mean a ghost," Annica said. "I hope we do."

~ * ~

Spring trembled in the air. It was almost time for her grand entrance, but traces of snow lingered in the woods where the sun couldn't reach. It was cold, but the stream had begun to thaw. Along its bank, the modest burst of pale yellow proved to be early daffodils. Very early. I hoped they wouldn't freeze.

The woods were indeed magical.

The Valentine heart between the house's twin gables had a dull shine in the weak sunlight. It appeared to beckon to us.

"Evanora's house," Annica murmured. "What a tale it could tell."

At some point, I had stopped thinking about the little girl for whom the house had been built. This was the secret meeting place of Evanora and Ned. If Evanora had passed on, it made sense that her spirit would haunt the place where she had been happy.

We would look for a ghost then.

Not that I expected to see a mint green wraith flitting up the stairs. But I thought I would know if something of Evanora remained behind.

An odd thought came to me. What if there were *two* ghosts— Evanora's and the child's? Would they be aware of each other? Would they possibly collide on the stairs?

We stood in the middle of the room, Annica searching the shadows in the corners while I listened for the voice I had heard before.

"We're here," I said for the benefit of the voice.

Silence.

I walked over to that part of the room in which a table had stood. A table with a scarf flung carelessly across it. A glove without a mate. In my dream.

"It's cold in here," Annica said. "Do ghosts feel the cold, I wonder?"

That comment didn't require a response. Still, I said, "If they did, they'd find a warmer place to hang out."

If only Lucy had come with us. She would have an explanation for the sense of unease that began imperceptibly to coil around my body.

"I feel like I've been here before," I said.

"You *have*," Annica reminded me. "We both have."

"Before that," I said.

The coil strengthened. It told a tale of loss and all aloneness. *Hath me bereft...*

"I think Ned abandoned Evanora," I said. "He did it quietly, without fanfare. One afternoon he kissed her, then walked back through the woods to the lane, never to return."

At that moment, my imagined sequence was as real as any scene in a movie.

'Don't go,' she had said.

But he went. He didn't look back.

I thought it might have happened that way. And after he was gone, when she knew he wouldn't return, she came to the house in the woods and remembered all that had transpired within its walls. Perhaps she wrote in her diary. And she waited.

"There's nothing down here," Annica said. "Let's check out the upper story."

~ * ~

Up the staircase. Hearing the ominous creak of a board. Reaching for the banister a moment before remembering it was loose.

We were there, level with the branches of the tree framed by the window.

"Brrr." Annica crossed her arms in front of her chest. "It's even colder up here. I read that a cold spot indicates a ghost is present."

She moved to the window, away from the spot. "It's still cold."

"Well, it's March," I pointed out. "And there's no source of heat in the house."

"Lack of foresight."

"I don't think a child would use a playhouse in the wintertime."

Or a pair of lovers.

Perhaps by the winter in Evanora's time, her love affair with Ned was over.

'Don't go.'

I heard it clearly. A low-pitch voice that might have originated downstairs. Or in another part of the room. I couldn't tell.

"Did you say something, Annica?" I asked.

"This window sill is covered with mold. Ugh. And these curtains. They're only fit for the trash."

I looked down at my right boot. A square of material slightly larger than a postage stamp adhered to the toe. It was light green in color. Mint green.

Where did it come from? And when?

I picked it up and held it in my palm. It was cold. Like an ice cube.

Evanora had left something of herself behind on one of those long-ago summer days.

No! The tiny scrap wasn't here the last time we stepped inside this room. I would swear to it.

Then...

She's here. Now. Wanting us to know she's returned.

I showed Annica the scrap of material. "Lucy will be coming with us the next time."

"Where did that come from?" she asked.

"My question exactly."

"Did you step on it outside? Bring it in on your boot?"

"I think we both know the answer to that. Evanora wore a dress she made to one of her trysts with Ned. It was this color. Mint green."

Annica stared at the material. "She tore her dress?"

"Possibly." Brushing against the jagged edge of—something.

"But you don't think so?"

"I don't know. If she lost it outside, wouldn't it have been swept away by the wind or washed away in the rain?"

"You'd think so. If it was outside. Could we have missed it when we were here before?"

"No. We went over every inch of this house."

"That's creepy. Maybe a squirrel or bird carried it in from outside."

"Possibly, but unlikely."

"Then we really do have a mystery," Annica said. "Not that I ever doubted it."

I slipped the scrap of material into my pocket. One would think that, having given us this sign, Evanora would take another step. Would show herself. But there was no indication of a spirit. We were alone in this icy shell of a house.

"Let's go home," Annica said.

I was suddenly overcome with a sense of confusion and pain. The emotions weren't my own. I wanted to escape them, to feel the cold and damp of the March woods, to shelter in my own home with my beloved collies around me. Ghost hunting was nerve-wracking.

Annica was already descending the staircase, rather hurriedly for safety. I followed, expecting to hear the poignant entreaty, 'Don't go' again, but the house was silent.

Twenty-eight

All the way home, all through the woods of the abandoned construction site and on the lane, strong emotions of sorrow and confusion followed me. They weren't my own, and that was unsettling.

The weather matched my mood. It had turned colder. The sky was a dull gray, and bloated clouds promised rain or snow.

Annica was uncharacteristically quiet. I imagined she was plagued by similar feelings, but when I questioned her, she admitted to being frightened by whatever lingered in the Valentine House.

"It's an unhappy spirit," she said. "Do you think it intends to harm us?"

"Heavens, no. Why should she? We don't pose a threat to her."

"You're reading her diary. That's intrusive."

"Yes, but why would she care now? She's probably dead. It's the only way we can know what happened to her. I think she wants that."

"You may be right."

I hoped I was. "Secrets don't keep in the afterlife."

"That scrap of material you found puzzles me," Annica said. "Where did it come from?" She waved her hand in a space above her head. "If it was torn from Evanora's dress, how did it get from there to here?"

"I like your idea of a bird or squirrel bringing it inside," I said. "and maybe the material didn't come from Evanora's dress after all. But I don't think that's what happened."

"Then what did?"

"That's part of our mystery. It's easy to get a stain on clothing or have a seam come apart," I said. "Maybe Evanora didn't even realize what had happened."

Or maybe she did. Find the answer in the diary.

"It might have been part of an entire scene that, for now, is hidden from us,' I said.

"It's important, isn't it?"

"I think so. Besides, it's our only clue."

Well, there was the diary, the most important of clues. Tonight after dinner I intended to read more of what Evanora had written. If it were possible to find answers to the questions that eluded us, the diary would be the place to look.

By now, the yellow Victorian and my own green Victorian farmhouse were in sight, and I could hear dogs barking. Slowly the emotions I'd carried with me had dissipated. Once I was home, dealing with ordinary chores and events, I suspected they'd be gone.

But I knew I'd soon return to the Valentine House. Its hold on me was strong and undeniable. It didn't intend to let me go.

~ * ~

There's nothing like a hale and hearty man to dispel the darkest of otherworldly shadows. Brent fairly radiated with energy and enthusiasm. With Brent-ness.

That evening, he asked what I was cooking, handed me a bag from Pluto's Gourmet Pet Shop, and dropped into the rocker. The collies gathered around him, Misty claiming the place of honor in his lap.

"Great news," he said. "I bought the house on Park Street for a new all-breed shelter. Now all I need is a caretaker."

I had expected Brent to make his new project a reality, but hadn't thought he'd act so soon. Still, I was delighted to hear that the old white Victorian would be a safe haven for all the town's foundlings again.

"There's one drawback," he added. "I had the devil's own time finding someone for the collie house before I thought of Letty and Lila Woodville."

That idea had been mine, but it was irrelevant. Brent had interviewed several people for the lucrative position of caretaker. Not one was remotely suitable. Then Fate stepped in. The Woodville sisters were about to lose their home after the death of their primary benefactor. Moving to the house on Loosestrife Lane to take care of Brent's geriatric collies was the best solution for everyone.

"The ladies left the house in tip-top shape," Brent said. "There's a fenced yard and the park across the street. It's an ideal location."

"It always was. I miss hearing dogs barking when I go to the library."

"But where am I going to find my caretaker?" he asked.

I said, "You can advertise in the *Banner*. You're offering free room and board and, I assume, a good salary."

"I am. With benefits. I want the very best for the dogs. But that's what I did before, and all the loonies in town turned up on my doorstep."

"Then be innovative. You want to attract the right kind of person. Ask Doctor Foster if you can post a flyer in the animal hospital. Or, better still, I'll talk to Sue Appleton. Maybe one of our Rescue League members would be interested."

If I didn't have my own happy place in life, I would be interested myself. Park Street was, as Brent said, an ideal location, with the library and a whole block of elegant vintage Victorians as neighbors, not to mention the woodsy park across the street.

I imagined Brent would have plenty of applicants lining up for the chance to manage the new shelter.

"How's Brownie doing?" Crane wanted to know.

"He fit right in. He's so smart and grateful for any attention. I don't know how anyone could abandon him. As soon as Jeff moves to the farm, Brownie will have his own acres to play in."

"If only all cast-off dogs could have kind new owners."

"That," Brent said, "is my goal. The new shelter will be a halfway home. Thanks for the suggestions, Jennet," he added. "Now tell me. What have you been up to?"

"Annica and I visited the Valentine House today," I said. "I found a scrap of cloth."

"Is that so unusual?

"In this case, yes."

I told him the rest, including my belief that the spirit of Evanora haunted the house. "I don't know her last name. It may be Sherbourne."

"You're becoming obsessed with that house," Brent said.

"Not really. At the moment, it's just a fascinating mystery."

Privately, though, I agreed with him, although 'obsessed' was too strong a word for what I felt.

"I'd like to check it out," he said

"Go ahead. You won't be trespassing, as far as I can tell."

"Does the property belong to the developer?" Crane asked.

"I assume so."

"Don't worry about him then, Fowler. He won't dare show his face in Foxglove Corners."

If he did, he would have to deal with the unfinished development in some way—-either raze the structures or rebuild them. As he had gone bankrupt, I didn't see that happening.

"I know you love mysteries," Brent said. "But exactly why do you find this one so fascinating?"

"I feel a connection to Evanora. We're alike in some ways."

"I hope you're not meeting a handsome policeman in the woods," Crane said, trying for a stern tone and failing. We both knew the idea was ludicrous.

I said, "Here's one similarity. Ned Douglas is a policeman. You're a deputy sheriff."

Brent's eyes sparkled. "You've really thought about this. What else?"

"I'm an English teacher. Evanora loved her English classes. We both discovered the house in the woods and wondered about it. We both have dogs—but Evanora hasn't mentioned Honey lately—and I bought her music box and diary. Green is my favorite color, too."

Mint green.

I showed them the scrap of material safely stashed in the drawer of a side table.

"It came in a mysterious way," I said. "I looked down and there it was stuck to my boot. You might say it materialized."

"Does Lucy have any ideas about why your ghost chose such an isolated place to haunt?" Crane asked.

"She hasn't seen the house yet. She'll go with us the next time."

"I want to go, too," Brent said, sounding like a little boy who didn't want to be left out of an adventure.

At that moment, Candy nudged me, and I remembered my roast. "If you gentlemen will excuse me, I'll check on dinner," I said.

And afterward, when Brent had gone home and the kitchen was back in order, I would have time to read more installments of Evanora's diary. Perhaps I'd discover another way in which she and I were alike.

Twenty-nine

EVANORA'S DIARY

A PERFECT DAY—Today was perfect in every way. Ned and I had a picnic in the woods by the stream. I packed a basket with fried chicken, strawberries, and lemonade. Mom was in bed with a headache so she didn't know what I was doing in the kitchen. Not so Sara.

"You're not meeting Ned again, are you?" she asked.

"Maybe," I said.

"Eva, what are you doing?"

"Being happy."

"This isn't right," she said.

"I think it is."

"Okay, but what would Dad think?"

"It's my life."

When everything was ready, I called Honey and we set out for the house in the woods. She ran ahead of me on a mission of her own, but when I reached the stream I didn't see her.

I spread the blanket on the grass and lay back to watch the puffy white clouds float by in the azure sky.

Would he come? Or would today be a repeat of that dreadful Sunday? I am always afraid something will go wrong, and I won't see him.

He was late, but he was there. Honey found him first and led him to the stream. He was surprised, happily so, I think, when he saw the picnic basket.

"I brought lunch," I said. "Fried chicken. My cousin Louise's recipe."

"Great!" he said.

"And fresh strawberries. I bought them at a stand, just up the lane. They're hot off the vine."

"How sweet," he said. "But they can't be as sweet as you." And he pulled me into his arms.

God's in his heaven. All's right with my world.

THE DREAM—It rained today. I stayed inside. Mom still has her headache, but she got dressed and disappeared into her sewing room. I don't know where Sara is. Nothing is happening. By that I mean I'm not seeing Ned. So I'll write about a dream I had. It bothered me. It was so real I remember every part of it, even now.

I was walking in the woods, carrying the picnic basket, when I came to the house. It looked different, old and tired, like a hundred years had passed since I last saw it. Usually it has a lovely glow, like a fairy house set down in an enchanted spot. Now even the heart between the gables was dull. Most puzzling of all, the ground was covered with snow.

I was suddenly inside, and the room was empty. Someone had stolen all the furniture and even my scarf that I left on the table and the glove I thought I lost! Just as suddenly, for this was a dream, I was on the second floor. It was like standing in ice. This room, too, had been cleared out.

I looked out the window and saw snow on the ground. The stream was frozen.

Had I somehow come to another house in the woods with a heart decoration on the front of it? Were there two of them, this one in hiding until now? It didn't seem possible, but what happened between then and now?

I was afraid. Where was Ned?

Then I heard a woman's voice: "She's probably dead."

That's all I remember of the dream.

THE DREAM AGAIN—I can't forget that horrible nightmare. What does it mean? Am I going to die? Is God going to punish me for loving Ned? But why would that be wrong? I'm not the first girl to wander into an enchanted forest and fall in love with a man who couldn't possibly be more perfect for her. And I do love Ned, with all my heart and soul. I think he loves me, but he never says so or talks about our future. I guess some men are like that.

Should I ask him? Not yet.

It's still raining. That means I can't meet Ned. Also I want to see if the house in the woods is changed like it was in my dream or if all the furniture is still there. If Ned is waiting for me by the stream. If everything is going to be all right. But I'll have to wait for another summer day.

~ * ~

Instead of turning the page, I read a certain line again: *Then I heard a woman's voice: "She's probably dead."*

Dear Lord. I'd said that when Annica had mentioned my reading Evanora's diary being intrusive. Could Evanora have traveled to the future in her dream and seen the Valentine House as it was today, all of the furniture gone, the ground outside covered with snow? It was too fantastic to contemplate.

So I told myself, but contemplate I did. Once in motion, my train of thought refused to stop. Had Evanora heard my voice in her dream? How was that possible? Could the walls have absorbed my words and tossed them back in time to her—in her dream?

Beyond fantastic!

What exactly had I said? Something about Evanora not caring that I read her diary because she was dead?

I could think of one explanation. The dream troubled her because, in her heart, she feared that one day Ned would leave her and never return. She couldn't imagine living her life without him.

I wished I could tell her that in all likelihood she would live on and find other loves. One day Ned would be only a memory with no more substance than a dream—if that. Because that was the way life worked. Like in the song from the musical *Oklahoma*: *A kiss gone by is bygone.*

Crane was quietly reading his paper. Misty lay at my feet asleep. I wanted to tell Crane about my new fear but decided not to. I wasn't even sure what to believe.

That in a dream Evanora had heard something I'd said earlier today? That I was a ghost of the future speaking in her past?

Fantastic, insisted my inner voice. *Consult Lucy, if you must. Don't obsess about something that couldn't possibly have happened.*

If I told Crane about my vague suppositions, he would undoubtedly insist I stay away from the Valentine House, and I didn't want to do that. But I had to discuss the matter with someone, and that person could only be Lucy.

She would understand, and, I hoped, would be able to advise me.

~ * ~

Fortunately the next day, school was relatively easy with cooperative students and lessons that provided momentarily respite from the fear that stayed with me even in the light of day.

How could Evanora have heard what I'd said to Annica? It defied the rules of logic.

"Would you mind if we stopped at Dark Gables on the way home?" I asked.

"Not at all. Let's do it. Jake is away this week."

Like me, Leonora had a kind neighbor who was happy to take care of her collies in her absence.

"Do you have any particular reason for wanting to see Lucy?" she wanted to know.

I must be transparent or Leonora knew me too well.

"There's something about the Valentine House that troubles me," I said.

When talking to Lucy, I would be more specific. I didn't want to verbalize my concerns twice.

"Maybe you should forget about it," she said. "A mystery shouldn't leach into your private life."

"This one does. I find I have a lot in common with Evanora."

I repeated the similarities I'd pointed out to Crane and Brent yesterday.

"Coincidences all," she said.

But she didn't seem convinced. And I didn't comment.

Thirty

I turned off Spruce Road and drove down the long, well-shaded driveway that led to Lucy's house. Mature conifers grew close together, forming a green-blue barrier that ensured Lucy's privacy and safety. Here she lived with her blue merle collie, Sky, and wrote horror stories for young people.

Dark Gables sat in a bleak surround of snow and woods. New additions were a life-sized stone statue of a sitting collie. It had a cheery grapevine wreath adorned with silk daffodils and jonquils around its neck, giving the porch a welcoming new look.

Lucy opened the door, as usual clad in a floaty black dress with gold chains and bracelets. Sky, the most mannerly of collies, stood at her side wagging her tail in a silent welcome. Visitors to Dark Gables were rare.

"I've been expecting you," Lucy said.

I was surprised, having decided on this visit at the last minute. "You have?"

"I've been thinking about you," she added. "I had a feeling you were in trouble."

"Oh, no," Leonora murmured.

"Or in over your head," Lucy added.

She led the way to her sun room in back. She had indeed been expecting me—and Leonora as well. Three teacups were set out on the coffee table, together with a pound cake which Sky, amazingly, ignored.

Lucy put the water on to boil. The cake was already sliced, and I could see it had candied cherries in it. Very festive indeed. All of a sudden, I was ravenous.

While we waited for our tea, I told Lucy and Leonora about my latest visit to the Valentine House and about the sentence in the diary that haunted me.

Throughout the tale, Lucy remained calm. "Surely you said more than, 'she's probably dead'."

"I've gone over and over that conversation. Annica had just mentioned that reading Evanora's diary was intrusive. I can't remember my exact words, but I think I pointed out that Evanora wouldn't mind my knowing her secrets, being dead."

I started as the teakettle whistled. It was new, and its voice was shriller than the one I was accustomed to. It was as if I'd forgotten we were waiting to hear it.

"Don't forget, Evanora was writing about her dream," Lucy said. "That voice may simply be an expression of what she feared on seeing the change in the playhouse. Deep down, she was afraid of losing Ned. From what you said, she keeps referring to the woods as enchanted and using fairy images to describe common objects."

"She was a romantic at heart. But there is something about those woods..."

I broke off, uncertain of the best way to describe their atmosphere without resorting to cliches like magical.

I said, "So I shouldn't be concerned?"

"I didn't say that. There's so much more to learn. What happened between Evanora and Ned in the end?"

"I haven't finished reading the diary," I admitted.

"Why not?"

I had no reason to give her except one. "That business about the voice frightened me."

"You *have* to know," Lucy said. "Keep reading and, whatever you do, don't insinuate yourself into Evanora's story. I agree with Leonora. All of these similarities are coincidental."

In my view, the similarities were too numerous to be insignificant.

As she brewed the tea, she added, "I'll be with you the next time you visit the house. The story has captured my interest, and I'm always up for investigating a haunting, especially if it's local."

"Not me," Leonora said. "I just want to be safe. I can hear about it after the fact. Jennet is the intrepid ghost hunter."

"Hardly. All I did was buy a pretty music box and some old series books."

Lucy handed each of us a cup of steaming tea. "Sometimes that's all it takes," she said.

~ * ~

I drove Leonora home and returned to my life with a lighter heart. After talking to Lucy, I felt a little better about reading the diary. She was right. I had to know what happened next in Evanora's life and how her romance with Ned ended—or flourished. I only hoped she continued to record its progress.

I remembered the fate of my own adventures in journaling— begun with enthusiasm but eventually abandoned. I flipped through the pages. of Evanora's diary. All were filled with writing except for the last pages.

I didn't allow myself to read ahead, though. *Day by day*, I thought. *Live Evanora's experiences vicariously and read slowly. Don't miss the slightest nuance.*

~ * ~

EVANORA'S DIARY

SUNSHINE AND SHADOWS—A cloudy day like today turns bright when I see Ned's face. I'm constantly amazed at how handsome he is. Like a god of the forest, he comes down to earth to consort with a mere mortal. Me.

I just read what I wrote. How corny! Simply said, when I'm with Ned, I'm happy. Only then. But our time together races by.

He finished his sandwich and started to get up. "I have to get back to work."

"Am I your coffee break?" I asked.

"You're my half hour of peace and sanity in this crazy world," he said. "The criminals and danger can't find us here in the woods."

"I pray you'll be safe out there," I said.

His serious mood changed, his moment of quiet introspection over. "Oh, I will. Foxglove Corners is a quiet little town. Besides, I'm invincible."

I wrapped the last piece of pie. "Take this with you," I said.

He gave me one last kiss and was gone.

IN THE STORE—We're always running out of milk and bread, and Sara is never around when it's time to go to the store. You'd think by now I'd be used to Maybelle's hostility. I've never understood why she dislikes me so much. It's more like she hates me.

Is it because I'm young and attractive with my whole life ahead of me while she's old and stuck working in a country store?

"Two loaves of white," I said, "one of cracked wheat, and a half gallon of milk."

She has apple walnut coffeecake today. I decided to add one to my order.

She rang up my items silently and, as usual, avoided making eye contact with me. The door opened and a black-haired woman in white stood there looking at me, then she stepped up to the counter. There was an instant change in Maybelle. She was all smiling and talkative. She called the newcomer Georgina.

I collected my change and listened.

"Are you back in Michigan to stay?" she asked.

"It depends on the climate, if you know what I mean."

"I do."

"He's like the spring wind. He blows hot, then cold."

"How true. What'll you have today?"

"A cup of your good coffee to go. I've missed it. And do I smell fresh doughnuts?"

"I just made a fresh pot—and yes, you do. How many?"

"Two."

Maybelle took off for the back room. Georgina read the headlines in the paper but didn't buy one. I left. What else could I do?

Could Georgina have been referring to Ned? Delilah, April, Georgina. How many former girlfriends does Ned have?

TROUBLE—Today Dad came in from taking Honey for a walk and said, "We need to talk, Eva. Sit down."

I could tell by his expression that whatever was coming wasn't good.

"I heard that you and this policeman, Ned Douglas, are spending time alone together in the woods."

"Who told you that?" I asked.

"It doesn't matter if it's true."

"Sara!"

He didn't answer.

"It doesn't look good, Eva. If you want to see him, you should invite him to visit you at home. Maybe even ask him to dinner again."

There was so much I wanted to say, so much I couldn't say.

"I sort of look on that old playhouse in the woods as my home."

He looked disappointed and angry.

"You know what I mean, Eva. You're my responsibility. I won't have you—compromised."

I wanted to laugh but was smart enough not to. "We're not living in Victorian times. Next you'll tell me I need a chaperone to be with my boyfriend."

"You're not even twenty-one yet. Just because all the young people in the country are abandoning their morals doesn't mean you have to. Bring your policeman friend home. We'll welcome him."

What could I say? "I will. I mean, I'll ask him."

Maybe Dad is right. I don't care what people think about me, except for Ned, but Dad cares. As for Sara, I'll get even with her for betraying me if it's the last thing I do.

Thirty-one

A combination of eight collies barking and a frantic pounding on the front door pulled me out of the murky spell cast by the diary.

The collies were gathered at the door, responding to the untoward noise in their peaceful afternoon. *Company! Friend or foe?*

A glance through the window revealed Sue Appleton's truck. How odd. At this time of day, she was usually busy with her equestrian students.

Quickly I marked my page and hurried to the door. Sue's right hand stalled in mid-air, prepared to knock again. In her left arm she cradled a dark brown puppy. The pup was trembling uncontrollably, pretty dark eyes glazed in fear.

"What on earth?"

"She isn't a collie, but this babe is in distress," Sue said. "Let me in. I'll hold onto her."

That was a good idea. Candy was blocking the entrance, teeth bared. Someone else growled. The puppy tried to disappear into the folds of the beige blanket that enveloped her small body. She was so small, like a little plush animal. I estimated her age in weeks. Perhaps three.

I shouted Candy's name. "All of you, back up."

They did except for Misty who, unaffected by my raised voice, nudged Sue's leg. Her tail was wagging. I could imagine what was going through her mind. *A baby? For us?*

"She needs water and something to eat," Sue said. "I didn't want to waste more time driving back to the ranch."

Which would have taken less than ten minutes. Sue was rarely so frazzled. Strands of strawberry blonde hair fell forward into her eyebrows, and the hand she lifted to push them back was shaking. "So I came to you."

"Bring her to the kitchen and tell me about it."

To my amazement, her eyes filled with tears. "Some woman let her out at the side of the road and drove off. She isn't even old enough to go to a proper home."

I handed Sue a tissue. She wiped her eyes and held the puppy tighter while I poured fresh water into the closest bowl I could find. But food? For a puppy this young? I didn't have puppy kibble. Milk then?

"So she just sat there in the middle of the road not moving, probably scared to death," Sue said. "She was crying. She let me pick her up."

"Did you get a good look at the car?"

"It was silver, pretty muddy. I couldn't see the license plate."

Darn. Another hard-to-trace vehicle.

"Luckily I had cancellations today, or I wouldn't have been there when she was abandoned."

All but one of the collies had retreated to the dining room. Misty separated herself from the pack and stood close to me as I filled the teakettle. I gave her a quick pat on the head, my mind on our guests.

Sue could use a drink herself. A cup of good strong tea. I looked around the kitchen, wondering, hoping. Good. I'd brought a loaf of banana nut bread out of the freezer last night.

I set the water on the table and Sue guided the puppy's nose to it. The little creature lapped loudly.

"She's too young to be away from her mother," Sue said.

"I wonder how that happened. Was she the only puppy in the litter? If so, what happened to the others?"

"Who knows?"

"Where did you find her?" I asked.

"On some country road or other. I didn't think to look for a road sign."

"They always dump them in the country."

I'd need more water. I opened the bread box. How about a mixture of white bread torn into baby-sized pieces and milk?

Sue was saying, "I turned on this road just in time to see the woman put the pup out of her car. She was wearing jeans and a brown jacket with a hood. The hood covered her hair, but I saw her face in profile, and I might recognize her again. She had a stocky build, and when she walked back to the car, I noticed she had a limp.

"It was a man who dumped the four collie puppies," I said. "There's more than one, then, working independently of each other."

"We have to find them or this will keep happening over and over again."

"Crane tells me he takes an average of two strays a day to the shelter in Lakeville. That's appalling. We can do better than this as a town."

I hadn't forgotten the four collie puppies abandoned in front of the unfinished construction site, even though apprehending their original owner had dropped to the bottom of my list. After all, what more could I do? The Blackwell man had apparently walked free.

There has to be something, I kept telling myself. *Think.*

My mind remained a blank.

Sue ran her finger along the baby's velvety head. "I'm happy to report that three of the puppies are in new homes. They're doing fine with treatment and growing like weeds. Unfortunately, we couldn't trace the lady who took her puppy to Blackbourne's."

"We have to assume she's taking good care of her."

"If she knows about the parvo."

"She will, if she took the pup to a vet."

"Let's hope she did. But we always have new strays to care for and try to place. This one's going home with me. I won't take her to a shelter."

"One day soon you may not have to."

I told her about Brent's plans to turn the former Woodville house into another all-breed shelter. "All he needs is a dependable caretaker. Do you know of anybody who would be interested?"

"Someone who loves dog and wants to help them? Let me think."

"Emphasize that they'd have a large house to live in, a salary with benefits, and all expenses for the dogs paid," I added.

"That would be ideal for the right person," Sue said.

I removed the puppy's bowl, now empty, and replaced it with an (appetizing?) milk-bread mix. She began to lap milk eagerly, drinking around the bread. That done, I poured tea for Sue and me and sliced the banana bread.

Sue said, "We have a new member, Rachel, who wants to get more involved with Rescue, but she lives in a gated community. She can only foster one dog at a time."

"Maybe she'd like the freedom of living in a house with a backyard," I said.

"I can ask."

"Can you call an emergency meeting of the Rescue League? Brent would come, and he has a way of charming women to get what he wants."

Sue smiled. "That he does. If all he needs is a caretaker for the new shelter, I could have a place to take this baby when she's a little bit older and stronger."

The puppy had finished the milk and was sniffing at a small chunk of soggy bread.

After a moment, Sue said, "Then there's Emma. I wonder if she would be interested. She rents her house. It's nowhere near as nice as those old Victorians on Park Street."

And we had more members, more possibilities, about two dozen.

"You get everyone together, and I'll bring refreshments," I said, encouraged at the thought of several likely caretaker prospects together in one room.

Sue nodded. "I'll start calling people. We'll aim for this Friday."

She broke off a hunk of banana bread for herself. The puppy came alive, licking her milky chops. Most dogs are alike; they'll do anything for a tasty treat.

"Maybe I shouldn't...Banana bread? What do you think?"

"Go ahead," I said. "If you hadn't rescued her, she'd have to eat berries or some other noxious stuff."

If she survived, which was doubtful. To a hungry coyote or ravening hawk, she would be a tasty morsel. Did the woman who left her on a country road think of that?

Misty whimpered. I gave her a piece of her own and sat back, satisfied at the latest development. If we were lucky, Brent's shelter would be up and running, possibly by the end of the week. When she was ready, little Milk Mug would have a safe place to go.

<h1 style="text-align:center">Thirty-two</h1>

After school on Friday, I baked three dozen cookies. Crane was bringing a pizza home for dinner. Now all I had to do in the kitchen was make a salad. I was growing weary of time spent in the classroom and kitchen. The prospect of doing something different, even attending a meeting, energized me.

With my baked offerings packed in a box, I drove the short distance to Sue's horse ranch.

It was a gorgeous afternoon with ample sunshine and a hint of spring in the gradually warming air. I would have liked to walk to Sue's house but remembered the bowl of stew that ended up as dinner for a thieving coyote.

Never again.

The number of vehicles parked near the ranch house was encouraging. Our last two meetings had been cancelled because of inclement weather, and everyone must be anxious to see one another and compare notes.

The door was ajar, guarded by Scarlet and Bluebell, two of Sue's rescues. Both were in a state of high excitement. A conversational hum and the enticing aroma of coffee drifted out of the family room. I followed it.

"Here's Jennet," Sue said. "Scarlet, Bluebell, stop that!"

Smelling the contents of the box, both dogs were leaping up, dipped ears flying back.

"I'll take it."

I knew that booming voice. Brent came up behind me. "Sure smells good."

"Fresh baked cookies," I said. "Orange chocolate chip."

"Come in, you two." Sue's gaze lingering on Brent. "Find a seat. We've been waiting for you."

"Where's the new baby?" I asked.

"Sleeping in her crate the last time I looked. My pack of hooligans intimidate her."

Brent handed the box to Sue. "I turned baker. What's the emergency?"

Sue rolled her eyes at me. To Brent she said, "You are."

"What?"

Apparently, she hadn't told him that he was the possible beneficiary of the meeting.

I sat and greeted my nearest Rescue friends and nodded to those who sat around the room. Dispensing with minutes and other League business, Sue opened the meeting with a request to Brent. "Tell us about your new shelter, Mr. Fowler."

Brent seemed surprised to be the center of attention but launched into a description of his project. He was comfortable in the spotlight and at home in his lord-of-the-manor persona. Needless to say, he held his audience—mostly female—in the palm of his hand, and his fervor was contagious.

In conclusion, he said, "The house on Park Street is in move-in condition, but I need to hire a live-in caretaker. Then we can fill it with dog food and start welcoming the dogs that heartless people let loose to fend for themselves."

His announcement met with murmurs of approval. He mentioned the salary and benefits the caretaker could expect, along with free rent in a gracious Victorian house.

Emma said, "That's incredibly generous, Mr. Fowler. It's practically irresistible."

"When I realized what I'd done by moving the Woodville sisters out of the shelter, I felt guilty," he said. "My home for geriatric collies is flourishing, but it came at a price. I've deprived so many other dogs of their safe haven."

"For those who don't know," Sue said, "just this week we've had a dog, Brownie, abandoned at the roadside with all his possessions. Two days ago, I rescued a poor little mite that was way too young to leave her mother. She was just thrown away. If I hadn't happened to arrive on the scene when I did, she would have died."

"Brownie is safe," Brent added. "One of the men at my barn adopted him."

"And our new baby is in her crate in the kitchen," Sue said. "But these are only two of many."

Rachel, our new member, spoke up. "It isn't just the old and young that are being booted out of their homes. A young Irish setter mix without a collar has been wandering into my yard every day. I've been feeding him. I can't catch him, though."

Brent addressed the group, taking care to look at each person directly. "If any of you know of someone who'd like a good job at the shelter, give me his or her name. Please."

He sat and reached for a cookie, found my eye, and nodded. I smiled at him and mouthed, 'Good luck.'

Brent was indeed a special man. He deserved every good thing life could offer.

Sue raised her coffee mug. "Let's all drink to the successful reopening of the Foxglove Corners Animal Shelter."

It was really going to happen! I thought of the former shelter's guiding spirit, animal activist Caroline Meilland, who had so loved all the creatures that shared God's earth with us. Lila and Letty Woodville had taken Caroline's portrait with her when they moved to Brent's collie home.

I felt certain Caroline's loving spirit would preside over the old white Victorian in its new incarnation. We'd have to have her portrait copied.

~ * ~

Even though Crane and I were eating a simple pizza dinner, I set the table in the dining room, and lit the tapers in the heirloom candlesticks. The salad filled a large crystal bowl, crisp and green with cucumbers, radishes, and red grape tomatoes. It looked festive. Well, after our Rescue League meeting, I felt like celebrating. I had no doubt that someone was already considering Brent's offer.

As I returned the box of matches to the drawer, my gaze fell on Evanora's treasured music box. I hadn't thought about it for days. Now the little Cupid seemed to wink at me. *Truly thine.*

On an impulse, I wound the key and listened to the poignant song, wondering how many times Evanora had done this while thinking of Ned.

But something seemed off. When the delicate fairy notes faded, I wound it again and listened intently.

Didn't the music box have two distinct melodies, both of which were vaguely familiar to me, neither of which I could identify?

Yes. Two melodies;but now I heard only one.

Although...Perhaps there were two, after all, a sub-melody caught in the middle of the major one? Like an arrangement I'd once heard of *Greensleeves* and *Lovely Joan.*

I wound it yet again and started when I heard heavy breathing. Misty stood at my side. She wasn't tall enough to reach the top of the credenza—which was good—but her eyes were fixed on the music box, and she appeared to be reacting to the sound it made.

Misty, my psychic collie.

Reacted how?

With curiosity? With apprehension? As if to reinforce my thoughts, she uttered a faint whimper.

None of the other collies showed any interest in the music box, nor even appeared to notice its music.

Don't get carried away, I told myself. *She thinks it's a toy like her stuffed praying bear. She'd like to play with it.*

"Nice music." Crane joined me, fresh from the shower, the silver streaks in his hair glistening in the candlelight. He'd never paid any attention to the music box, and I hadn't mentioned that I thought it played two melodies.

"I wish I knew what that song was," I said.

He kissed me. "I can't help you with that."

Any identifying tag had vanished long ago. Even Evanora hadn't been able to name the melody, and presumably it was new when Ned had given it to her. Maybe there had never been a tag.

The last note faded. Time to let this minor mystery fade as well, for the moment, anyway.

"Everything's ready," I said. "I'll get the pizza out of the oven."

"And I'll pour the wine."

Which we only drank on festive occasions. With the reopening of the animal shelter on the horizon, this evening qualified as special.

Happily, I stepped out of the *Twilight Zone* into my own life. Even those of us who come in contact with otherworldly matters need occasional sustenance.

Thirty-three

Pizza for dinner translates into a longer evening. Quickly, I restored the kitchen to its customary order, treated the dogs to a snack of crusts, and opened Evanora's diary. It was high time I finished reading it.

In her last entry, Evanora had been angry with her sister for telling their father about her ongoing affair with Ned. She had vowed to get even with her. What happened next? Did she seek revenge or have a change of heart?

I opened the diary and removed the bookmark. The next entry was titled 'Reconciliation' which answered my question.

EVANORA'S DIARY

RECONCILIATION—Sara said, "You're my sister, Eva. I love you. I don't want anything to happen to you."

"You didn't have to go blabbing to Dad."

"He already knew. Mrs. Baker told him. She's seen you going into the woods with your picnic basket. Then she's seen Ned's car. It

would be hard not to. He parks in front of her house. He drives away, and you come out of the woods. So she drew her own conclusions."

"The miserable old snoop."

I was so angry. All the times I carried Mrs. Baker her dinner on a tray and sat with her while she ate. And this was how she repaid me.

"She doesn't have much entertainment," Sara said. "Only her stories on television."

"I'm nobody's entertainment."

"You were looking forward to college this fall," Sara reminded me. "You were going to make new friends and take all the English classes you could. You bought all those new clothes."

She glanced at the closet where my new plaid skirt hung. I had a forest green cashmere sweater to go with it. What Sara said was true, but my college was a two-hour drive up north. I'd have to leave Foxglove Corners and Ned. Could I do it? If I did, would he find someone else?

"That'll still happen," I said, but I didn't believe it. I didn't know what the future held. Maybe I wouldn't go away to college after all.

"Don't forget your dream," Sara said. "You always wanted to be a teacher."

A toy chalkboard. Stuffed animals sitting in tiny chairs. A pretend classroom in the basement. At one time, that was all I wanted. Before Ned.

"I haven't forgotten," I said.

But my hope for a happy life with Ned overshadowed all those dreams.

Sara hugged me. "Am I forgiven, Eva?"

What could I say?

"Of course. Just don't interfere in my life again."

NEWS—When I went to the corner store today, I found that it was locked with a note on the door. 'Closed indefinitely'. Indefinitely? What was going on? I found out later that day. The story made the front page of the paper. There'd been a robbery the previous evening.

Maybelle had been shot trying to keep a paltry twenty dollars away from the thief. She was in the hospital in critical condition.

Maybelle. Ned's aunt.

The only suspect was a high school drop-out, Jimmy Redmond, who had previously robbed the jewelry store—or so the story went. No one knew where to find him.

I learned later that Maybelle wasn't just a clerk. She had owned the store, inherited from her late father. Before I'd left, I looked through the window. Loaves of bread on the rack, coffeecakes in the display case. Yesterday's unsold baked goods. Everything frozen in time.

What would it happen to it now?

I'd never been comfortable in Maybelle's presence, but the corner store had been an important part of my life in Foxglove Corners. Gone forever.

AFTERMATH—Maybelle died last night. Such a senseless death. All because she made a snap decision to guard her twenty dollars. May she rest in peace.

I haven't seen Ned since the news broke. He must be busy with a death in the family, and he'll surely want to catch Maybelle's killer. I wished I could tell him how sorry I am for his loss. I wonder if I could go to the funeral.

~ * ~

Shocked by the unexpected news, I forgot that what I was reading was practically ancient history. The next page contained only two words: 'He's gone.'

Here was a further shock. Surely Evanora had meant to write 'she.' The next page was blank. Then instead of resuming her narrative, Evanora had copied four lines of a poem. She used a pen with black ink and printed the words:

Cold blows the wind to-day, sweetheart,
Cold are the drops of rain,
The first truelove that ever I had
In the green wood he was slain.

Ned slain? Along with Maybelle? What had I missed?

I looked for evidence of a section torn out. But the diary was intact. I turned the page and read:

GRIEVING—I haven't written in my diary since that day when my world ended. Ned lost his life, gunned down by the very stream where we spent so many happy hours.

So much has happened since then. All of it bad. Nothing good. For a while, it looked like they were going to suspect me because of something Mrs. Baker said, that I had killed him because he broke up with me. How ludicrous. What would you expect from an old woman who watches soap operas all day?

Sara confessed that she wondered if Dad had shot Ned because he continued to see me, but then admitted that it was unlikely. At the same time, I wondered if Sara had chosen to eliminate Ned for the same reason. Sara with no knowledge of firearms? She never went near Dad's gun collection. Or someone else, a jealous ex-girlfriend, perhaps? There were at least three to choose from.

As long as the killer remained at large, people would wonder. After careful consideration, I decided the shooter had to be Jimmy Redmond. Ned had been determined to find him and arrest him for murder. Redmond retaliated. Nothing else makes sense.

Something continues to bother me, though. Why was Ned's body found beside the stream? It was almost like someone knew it was special to us. Like someone was sending me an ungodly message.

LOOKING BACKWARD—Tonight while the rain comes down in torrents, I read what I wrote from the beginning, from the night I met Ned. The night of the bat. I also remember the last time I saw him.

I think I may have heard the shot in my dream.

I only remember that I was awake every hour or so during the night, and when the alarm went off, I had a headache. I got up, ate a piece of toast, and took two pills with coffee. It only got worse.

Later that morning, I found his body.

We were planning to meet at the house in the woods. I'd packed the basket with sandwiches, cupcakes and lemonade. Honey ran on ahead of me, and I heard her barking. It was a different sound from the excited one she usually makes when she discovers something delightful on the forest floor.

Her bark turned into a howl.

As I approached the house, she ran to meet me, taking the edge of my skirt in her mouth, leading me to the stream.

He lay there, a nightmare vision in blue, one hand resting in the water, his head at an unnatural angle. It rested in a pool of blood.

After that, everything that happened is a blur. I ran back to the house, called the police—Ned was the police—and waited...while my world, and my heart, broke apart, piece by piece.

So much joy lives on in this little book and so much pain. Memories to cherish for a time when this golden summer ends, and that will be soon.

The woods were filled with magic once. Now Ned is gone. He took the magic with him. Leaves are turning and falling, and it's too chilly to sit by the stream. It's cold in the house in the woods. All the warmth has gone.

How could it end like this?

FAREWELL—I didn't go to the funeral. Ned was buried beside his aunt. They said his fellow policemen all turned out to pay their respects. I had a headache and stayed in bed that day. I kept telling myself, 'He isn't in that casket. He's somewhere else. My dear love.'

GHOST?—Today something happened. I don't believe in ghosts, but now I wonder.

I thought I couldn't bear to walk in the woods again, knowing I wouldn't meet Ned, but their pull was too strong. I gathered a bouquet of wildflowers to take to the stream, which is where I think he really is, not that dreary cemetery, and soon I was following the familiar path to the house in the woods.

How beautiful it was beneath the rustling leaves, how cool and quiet. The woods didn't care that Ned had left the earth or that the last piece of my heart was hanging by a thread.

The leaves seemed somehow less colorful. Even the flowers I carried weren't as vibrant as they should be. All my tears must have harmed my vision as well as my sense of smell. The sweet fragrance of lilacs was gone.

For the first time ever, the valentine heart on the front of the house seemed tacky. I never noticed before, but it's the color of blood. I pushed open the door, took one step inside, and immediately became aware of a presence.

Ned was inside waiting for me, just beyond my peripheral vision. I knew it. I could smell his aftershave. Old Spice.

He had come to say goodbye.

Then, too soon, whatever I sensed disappeared. It was too fragile to last.

"Don't go." I said that aloud, willing him to hear me.

But he'd gone. I knew I was alone in the house. In place of the presence and its attendant scent, there was—nothing.

Thirty-four

My tears fell freely as I closed the diary and pulled a tissue out of my purse. I had no idea when they'd started. I dabbed at my eyes while Misty and Velvet stared at me, dark eyes filled with concern and vague guilt.

Did we do something wrong?

Crane was looking at me, too, above the pages of the *Banner*. "Why are you crying, honey? Did the dog die?"

Crane knew me well. If a dog died in a movie or a book, I cried for him. I rarely cried for the human who had met the same fate.

"It was a man who died," I said.

"Why the tears?"

"Ned was a policeman and Evanora's true love. She wrote about his death. I can feel her sorrow as if it were my own."

"True love? Why do I feel we've gone back in time?"

"That's how she referred to him," I added.

"How did the man die?" he asked.

"He was shot in the woods. Evanora discovered his body by the stream. She wondered if the killer meant to send her a message."

He looked puzzled but interested.

"By the stream that runs alongside the Valentine House," I said. "Evanora used to meet Ned there and in the house."

I moved the diary to the coffee table. I couldn't read any more. Not yet.

Because suddenly I remembered all the ways in which Evanora and I were alike. She loved walking in the woods where we'd both discovered an enchanting little playhouse. She had a dog, Honey, who accompanied her. She planned to take English courses in college and major in education, my own profession.

Most important, she loved a handsome, beguiling policeman. Crane was a deputy sheriff.

"Did some hunter mistake him for a deer?" he asked.

"No. No, it was in the summertime."

But that was a possibility I hadn't considered. A careless hunter stalking his prey out of season.

"He might have been killed by a thief he was pursuing," I said.

"We lawmen make enemies."

I sighed. It was a simple fact of life. They could make enemies and never even be aware of them.

I longed to join Crane on the sofa and wrap him in my arms. Well, why not do it? I crossed to the sofa and leaned into his ready embrace. The paper fell to the floor. I felt safe for the moment. We were all right. For now.

Every time Crane left the house, I said a silent prayer that he would return to me in one piece. He had been shot once. It could happen again at any time. Any bright new morning when he set out in his patrol car, he could be waylaid by a careless bullet.

In the greenwood he was slain.

We had made an unspoken pact not to speak of the danger that rode with him on the roads and by-roads of Foxglove Corners. I consoled myself with the thought that our town was an extremely safe part of Michigan, mostly rural.

Not that crime was unknown to us. I had been in danger of losing my life more often than my law-enforcing husband. Facing a gunman, thankfully emerging from a confrontation unscathed, often helped by one of my collies—at times my life seemed to consist of one threat after another.

It came to me that perhaps Ned hadn't been shot by Jimmy Redmond. Perhaps the motive was more personal. Could it have had its root in the semi-secret love affair between Evanora and Ned?

Evanora, herself under brief suspicion, had speculated about possible killers. A disgruntled former girlfriend, bent on revenge? Sara had wondered if their father could have killed Ned in an ill-advised desire to protect her. Evanora had questioned her sister's role in the tragedy. The shooting could even have been random.

Had they ever found out who'd pulled the trigger? The diary would have the answer, and if a member of the Foxglove Corners Police Department had been slain, a record of the event would exist somewhere. Miss Eidt might have a clipping in her vertical file.

If only I could tie Ned's shooting to a specific year. Even a decade would be helpful.

Then I remembered the scent of Ned's aftershave.

"Do men still use Old Spice shaving lotion?" I asked Crane.

"My grandfather did. My father—I don't think so. Why?"

"That was Ned Douglas' brand. Evanora mentioned it."

"Old Spice has been around for a long time."

I nodded. "I'm sure. I'd like to read an objective account of Ned's murder. Evanora's writing is filled with emotion, which is only natural. It would help if I knew the year Ned died."

I could search the history of Old Spice on the Internet. But years? I needed to be more specific.

"What happened to the girl who wrote the diary after she lost her so-called true love?" Crane asked.

I glanced at the diary. My intention had been to finish reading it tonight, but I didn't think I could absorb any more second-hand grief. I'd let the shocking revelation settle a bit and resume reading tomorrow.

I wondered. Certainly Evanora wouldn't have mourned forever. That happened only in fiction and poetry.

Twelve months and a day?

I remembered the lines she had copied into her diary from *The Unquiet Grave.*

The ballad was one of my favorites, bound to appeal to a lover of Gothic novels. Having lost her true love, the speaker couldn't stop mourning. Eventually, her lover spoke to her, telling her that her grief was preventing him from seeking eternal rest. There was more, all of it grim and heartrending: withering stalks, frost, kisses cold as death.

Tomorrow was Saturday. My lesson plans for the following week were written and my preparation done. I could devote the entire weekend to the mystery of Ned Douglas' murder. If nothing happened to prevent it.

~ * ~

Annica looked upset. She unloaded plates filled high with pancakes and bacon, poured coffee, and stepped back from the table she had just served, all without her usual bright smile or even a cheerful word to her customers. Her deep pink dress only served to bring out her unaccustomed pallor.

She saw me and nodded toward the booth by the window that I considered reserved for me. I sat and noticed the vase of brilliant orange roses on the counter. Another offering from Colton Reeves, I assumed.

"What'll you have this morning, Jennet?" she asked.

I didn't need to consult the menu, having been fantasizing about my second breakfast at Clovers all morning.

"A cinnamon bun and a pot of tea."

"Coming right up. I'll join you."

She nodded to Marcy, their signal to cover for each other.

While I waited, I looked out the window. The woods on the other side of Crispian Road had a faint, barely discernible tinge of green. The buds were still tight, but they were there. Spring was on the way, obviously in no hurry.

Soon we'd be able to hike out to the Valentine House without trudging through mud. After reading Evanora's last entry, I was anxious to know if I would hear her plaintive entreaty again. If so, I would be hearing her voice or, rather, that of her spirit. If she rested in an unquiet grave of her own.

Thirty-five

Annica brought two pots of tea to the booth, along with cinnamon buns, each on a plate decorated with spring blossoms. Clovers was different from other restaurants in many ways, among them with its hand painted season-changing china. I could almost believe I'd come to a quaint tea shop.

"Now tell me what's wrong," I said.

"Waitressing. It isn't exactly a bowl of cherries. Except during cherry season," she added with a weak attempt at a smile.

"Seriously."

"I tangled with the customer from hell this morning," she said. "She yelled at me and called me a stupid tramp. Everyone in the restaurant heard her."

I paused in the act of pouring my tea. "What?"

"I am not stupid," she said. "I am not a tramp."

I was truly shocked. With her friendly manner and sunny appearance, Annica was a favorite at Clovers. Who had dared hurl those insults at her?

"Of course you're not," I said. "What was this person's problem?"

She shrugged. "Who knows? She's just crazy, I guess. As soon as I brought her order to the table, she took one bite of it and called me back. She claimed the French toast was burned and the egg batter was raw."

"How could the toast be burned and undercooked at the same time?"

"It makes no sense. And it gets worse. She threw the plate at me and walked out without paying her bill."

Annica touched a spot on her dress that still looked damp but, fortunately, not stained.

"That's assault," I said. "I'd report it to the police if I were you."

"I'd just like to forget it, but I may do that. The French toast was perfect," she added. "That woman just wanted to attack me verbally for something. It didn't matter what."

"And you let it upset you," I said.

"It happened less than an hour ago. I guess I should be glad she hadn't poured syrup on it."

Her eyes were brighter than usual. I suspected she'd shed a few tears in private. Over the years, I'd been verbally attacked in my classroom and shed a few tears of my own.

I said, "But why would she call you a tramp?"

"She was here when Colton came in with his bouquet of the day." She indicated the roses on the counter. As she left, she threw out a question to the other customers: 'What do you have to do to get a decent breakfast in this place? Bring the waitress flowers?'"

"Mary Jeanne should ban her from Clovers," I said.

"Probably she will. She isn't in today. I don't remember seeing this woman in here before this morning. The day started off so well, too, with sunshine and spring in the air."

"Don't let that hateful hag ruin it for you," I said. "If Mary Jeanne doesn't ban her, refuse to wait on her. Tell Marcy to ignore her, too. But I'll bet after that shameful display, she won't show her face in Clovers again."

Annica cut her bun into quarters and took a sip of her tea. "I feel a little better after talking to you. I think I can actually eat this."

"What does she look like, in case I run into her?" I asked.

"She has short curly hair dyed a carroty shade of red and gray roots. She was dressed in black jeans with a tight black top. Oh, she's on the chunky side, and she limped."

"That sounds exactly like the woman who dumped the puppy," I said.

"I'll bet it is."

"I wish you didn't have to put up with abusive customers," I said.

"Me, too, but overall, I enjoy working at Clovers. It's like a second home to me."

We needed a happier subject. "Is Colton still bringing you flowers?"

"Every third day or so. He's the most persistent guy I know."

She needed to redirect her focus. "Did you hear about Brent's latest project?" I asked.

"I haven't seen him in days. What is it?"

"He bought the old animal shelter on Park Street and is going to reopen it as soon as he finds a caretaker."

She wiped icing off her fingers. "He just bought the house on Loosestrife Lane for geriatric collies."

"This one will accept all breeds, like it did when Lila and Letty were in charge."

"Brent is a good man," she said quietly. "The best. But I'm sure he knows that."

"He might like to hear it from you," I said.

I knew I was interfering but didn't care.

"I'll tell him," she said, "if I ever see him again."

"Sure you will. He's just been busy."

Was I missing something? Neither Annica nor Brent had given any indication that their relationship had encountered a roadblock. If Brent had been in Clovers this morning, he would have wiped the floor up with Annica's antagonist.

I wondered why Colton Reeves, the bringer of roses, hadn't leaped to Annica's defense.

"Let's hope that horrid woman is just passing through Foxglove Corners," I said. "I like to think we're surrounded by nice people."

~ * ~

At the library an hour later, I found the objective news story I sought, as well as the date of Officer Edward Douglas' death: August 30, 1968. I stared at a grainy photography of him while Miss Eidt peered over my shoulder and sunlight danced across the diamonds in her engagement ring.

"What a fine-looking young man," she said. "Why did he have to die?"

Why should the beautiful die? Stephen Foster had asked that question in song, probably knowing it had no answer.

The article repeated information I'd already gleaned from Evanora's diary. Ned had been shot by an unknown assailant who subsequently fled the scene, leaving no clue behind. It ended with a plea to the public for information leading to the arrest of the shooter.

"If they'd found Ned's killer, there'd be another article," I said.

I had sifted through the folder labeled 'Criminals of Foxglove Corners' several times but failed to find another clipping.

Ned had died in another century, but because of Evanora's impassioned writing, the tragedy seemed as immediate to me as if it had happened recently to someone I knew. I felt that I had been there in 1968 trying to solve a murder with no clues. A murder destined to become a cold case.

As for Evanora, I hadn't been able to find a shred of evidence that she existed, although, of course, she must have. The name 'Sherbourne' was a dead end. There were no Evanoras on the Sherbourne family tree.

If I hadn't read the brittle clipping, I would have thought Evanora's diary was a work of fiction penned by a romantic young girl who had fixated on a handsome policeman. She might not even have known him.

I took a moment to examine that thought. Could it be?

No. I had my own evidence in the knowledge that a sorrowing spirit haunted the Valentine house mourning the death of her lost lover. And I had something else. A scrap of mint green cloth.

<h1 style="text-align:center">*Thirty-six*</h1>

That evening I settled myself in the rocker, determined to finish reading the diary, come what may. Misty and Velvet lay at my feet. Velvet held her gingerbread man toy in her mouth, her eyes filled with hope.

"Later," I murmured, and she dropped it, resting her chin on the toy's little head.

Crane opened the *Banner,* and I began reading. Evanora had stopped writing in her diary for a while. She resumed her entries with black ink. Was that significant? I wondered. Probably, as she'd drawn black ribbons around the pages.

EVANORA'S DIARY

SEPTEMBER SONG—After I lost Ned, I thought my life couldn't get any worst. I was wrong. I should have known this might happen. I should have known better, but I honestly never anticipated it. I didn't look beyond the moment.

What's done is done. Now what am I going to do? What <u>can</u> I do?

I've been reading, poetry mostly. It gives me some little comfort. My old favorite, John Brown's Body, has a section that seems to have been written especially for me. One of his characters, the gentle Melora, discovers that she is pregnant. Her words are "go with child".

ALONE—"Go with child." That phrase sounds so much more refined than any modern expression. But archaic words don't change meanings.

I've gone walking in the woods many times since I first felt Ned's presence in the house by the stream. Sometimes, I think he is there waiting for me. Other times he isn't. I talk to him. I tell him that I love him and ask him what I should do, and I weep for everything that was stolen from me. We would have been married. I know it.

"Eva?"

Sara was standing in the doorway. She must have followed me and heard me talking to Ned.

"Who's here with you?" *she asked.*

"No one. I was talking to myself," *I said.*

"In this dreary old house? Really, Eva. Come walk with me and get some fresh air. It's a beautiful day."

I agreed. Ned was elsewhere today, anyway.

"You don't look well," *Sara said.*

"I have a scratchy throat," *I said.* "I may be catching a cold. The season is changing."

"It isn't that."

"How do you know? Are you a doctor?"

"He's gone," *she said quietly.* "You have to forget him and find someone else. It's not like you were together for years."

How can she be so cruel?

"I won't," *I said.* "I can't."

"I didn't mean that the way it sounded," *she said.*

We passed the stream, found a clearing a little further on, and sat on a thick trunk of a tree that had come down in the wind, checking first for ants or other loathsome bugs. For the first time in days, I smelled the scent of lilacs. Was that good? Did it mean that elusive plant was near?

"You have to move on with your life, Eva," Sara said. "It's terrible what happened, but you can't bring him back."

I didn't answer her, but I thought, I can. I've already done it. He's waiting for me in the playhouse. Sometimes. Not today, though.

"This is unhealthy, Eva."

"What?"

"This depression you've fallen into. There'll be lots of nice guys at college. Maybe you'll meet a special one."

"I've been thinking," I said. "I may not go to college, after all. I can get a job in an office instead. I can type fast and take dictation."

"That would be a mistake," Sara said. "You've been accepted, your tuition is paid, you have a room in the dorm. You're ready."

My new skirts, straight and form fitting. How long can I wear them?

We were quiet for a while. Sara studied the scenery and said she should have brought her camera. I wondered if I should get up and look for the lilac flower.

"I wish I were going to college," Sara said. "Next year, I'll join you. We'll be together."

I swallowed. My throat was scratchy. I shouldn't have tempted fate by saying I was catching a cold.

I didn't need a cold on top of everything.

Except for birdsong and twitterings in the shadows, it was quiet in the woods. The silence was unnerving.

Did I dare confide in Sara? She had betrayed me once.

I looked over at her and saw that she was crying.

Somehow she knew.

"I'm so sorry, Eva," she said. "You have to tell Mom."

TELLING MOTHER—So I did. I invited myself to her sewing room after dinner. Sara was right. Mom had to know. Maybe she could help me decide what to do. I hardly thought she'd throw me out of the house like an outraged Victorian parent.

Her look of shock and disappointment was fleeting, leading me to believe she might have suspected this unwelcome development.

All she said was, "Are you sure?"

"Pretty sure," I said.

"You have to see Doctor Simms."

The thought appalled me. Sara knew my secret. Now Mom did. But I didn't want anyone else to know. Not even Dad, although eventually he'd have to be told.

"Not yet," I said.

"Soon then. I'll go with you."

I longed for her to say, 'Everything will be all right, Evanora.' But she didn't. Why should she? How could it possibly be all right?

"What am I going to do?" I asked her.

"What we planned all along. You'll leave for college next week. You'll study hard and get good grades so you can earn your teacher's certificate. You'll have to support yourself and your baby now that you're alone."

LOOKING FORWARD—Stephen Vincent Benet isn't popular with modern readers. Few people have heard of his book-length narrative poem, John Brown's Body, let alone read it. Alone in my room, I've escaped from my present situation by reading it again and am constantly amazed by how perceptive he is. Some passages might have been written especially for me. I feel a special kinship with Melora.

Reading poetry is good for a few hours' escape, but sooner or later, I have to make a plan. Only why do I have to make it alone?

~ * ~

The next page was blank. I turned to another. Also blank. I counted nine more pages in the diary. And not a single written word.

"No!" I cried. "No, no, no!"

Crane looked up from his paper. "Did someone else die?"

Misty and Velvet were looking at me, Velvet with her gingerbread toy in her mouth.

"I just read the last page," I said. "Evanora stopped writing. Now I'll never know what happened. She discovered she was pregnant," I added.

"Do you think there's another diary somewhere?" Crane asked.

With empty pages left in this one? I doubted it. Still anything was possible. But I had checked the box of series books after finding the diary. There wasn't a Volume II in it.

"Maybe there's one at the Green House of Antiques packed in another box," I said.

If it wasn't so late, I would drive straight to the antique shop with possibly the strangest request they'd ever heard.

If Volume II didn't exist, or if it had been destroyed, what could I do? Redouble my efforts to trace Evanora? Inquire whether any items from the Sherbourne estate sale remained unsold? My options were limited and not that good.

"I hate not knowing," I said. "Did Evanora keep her baby? Did she meet another man? Did she realize her dream to become a teacher?"

"You'll solve the mystery with or without another diary, honey," Crane said. "I have faith in you."

I smiled at him, wishing I shared his optimism. Feeling bereft, I closed the diary. It was a little like closing a door.

After all we'd been through together, was Evanora now irretrievably lost to me?

Thirty-seven

The dream was short but terrifying, and more real-seeming than any dream had a right to be. I was walking in the woods looking for the flower that smelled like lilacs.

A deadly chill seeped out through the encroaching trees. I felt the sharp sting of wood on my ankle as I stepped on a branch, snapping it in two. The air smelled of smoke rather than flowers, and my arm itched where a mosquito had bitten it.

At last I came to the Valentine House. The heart between the gables was brilliant in the sunlight and dripping huge splotches of red as if it had been freshly painted.

I didn't go inside but walked on to the stream.

A man in uniform lay on his side in a bed of tall grasses. From a wound in his head, a pool of blood flowed into the still water, turning it a sickly shade of pink.

The man was Crane.

"No!" I cried. "The dream made a mistake. Ned Douglas was slain in the greenwood, not Crane. Rewind it!"

With a dream's illogic, I found myself back at Jonquil Lane beginning the walk again. Before I reached the stream, the dream ended.

Thank God.

I lay in bed beside Crane, cold and trembling. The thread that connected my life to Evanora's was as thin as gossamer. I could easily sever it and end this affinity I felt for a girl whom I didn't know, whose face I'd never seen, a girl who was only a name in an old diary.

So do it. Cut the thread and let it drift away.

But that was a matter for the day. Another day. I was wide awake now, my brain in spin-mode, sleep a thousand hours away.

It was still dark with plenty of time until first light. Plenty of time to dream again, for the dream to correct its mistake.

But I couldn't fall asleep.

Crane stirred. I touched his arm lightly, not wanting to wake him but needing to feel he was still with me.

Unyielding to control, my mind drifted back to Evanora. I had been spending too much time thinking about her bereavement and new predicament. And what did I have to show for it? A story without an end.

Oh, it had an end. I just didn't know what happened next and had no idea how to find out.

Clever detecting, I told myself, having already abandoned the idea of severing the gossamer tie.

I had possible sources in the Green House of Antiques and the Sherbourne estate sale.

The Valentine House was another avenue to explore. The woods were easier to navigate now that spring winds had dried the everlasting mud. We needed to visit the house again, Annica and I, for that was where we had the best chance of finding Evanora.

~ * ~

As often happens after a vivid nightmare, distressing images lingered long after I'd wakened and dressed for the day. As I mixed pancake batter, a picture of the man lying dead beside the stream invaded my thoughts.

Ned. Not Crane. Never Crane.

I closed my eyes, concentrated on stirring batter, and the picture faded.

Today was Sunday. Crane would soon set off for his patrol of Foxglove Corners. God keep him safe. I had another day to chase my elusive mystery. The Green House and the library were closed, but the house in the woods would still be there, open to all comers, waiting with its promise of a solution, of sorts. I'd take Misty with me and Annica, if she was available.

Crane opened the door and the dogs trooped inside, eight collies racing to two large water bowls. My family.

He pulled me into his arms for a quick kiss, then poured a cup of coffee and sat at the oak table. His frosty gray eyes sparkled. "I'm starving. Must be all that fresh air."

My love. My true-love.

"What are you going to do today, honey?" he asked.

"I'm going to take a walk in the woods," I said.

"It's a nice day for it, but be careful. The coyotes are starving, too."

"I haven't seen any lately. Can we hope they've gone away?"

"We can hope, but didn't you hear them howling last night?"

Surprisingly, I hadn't, in spite of the hours I'd lain awake, turning, trying in vain to find those few minutes of complete relaxation that would send me sleep to me again.

On the other hand, maybe I'd heard the coyotes and didn't remember. Their howling could have inspired my dream of the woods.

"I'll take Misty with me," I said.

"Don't forget the change jar. Just in case you come across one."

I felt silly rattling that jar and screaming at an animal, but, as Camille said, 'Whatever works.'

"I'll be all right," I promised him. "I want to see if there's any sign of supernatural activity in the Valentine House."

"That sounds dangerous," he said. "Weren't you going to take Lucy with you?"

Lucy! I'd forgotten. Would she be interested in a woodland jaunt now that the weather had moderated? On our way, we could look for spring flowers. Maybe the ones that smelled like lilacs. And, remembering the scrap of mint green material that had appeared seemingly out of nowhere, maybe there'd be something else left behind—or dropped by a ghost.

My plan for the day energized me, but I'd need fortification, more than toast and tea could provide. Serving myself the last three pancakes, I joined Crane who was drinking his grapefruit juice. I had high hopes that in the Valentine House I'd find the answers I sought.

~ * ~

Brent stood in the vestibule, waving a bag of treats above the noses of my collies.

"It's raining cats and dogs out there," he said. "Literally."

I looked out through the bay window on a sunny, clear day.

"Literally?" I asked.

"There was a little white pup hanging out in Camille's garden with a black cat. The cat ran away, but I caught the dog. He's in the Plymouth. You have to see him, Jennet. He has the most incredible blue eyes."

Now that he mentioned it, I heard Twister and Holly barking across the lane. Mine were fixated on their visitor and the present he'd brought them.

"I have good venison tarts," he said. "Can they have them now?"

"Yum," I said with a grimace. "Actually, ugh. In the kitchen," I added.

Rather than spreading them on paper, I gave each dog her tart lest Candy gobble them all.

"One puppy and one cat don't add up to a shower," I said.

"No, but think of all the dogs we've rescued lately."

"Christmas presents that wore out their welcome, I suppose. If only people would band together and agree not to sell dogs during the holiday."

"That black cat may be feral," he said. "I've seen four others, kittens."

I thought of the coyotes with horror and wished the little cats well.

"Can you domesticate a kitten born to a feral cat?" Brent wanted to know. "I'm asking for Jeff. He wants a good mouser."

"Sure." I poured him a cup of coffee and, at his request, a glass of water. "You have to start when they're young and be patient. Miss Eidt's Blackberry was a feral."

He didn't even ask whether I had cookies or a cake. Taking a long sip of coffee, he said, "I've come to share my good news. The little snowball in the car will be the first pooch in the new shelter."

"You found a caretaker!"

"Two of them. You give good advice, Jennet. Both Emma and Rachel are interested in my job. I'm taking both. They'll work together. In fact, I have about a ton of kibble in the trunk and other stuff, too. We'll be open for business tomorrow."

"That *is* good news. It'll be like having Lila and Letty back. We should celebrate."

"I think so, too—with a dinner at the Hunt Club Inn."

Caroline Meilland would be happy. I could almost see her smiling down on Brent who had given her shelter new life with one white puppy and two caretakers. *I* was happy. Something was finally going my way.

Brent lifted his glass of water. "To the shelter. Long may it live."

Thirty-eight

Once Brent learned about our proposed trek to the Valentine House, he declared he was coming with us.

"There's nothing like a good ghost hunt to liven up a dull Sunday," he said. "But why are we going?"

"Evanora's spirit may be there." I summarized her story for Brent, marveling that all those pages, all her impassioned words, could be reduced to a few sentences:

"After Ned was killed, Evanora discovered she was going to have a baby," I said in conclusion.

The story had caught his interest.

"And…?"

"That's all I know. At that point, she stopped writing in her diary. I think she haunts the house."

"If she turns out to be dangerous, I'll protect you," he said.

"I don't think she's evil. Just sad and pathetic."

"Don't you remember how you fell down the stairs in the house on Loosestrife Lane? You could have broken your neck."

"Of course, I remember. This is entirely different."

"How?"

Stairs leading to an empty second floor, a loose banister, an unseen, unheard presence. Perhaps the hauntings weren't so different after all. But Evanora had no reason to consider me a threat. Hadn't she allowed me to hear her anguished plea, 'Don't go?'

"I guess it isn't so different, after all," I said. "Welcome to our expedition, Brent."

We met in the early afternoon, a party of four. Lucy had agreed to join us, and Annica had the afternoon off. Because I wouldn't be alone, I decided to leave Misty at home, a decision I hoped I wouldn't regret.

Annica wore beige slacks and a dark green cardigan with a pair of jade earrings, but in her long black skirt, Lucy was severely underdressed for dodging grasping branches. I linked my arm in hers as we entered the abandoned construction site.

It looked as if had been ravaged by a tornado, houses torn away from their foundations, sticks and stones melded to the forest floor. One day, I imagined, all vestiges of the unfinished houses would have vanished.

Before long, the Valentine House swam into sight, veiled in a light fog that had just become apparent.

And why was that? I hadn't noticed even a trace of mist over Jonquil Lane or the woods.

'Enchantment,' Evanora would have said.

"Ghosts love mist and fog," I would have told her. "They make it easier for them to come and go."

My heartbeat began to race. I was certain we'd find evidence of Evanora's spirit in the house or maybe even another piece of her life, like the scrap of material.

My gaze fell on the Valentine heart. Like a lightning bolt, images from my dream flashed in my mind. Unnatural brilliance, drops of paint. Drops of blood. I didn't want to look toward the stream, but I did. No well-loved man lay beside the silvery water. I breathed more easily. The heart was merely a painted decoration on a playhouse, the stream a tranquil woodland waterway.

"It looks peaceful enough," Annica said. "Did you leave the door open, Jennet?"

"I don't remember. I don't think so."

"You girls stay here," Brent said. "I'll go in first. It wouldn't be the first time a vagrant moved into a deserted cottage."

Before he could do so, a sleek medium-sized animal the color of wheat burst through the door and took off into the woods. For the merest fragment of a second, I thought it was a fawn. Then I noticed the floppy ears.

"Not another one!" Brent exclaimed. "Like I said before. It's raining cats and dogs."

"You'll never catch that one," Annica pointed out.

"I'll wait till he comes out of the woods," he said.

We stayed close to the doorway while Brent went inside, announcing his entrance with stamping feet.

"All clear down here!" he said.

We entered cautiously, conducting our own surveillance, but there was no hiding place in the large, empty room.

"I'm going up," Brent added.

In that moment, I imagined him tumbling back down the stairs, as I had done in another house.

"Don't put weight on the banister," I said. "It's loose."

"Be careful." Lucy paused at the bottom of the staircase. "There's something up there. It's like a cloud. Or smoke."

"I don't smell anything," Brent said.

I almost said, 'Neither do I,' then realized I did. A faint fragrance drifted through the musty air of a mostly shut-up house. A scent of lilacs.

Lucy peered up the staircase into the dimness above. Brent had reached the top. "Be careful, Brent," she repeated. "Something malevolent is trapped up there."

"If I see a dark cloud, I'll send it on its way. Right through the window."

"Good luck with that," Annica said. "You're scaring us, Lucy," she added, eying the open door. "If this thing is above us, is it going to stay there or should we get out of here?"

"I don't know. It might be best if we left. Brent. Come back down."

"We're supposed to be ghost catchers," I said. "We don't run the other way."

"Yes, but we're not professionals," Annica reminded me.

"If there's a malevolent presence in this house, I want to know who it is," I said.

"Too late," Lucy said still looking upward. "It's fading away—it's gone."

I didn't want to leave, perhaps because I didn't have Lucy's ability to detect the presence of an evil entity residing in the house. All I sensed was sorrow, and I'd heard its lament: 'Don't go.' Before, that is; not now.

Again I wondered if a place could be host to multiple spirits: a happy child, a grief-stricken young girl, and an evildoer.

I still smelled lilacs. Freshly opened on a dewy spring morning, their light fragrance at its most potent, they had a curious hold on me.

Brent stamped his way downstairs. "There's nothing up there but dust and cobwebs, Lucy. Your ghost-a-meter needs a new battery."

"There was," she insisted. "It's gone now."

Gone…I was conscious of the lilac scent moving away, evaporating into the musty air.

"Maybe the malevolence you sensed was Ned's killer." I looked out the window at the stream. The grime of countless years distorted the view, but in my mind I again saw the man lying dead in the tall grasses. Ned, not Crane. "He committed murder. Either here or outside."

It made sense. A ghostly presence doomed to haunt forever the scene of his or her crime. He would have no quarrel with us, though. I didn't think we had ever been in danger. But how could I know for certain?

The stillness in the house was palpable. It seemed to have a life of its own.

I had a feeling that every ghostly thing was gone, even the haunting, unnatural scent of lilacs. Had we frightened Lucy's malevolent presence away? Or had it only materialized for a short time? I wondered if the dog had sensed it and run from the house?

Suddenly, I longed for a breath of fresh, reviving air, and had an irrational desire to gather a bunch of stems from a lilac tree and bury my face in the flowers.

~ * ~

Brent insisted on treating us to a late lunch at Clovers. "We have to talk about what just happened," he said.

"Nothing happened," Lucy pointed out. "An angry spirit haunts the house. As Jennet says, it could well be the ghost of a man who committed murder in life."

"Man or woman," I amended. "Would the killer still be angry?"

Lucy gave me a patient smile. "I don't have all the answers, Jennet. Perhaps if he was angry at the moment of his death, the emotion went with him into the afterlife. I just don't know."

"The man who killed Ned must have been angry," I said.

"Who had reason to be mad at him?" Annica asked.

"The guy he was chasing," I said. "Sara, some cast-off girlfriend, Evanora herself, her father..."

To my knowledge, the murder of Officer Ned Douglas was a cold case. If the killer hadn't been apprehended in the past, how could we hope to solve the mystery so many years removed from the incident, with practically no information?

"I'm disappointed," Annica said. "I thought we were going to see Evanora today. We didn't even see Lucy's cloud."

Should I mention the scent of lilacs? Why not?

When I described it, Brent said, "It's too early for lilacs."

"Not for ghostly lilacs."

"I didn't smell anything. Did you, Annica?"

"Just the stuffiness of an uninhabited house," she said.

"So Lucy senses an evil cloud, or smoke. Jennet smells lilacs. Annica and I don't smell anything. Where does that leave us?

"With two psychics and two normal people," Lucy said.

Brent's booming laughter drew curious stares from people at nearby tables.

"I should have taken Misty," I said. "Then we'd have three psychics."

Brent tapped his glass with a spoon.

"That reminds me," he said. "I have another dog to catch."

Thirty-nine

Annica said, "It's great to have others wait on me. What is everybody going to have?" She recited the Sunday menu for us, saying she'd made it out herself yesterday.

We decided on hot turkey sandwiches with mashed potatoes, and I ordered a take-out dinner of the same for Crane.

Lucy took a sip of water. "Ghost hunting makes me thirsty. We need to know more about Evanora."

"I'll stop at the Green House after school tomorrow," I said. "The next day I'll go to the library. I may have missed something relevant. Other than that…I don't know."

Annica stifled a gasp. "Did you see who just came in?"

I looked toward the door where a woman stood surveying the room, as if searching for an empty table—or someone. She wore a long black raincoat, and her hair was a garish shade of orange-red.

Marcy intercepted her at the dessert carousel and gave her a sweet, preemptive smile, obviously remembering her. "Table for one?" I heard her ask.

"Somewhere private," the woman said.

Marcy led her past our booth to the back of the restaurant. Neither one looked our way.

"It's that woman who was so rude to me," Annica said when they were out of earshot. "I didn't think she'd have the nerve to come back to Clovers."

"How was she rude to you?" Brent demanded.

"She threw a plate of French toast at me."

Brent started to rise. "That's more than rude. I'll take care of her."

Annica grabbed his sleeve. "No, you won't. It'd be like hitting a dog for chewing your remote a week after he did it."

She didn't mention the woman's parting insult nor Colton Reeves' roses. Come to think of it, there were no roses on the counter today.

"Nobody I know would hit a dog," Brent said, settling back down in his chair.

Annica withdrew her hand. "Don't get upset. It was just an example."

"From just one glance, I can tell she's mean-spirited," Lucy said. "She's the kind of person who would take pleasure in harassing somebody who can't strike back."

"Like a waitress." Annica gave Marcy a sympathetic look as she passed by our booth en route to the kitchen. "I remember wishing I could pick up a piece of French toast and smash it in her ugly face."

Brent laughed. "You should have."

"I'm not that daring."

"I thought Mary Jeanne was going to ban her from the restaurant," I said.

"Once again, Mary Jeanne isn't here."

"If she gives your friend a hard time, I'll step in," Brent said.

Dear Brent, always ready to defend a damsel—or a dog—in distress. But I hoped he wouldn't do anything he could get arrested for. Carrot Top simply wasn't worth it.

~ * ~

Sometimes, it's futile to make plans. Monday's visit to the Green House of Antiques fell by the wayside when Principal Grimsley called an impromptu staff meeting that showed signs of lasting forever.

When he had finally covered all the items on his agenda, it was too late for any after-school activity.

The next day, a volatile confrontation with a student in my American Literature class resulted in a headache, which only worsened as Leonora drove us home to Foxglove Corners. She had planned to go with the library with me, my tales of Evanora having stirred her interest in the mystery.

I couldn't approach a research project, however tantalizing, with pain lodged behind my eyes.

"If your headache doesn't go away, call in sick tomorrow," Leonora said as we entered the northbound freeway. "You need all your faculties to match wits with a rebel student."

"He insulted me and called me a rude name. I sent him to the office."

That was the bare bones version of the incident. The boy's hateful words had continued to play in my mind, effectively ruining the rest of the day for me.

Remembering Annica's experience with the orange-haired customer, I wished I could have retaliated in some way. Sent a book flying toward his head? But that would be unthinkable, and the school day was over, the student likely removed from class for a day or so.

Forget him.

I concentrated on all the comforts and remedies I could use to banish my present pain. A cup of hot tea with maximum strength medication, a hearty but easy-to-assemble dinner, eight hours of sleep undisturbed by ghastly dreams.

"I should feel better tomorrow," I said, resisting a childish urge to cross my fingers.

But I wasn't.

As soon as I woke the next morning, I took Leonora's advice and called in sick. Crane came in from taking the dogs for their first outing of the day. His bacon-and-egg breakfast was ready. Still in my nightclothes, I could barely face toast and tea.

"Stay home and rest today," he said. "All day. That's an order."

"Of course."

"I'll bring a pizza for dinner."

"I hate headaches," I said.

As pleasant as complete rest sounded, I'd rather be dressed and ready to take on another day, especially as the weather promised to be mild and even warm. Experience had taught me that no matter how bad a day at school was, the next day was invariably better. It was almost as if the class as a whole wanted to atone for the heinous act of one of their number.

Crane laid a gentle hand on my head. If only he could stay home, too.

You can't have everything, I told myself.

He kissed me goodbye and left for his patrol. Velvet nudged my knee.

Play with me?

She always wanted to play and favored a human playmate over one of her collie sisters.

"Later," I told her, tamping down the guilt, and settled myself in the rocking chair with a new mystery I had no intention of reading. My eyelids felt heavy. They began to close.

In the dream, my book had undergone a startling transformation. It was smaller, lighter, and blue. The dust cover had disappeared.

Eagerly I opened it and discovered I held Volume II of Evanora's diary in my hand. Drum roll, please...I'd soon know what happened next.

The pages were blank, however. I was holding one of those popular 'Anything' books, the kind you can use for any purpose under the sun.

A sharp sense of disappointment followed me into wakefulness. The book in my lap had turned into a mystery again.

I sighed. Life was maddeningly frustrating. I'd missed my chance to visit the antique shop where I might find more of Evanora's property. I would probably have to wait until the weekend to go to the library. In the meantime, I was wasting an entire day.

My mind began to teem with possible plans. If by happy chance my headache went away, I could take Misty and return to the Valentine House.

With a malevolent spirit who resembled a cloud inhabiting the second floor?

Yes. I knew I wasn't going to do it, but what was the harm in creating this bold scenario?

Apparently ghosts didn't do their best work in crowds. The four of us, especially Brent, the king of bluster, had scared the spirits, good and bad, away. Evanora hadn't said 'Don't go.' She'd have been happy to be left alone in the silence of the house.

And this time, exploring the Valentine House alone, I might find evidence that would lead me to Evanora. Misty would protect me...

Wishful thinking. I wasn't going to leave my own home.

Regardless, I should get dressed. Do something constructive. Write another set of lesson plans for my substitute folder or tackle some light housekeeping.

All worthwhile goals, but I stayed in the rocker and, occasionally, watched the hands of the clock. They seemed to have frozen.

I wondered if my dream had a message: *There is no other diary. There's no point in looking for it.*

Forty

Through my dream, a high wind blew. It wailed and howled around the house and yanked tall trees out of the ground by their roots. One of them fell on the roof, and the room filled instantly with cold air.

I reached for a cardigan or shawl, anything to stave off the deadly chill. There was nothing, not even a throw tossed over a chair.

I shivered into wakefulness as the clock struck three. If you're cold in a dream, chances are you'll be cold when you wake up. I hadn't planned to fall asleep again, but it had happened. This day was interminable, every hour twice as long as it should be.

I rubbed my forehead and realized my headache had miraculously vanished. Two brief naps had been more beneficial than any pain pills. I felt like myself again, only a little drowsy. I resisted the temptation to let my eyes close.

The wind was still blowing around the house, mighty gusts that might have escaped from my dream.

Misty raised her head and yawned. Stretched out next to her, Velvet rolled over, hind legs in the air, front ones folded over at the elbow. She had been sleeping on her yellow dragon toy.

I was the worst collie mom who ever lived. The dogs needed fresh air and exercise. On a normal school day, Camille would have let them out by now. As she knew I was home, she would let me take charge of my own dogs' welfare, and I had slept through their exercise time.

I looked out the window. The wind whipped through the woods across the lane, causing tall trees to bend as they had in my dream. It was no day to be out and about, but we had no choice. Just a quick break. Out and in.

Knowing I was awake, the dogs gathered in the living room which instantly filled with wagging tails and plaintive whimpers. How could we all have slept through the raging wind?

I gazed out at Jonquil Lane. To my surprise, Camille appeared on the porch of the yellow Victorian, a fragile figure bracing herself on one of the posts. She paused for a moment, as if calling on hidden reserves of strength. Then, carrying a basket covered with a blue-checked napkin, she made her way through the wind out to the lane.

Go back, I thought. *Stay home. It's dangerous out there.*

A strong sense of *deja vu* stabbed at me. I had lived through this moment in time before. Or through one just like it. One neighbor visiting another, bringing food, a silent watcher...

At the edge of the woods stood a scrawny coyote, his eyes fastened on the human and the basket.

The coyote! I hadn't seen it in days. Once again it was alone, detached from the rest of the pack. Still dangerous.

Unaware of the creature's surveillance, Camille proceeded across the lane, struggling to stay upright.

In the house, eight collies sprang into action. *Coyote! Enemy!*

Misty leaped over Velvet and pawed at the glass, barking frantically. I was dimly aware of Twister and Holly barking across the lane in the yellow Victorian. All of the dogs were aware of the danger; Camille was oblivious.

"Look behind you!" I cried.

She couldn't hear me, of course. I rushed to the door. As I opened it, a gust of wind snatched the napkin from the basket. She made a grab for it but grasped the air. The cloth went flying back across the lane right into the path of the coyote. At the same moment, Camille lost her grip on the basket. It fell, spilling its contents spilled out onto the gravel. They looked like muffins.

The coyote moved.

Finally noticing the danger, Camille hurried, almost ran, up the walkway to the door. Shooing Candy and Misty back, I took her wrist and pulled her into the house, while the coyote pounced on the muffins. Before I could close the door, they were gone. As was the opportunist thief.

Camille stood in the vestibule, catching her breath and patting down her windblown hair.

"They're gone," she said. "My good orange-nut muffins. I made them for you. And my basket... It was my favorite. I forgot that we agreed not to bring food outside anymore."

"I'll get it for you." I'd had a quick glimpse of the basket, now, alas, empty, caught in a tangle of dried sunflower stalks. "We can still have muffins. I have some in the freezer..."

"Don't go out!" she cried. "That creature may be rabid."

"He's gone," I said. "With a stomach full of homemade muffins. I don't think he'll be hungry for wicker."

So saying, I moved toward the basket, just as a motor added its hum to the wail of the wind.

The dizzying sensation of *deja vu* struck again and maintained its hold, flooding me with memories.

I set my pot of stew down on the ground and watched the car come to a stop alongside the abandoned construction on Jonquil Lane, watched a hooded person unload four precious collie puppies as if they were trash left over from lunch.

A silver car with unmelted snow still clinging to its windows. It had taken off, leaving the castaway babies behind.

Camille's basket momentarily forgotten, I waited to see what sort of vehicle traveled the road on a day when the strong wind could hurl a hapless vehicle onto its side. Moments later, a silver car rounded a curve and passed by my house.

The same Honda? I couldn't be sure. The woman behind the wheel wore a dark hood, eyes fixed on the road ahead. The same woman? Her lone passenger, a sable collie, sat in the backseat, head half out of the open window.

In that moment, it seemed to me that the dog's eyes met mine. I could almost hear the unspoken plea: *Help me!*

I rushed out to the lane, like Camille struggling to withstand the wind's buffeting.

The car had stopped in practically the same place it had before.

It was happening again!

The driver opened the back door and yelled something I couldn't hear. The collie jumped down to the ground. Wagging its tail, it waited for the next development. Something pleasant? A walk in the woods?

The woman picked up a stick and tossed it into the woods; and the dog ran after it, not suspecting the vile trick.

I knew what would happen next—and it did. In a heartbeat, the woman was back in her car and driving away. All in the space of minutes.

The dog came bounding out of the woods, the stick in his mouth, and stood in the middle of the lane staring after the car. His tail was still wagging.

I knew what I was going to do, and there was no time to waste. The driver already had a good head start.

Camille was waiting in the vestibule, surrounded by eight excited collies and looking puzzled.

"Did the basket blow away?" she asked.

"It's caught in a vine."

I saw my shoulder bag on the coffee table where I had left it last night and swung it over my shoulder. My keys were inside along with my cell phone.

"Can you watch the dogs for me, Camille?" I asked.

"Sure, but..."

"I'm going to follow that car. There's a collie stranded in the lane. I hope it's still there. Oh, and the dogs have to go out..."

"That coyote may be hanging around."

The coyote was the least of my worries. I had only a moment to regret the multiple problems I was handing Camille.

"You'll sort it out," I said and went back through the door, praying I wasn't too late.

~ * ~

This is madness, I told myself. *You'll never catch that woman. And if you do, what then?*

I passed the abandoned development, passed the collie who still stood in the lane, looking lost, as he had every right to be.

I had faith in Camille. She would take care of my dogs and coax the abandoned collie inside. Which wasn't ideal, but the wretched woman hadn't left me a choice.

I'd let the man who dumped the puppies drive off the last time and lived to regret it. I couldn't waste this heaven-sent opportunity.

When I reached Squill Lane, I hesitated. Turning left would bring me to a cornfield and the yellow cottage at Lane's End that, so far as I knew, was uninhabited. If the woman was familiar with the local geography, she would have turned right, which would take her past Sue's horse ranch.

I turned right and surveyed an empty lane brushed in pale sunlight. Once I reached the end of Squill Lane, where would I go?

Deal with directions a moment at a time.

I'd never thought of apprehending her. The woman would deny ever having had a dog in her car, in spite of inevitable fur trapped on the cushions. But if I could find the car, copy the license plate, she could be stopped and questioned. Perhaps she would be unable to continue her abominable activities.

It'll be her word against yours, I reminded myself, then had a more cheerful thought. At least she'd be warned that somebody knew about her activities. Maybe that knowledge would be enough to convince her to curtail them.

I drove on, pushing negative thoughts away, happy that I was finally doing something proactive.

Forty-one

A drop of precipitation landed on my windshield, then another, then several.

It was that dreaded rain-snow mix that had been so prevalent this year. In a heartbeat, I was passing through a snow squall.

Now? In April? I had hoped Mother Nature would be on my side today. But nobody dictates to the lady, and my snow scraper was handy. Knowing my state, I didn't move it to the trunk until Memorial Day.

I turned on the lights and windshield wipers and slowed to a reasonable speed. Not that there was any traffic to speak of on Spruce Road, but ice was likely already forming on the pavement.

Those negative thoughts I'd pushed aside returned to taunt me. I had lost the woman, lost my chance to give her license plate number to Lieutenant Dalby. The next time she drove up Jonquil Lane with a dog to get rid of, I might not be on hand to witness the incident.

I should have taken a picture with my phone. Why didn't I?

In the meantime, the spring day had grown hazardous. It was a struggle to see through the wind-driven snow-mix. I might as well be on Huron Court, the road of impossibly changing seasons.

Then, in the blink of an eye, my luck changed. Through the swirling mix, I spied the Universal Gas Station ahead. A silver Honda was just pulling up to the self-serve pump. Its front right tire looked low to me. A woman in a dark hooded jacket exited, and, without looking at the tire, limped to the office. The same woman who had just abandoned the collie.

Improbable coincidence? Yes, but I'd take it.

I turned into the gas station, brought the car to a stop alongside the white fence that separated it from a row of houses, and quickly jotted down the license plate number. A black and white sticker affixed to the rear window advertised: 'Relocations, Inc.' and contained a phone number.

Relocations?

I added that information and, my goal achieved, should have driven on.

But when had I ever left well enough alone? And lived to regret it? I turned off the engine and followed the woman inside.

She was at the counter, pre-paying for her gas. She had pushed her hood back to reveal a birds' nest of short carrot-red curls threaded through with gray. She could be described as stocky if one were inclined to be kind. I wasn't, as she was obviously Annica's tormenter from Clovers. It was a day for coincidences.

She grabbed a handful of snacks in a display under the counter: a bag of barbecue-flavored potato chips, a chocolate bar, a package of gum, and a bottle of grape drink.

"Ghastly weather," I said.

She glanced at me but didn't reply.

"Not fit for man or beast," I added.

It was the clerk who responded to my comment. "It came on all of a sudden. Be careful when you go back out there."

I took a twenty-dollar bill from my purse. "I'm guessing it'll take ten dollars. I have a long way to go, and I don't want to run out of gas."

"I don't blame you."

Bracing for a rebuff, I gave Carrot Top a tentative smile. "I saw what happened back on Jonquil Lane. Your dog got away from you. Hopefully, he's still there."

Anger flashed in her eyes. She glared at me. "I don't know what you're talking about. I don't have a dog."

"I'm sure the car I saw was yours. An older model silver Honda." I pointed to the only vehicle parked beside the pump. "Like that one."

"You saw somebody else. I don't even know where Jonquil Lane is and, like I told you, I don't have a dog."

"There aren't many cars on the road today. I saw what you did," I added.

Ignoring me, she pushed her snacks toward the cashier. "I'll take this stuff, too."

Well, I'd tried, and I had valuable information about Carrot Top in my notebook. I tossed my parting shot at her.

"You'd better check your tire, front right," I said. "It looks low to me."

She didn't thank me and didn't seem surprised. "Damn country roads."

She dropped her purchases into her oversized handbag and left me standing at the counter.

Now to buy gas I didn't really need.

~ * ~

By the time I reached Jonquil Lane, the snow squall had dissipated, along with the faint hint of spring. I made a detour to the front yard and retrieved Camille's basket. Then, shivering, I walked carefully up to the side door, stepping around a patch of ice and wondering how Camille had fared in my absence.

The dogs were barking, falling over one another in their race to be the first to welcome me home. Eight collies. Where was the newest foundling?

Camille sat at the oak table drinking tea. She'd brought a cup down from the cupboard for me and taken apple muffins out of the freezer to thaw.

I set her basket on the table. "Good as new. I didn't see the napkin, though."

"It must have blown into the woods. Maybe it'll turn up in the spring."

"Couldn't you find the collie?" I asked.

"I thought I'd save time and called Sue. She picked him up on the lane right where you said he'd be and took him to the ranch."

"He's safe them."

"Sue says he's an older dog. She's going to take him to Lila and Letty at Brent's new home for geriatric collies."

The newly-abandoned dog would be in good hands. Still, my happiness was mixed with sorrow at the fate of aging pets whose owners lost interest in them. It was so unfair.

With a sigh, I sank into a chair, suddenly exhausted, while Camille turned the heat on under the teakettle and heated the muffins in the microwave.

"Are you all right, Jennet?" Camille asked. "Crane said you stayed home with a headache."

Crane...He would be upset that I'd confronted a possible criminal and, not at all pleased that I hadn't spent the day resting. I couldn't *not* tell him, though.

"It went away," I said, "and I had a stroke of luck following that car."

I told her about catching up with Carrot Top at the gas station. "She denied having a dog, but I know what I saw. And she's the woman who insulted Annica at Clovers the other day."

"She may live locally then."

"I was hoping she was just passing through. No such luck."

Camille took the muffins out of the microwave and dropped them into the basket.

"That could have been dangerous," she said. "But wasn't the person who dumped the little collies a man?"

"That's true. A man in a silver Honda. They may be working together."

"Or there may be two people in different cars, dumping dogs independently of each other. The man could be her husband. You can't know."

"You may be right," I said.

But I felt I was the one who was right. A person who would hurl mean-spirited words at a waitress wouldn't hesitate to get rid of an unwanted pet.

Something nagged at me. I tried to make my mind a blank slate to think about it. Darn. It was gone.

"Cars today are either beige or gray or black," Camille was saying. "Or plain white. Bland. I remember a time when they painted cars pretty colors like sky blue."

"I don't," I said. "But I'd like a blue car."

Then the idea reappeared, and happily it made sense. What if Carrot Top and the man who had shoved the puppies out of his car weren't getting rid of their own dogs, but providing a service for those who didn't have the heart or stomach to do it themselves?

"I noticed a sticker on the rear window for a company called Relocations, Inc." I said. "It may have nothing to do with dumping collies, but think about the name for a minute. Could there possibly a business that relocates dogs?"

"From a comfortable home to a country road? It's possible. But I always assumed people took care of their own dogs, one way or another."

"I'm going to call them." I glanced at the kitchen clock. I hadn't realized how late it was. In spite of all that had transpired, it seemed as if I'd only wakened from my nap an hour ago. "I'll call them in the morning."

Dumping a pet was illegal, an act best done without witnesses. Who would start a business devoted to such an outrage? And who would be stupid enough to advertise it with a sticker on a car window?

Forty-two

Crane didn't lecture me about reckless behavior. On the contrary, he was happy to have Carrot Top's license plate number.

"I'll pass it on to Mac," he said. "I came across two strays earlier today. Abandoned dogs have become an epidemic in the Corners. If this woman is contributing to the situation, I want her stopped."

He set the pizza box down, a simple act which drew the collies from far and wide. Candy placed her paws on the table and gave an impervious woof.

"I can't believe so many people want to get rid of their pets," I said.

"You should hear the excuses people give for surrendering a dog. 'He sheds all over the new furniture.' 'She barks at everything, even her shadow.' 'The puppy bites.'"

"I've heard them all," I said. "I'm so glad Brent's new shelter is open."

"The ladies are taking care of ten dogs already, including the ones I brought them today."

"I'm going to stop in and visit them soon," I said.

It would be strange to see Emma and Rachel in the old white Victorian instead of the Woodville sisters. Come to think of it, I hadn't called on Lila and Letty at Brent's home for geriatric collies either. I'd been too busy.

With the dead.

~ * ~

In the middle of the night, the dulcet notes of Evanora's music box woke me. So much for it being broken. It simply preferred to play on its own schedule rather than mine and to come to life in the dark.

I lay still listening to the unknown melody. Inevitably, my thoughts turned to Evanora. Had its music provided her with any comfort in the aftermath of Ned's passing? She would listen to the sweet air over and over again and remember the day he'd given it to her as a birthday present. That was all she had left of him, except for the baby.

I imagined her wandering the night looking for her music box. From her home in the Valentine house, she would hear it playing and glide unseen down the lane until she reached our house.

Being a spirit, she could walk through walls, following the music to the credenza in the dining room. Only Misty would be aware of her presence. When I woke in the morning, would I find it missing?

If I continued with these eerie imaginings, I would be awake for the rest of the night. I told myself that the ghost of a girl in mourning wouldn't have that power.

Would she?

I'd had the music box in my possession since Valentine's Day and, although I hadn't realized it at the time, the diary also. I should have wrapped up the mystery by now. A house where a ghost continued to mourn, a temperamental music box that had the power to turn itself on at will, and a story without a proper end—all challenging but not impossible.

As I drifted off to sleep, I promised myself that this weekend I would tackle the mystery anew, and I wouldn't stop until I solved it.

~ * ~

After a sick day, classes can be doubly difficult, especially when a sub allowed the students to run amok.

I found a detailed report on the day's activities or a lack thereof on my desk the next morning, along with a stack of disciplinary referrals for the usual suspects, and a note from the principal's office. He wanted to see me during my conference period.

That was ominous. Could I be blamed for mayhem that transpired in my absence?

Apparently. I had six hours to wait and worry and steer my wayward students back in the right direction.

In general, I had a tenuous relationship with Grimsley. He gave the appearance of friendliness—you know, the principal is your pal—but it was as phony as the smile he pasted on when it served his purposes. He opened the conversation with a comment that seemed kind and caring. How unusual.

"I trust you're feeling better, Mrs. Ferguson. You look well."

"I'm much better," I said, thinking of closing in on Carrot Top in a snow squall.

He indicated his own stack of disciplinary referrals, the green copies.

"It wasn't a good day. I've instructed the board not to hire Miss Cannon in the future. You're lucky you had a classroom to come back to."

That was news to me. Our excellent custodians would have given the room a thorough cleaning. At least I hadn't noticed anything missing from the bulletin boards or obvious damage.

"Yes," he said, "and I think you'd better make sure you have more challenging lesson plans in your folder. More than enough to keep the classes busy."

I refrained from saying that I considered my plans adequate. They were, but in order to accommodate him, I'd have to make subsequent plans super adequate. And what if the malcontents refused to do the work?

I had nothing to be gained by asking that question. He would probably tell me that I hadn't demanded respect and industry from my students on a daily basis, so how could I expect them to behave for a substitute?

According to rumor, Grimsley had never taught a class.

Welcome to my world, I thought.

"I'll try not to get sick, anymore," I said.

The phony smile flashed on. "That's the spirit."

And the meeting was over.

~ * ~

Saturday dawned with another promise of spring and no snow squalls in the forecast. As soon as Crane left for his patrol and I'd walked the dogs, I invited Annica to accompany me on a sleuthing trip.

"Where are we going?" she asked.

"To Maple Creek. I want to go to Sherbourne's Bakery and check out a place called Relocations, Inc. I suspect they're in the business of dumping dogs."

After expressing her dismay and disgust, she said, "I have the day off and I'm caught up on my reading for once. We can have lunch out," she added.

"I'll pick you up at eleven," I said, which gave me a half hour to find my mystery notebook and make sure I had the cell phone in my purse As it turned out, I picked Annica up early, both of us eager for our adventure to begin.

She had dressed to welcome spring in lime-green with a yellow jacket. Both colors were immensely flattering for her red-gold hair, and her earrings were miniature suns.

"Where to first?" she asked.

"The bakery," I said.

"If we have time, can we see if Valentine Villa is still for sale?"

I recalled the pink Victorian house in which Annica had previously expressed an interest.

"Why not?"

On the way, I told her about my confrontation with Carrot Top.

"My arch-enemy strikes again," she murmured. "It looks like she's more than just evil-tempered. But do you think you should have accused her of dumping the collie to her face?"

"Well, I did. It's done."

"You've just made an enemy," she said.

I had considered that. But Carrot Top—I wish I knew her name—wasn't my first enemy, and I suspected she wouldn't be the last. In any event, I'd done it for dogs everywhere who were in danger of losing their homes.

"I hope you don't run into her again," Annica said.

I smiled, safe in my car with my friend for backup and the vile abandoner probably miles away.

"I hope I do," I said.

<h1 style="text-align:center">Forty-three</h1>

It was always a pleasure to visit Maple Creek, especially on a sunny day when the world trembled on the brink of spring. I hoped to find answers to the double mysteries that had taken over my life, but if I didn't, just being out and about was satisfactory.

Sherbourne's was a charming bakery, its window decorated with an Easter theme. Trays of hot cross buns and festive Easter breads shared a wide sweep of faux grass with a collection of vintage rabbit figurines. There was even a basket of brightly colored eggs—imitation, I assumed, as the window wasn't refrigerated.

Inside, a smiling young clerk in an enormous white apron was transferring powdered fried cakes from a baking sheet to a display case. She wished us a good morning and agreed that it was a beautiful day.

"Is Mrs. Sherbourne in?" I asked.

Her smile faded. "Oh, no. She won't be in—ever. She passed away a week before Christmas."

I should have remembered. The Sherbourne estate sale.

"That was Mrs. Evanora Sherbourne?"

"No, Miss Sara."

"Is the bakery going to stay open?" I asked.

She nodded. "Under new management. Sherbourne's has been a fixture in Maple Creek since 1975. A relative took over."

"Do you know her name?" I asked.

The girl's eyes narrowed. She must be wondering why I was asking so many questions.

"I don't recall it," she said. "What can I get for you, ladies?"

Interrogation ended.

I bought a half dozen cream puffs, and we set out to look for Relocations Inc., making inquiries in stores on Main Street. No one had heard of it, but one gentleman thought it was a moving company. That made sense, given the name, more sense than the idea that some unscrupulous person had started a company to dump unwanted pets.

"It looks like there's no such place," I said after we'd walked up and down the street twice and talked to several pedestrians.

"But you saw a sticker on that car," Annica reminded me.

"Yes, but maybe it was for a company that went out of business. Some people put stickers on their windows and never remove them."

Still, the sticker in question had looked crisp and new, in so far as I could tell, having seen it through a snow squall.

"I should have seen the writing on the wall when I couldn't reach them by phone or find them on the Internet," I said. "But I have a feeling that woman will turn up again."

Annica suppressed a shudder. "Not at Clovers, I hope."

I sighed. "And not on Jonquil Lane, dumping another dog."

"So the mystery continues, but all isn't lost," Annica said. "We have cream puffs and this absolutely gorgeous day. Let's have lunch and drive by Valentine Villa."

~ * ~

Over soup and sandwiches at a restaurant near the park, Annica said, "I've taken a virtual tour of Valentine Villa. It's lovely inside, too. I wonder if there's a story connected with it. A mystery maybe?"

"Is that why you're obsessed with it?"

She looked startled. "I'm not obsessed, no more than you are with the Valentine House. It's just that this is the only house I ever saw that called to me. I can see myself living there with someone special. Forever after, like in the fairy tales."

Brent, I assumed. She didn't have to say his name.

"It's your dream house then," I said.

"You could say that. If I had half a million dollars, I'd snap it up in a heartbeat."

I didn't remind her that if she had that much money, she could resign from her waitressing job at Clovers and concentrate on her college courses.

"Someday…" She left her thought unsaid.

I understood. I had felt the same way about the green Victorian house on Jonquil Lane. It had been love at first sight. Everyone is entitled to hold fast to a dream.

~ * ~

Valentine Villa lived up to Annica's lavish descriptions. It was an elegant nineteenth century Victorian with graceful lines, soft pink siding, and lacy gingerbread trim. Its most eye-catching feature was the heart-shaped stained-glass window that adorned the highest gable.

I found myself comparing it to Evanora's house in the woods, on a grander scale, of course. For this was a house meant to be lived in, not designed for child's play. Or lovers' meetings.

"It's exquisite, but it looks lonely," I said.

"Do you think so?" Annica asked.

She had taken several pictures of the house from every angle. Anyone would think she was a serious prospective buyer.

She slipped her phone into her purse. "It reminds me of a Valentine cake," she said. "See how the window shines in the sunlight? Did you ever see anything prettier? It looks like a gigantic ruby."

The window fairly sparkled, invoking an image of the painted heart on Evanora's house. An idea tried to rise to my consciousness, then escaped before I could grasp it.

"Whoever lived here must have loved Valentine's Day," I said. "I've only seen heart-shaped stained glass in sun catchers."

"This was obviously a special order, and it isn't the only Valentine decoration in the house. I took a virtual tour of the interior. The crown molding has a heart and scroll design, and the walls are different shades of pink. I wish I could have seen it when it was furnished."

The elusive idea reappeared. It was probably irrelevant, but maybe not.

I said, "I wonder if Evanora was the one who painted the heart on the playhouse, maybe in memory of Ned."

"Then after he was killed, she would go there and dream about him? We'll never know, Jennet, but I always thought the Valentine was part of the house from the beginning. Things for little kids are cute that way, illustrated with birds and ducks and flowers."

And hearts.

But Evanora, as I had come to know her through her writing, didn't seem like the kind of girl who would paint a decoration on a house. She would have had to take a ladder, a can of paint, and a brush to the woods, and how could she do it in secret? Sara would certainly intercept her.

Also, Evanora was on her way to college, and she was pregnant. The facts, as stated in the diary, didn't support the idea. Reluctantly, I let it go.

"We'd better move on before someone notices us and calls the police," Annica said.

"Don't be silly. The house is for sale. We'll say you're interested in buying it."

Still, I looked around. It was a singularly quiet street, and there was no one in sight.

"I hate to leave," Annica said. "I just love this house."

I glanced at the 'For Sale' sign. "Why don't you call the realtor and make an appointment to see it—in real life. He won't have to know you're just looking."

"Will you come with me?" she asked.

"Sure. I'm interested in Victorian houses, too."

"I'll do it," she said. "Quickly, before someone makes an offer."

For some reason, I didn't think that was likely.

"Well, nothing we did took as long as I thought it would," I said. "Would you like to top off our day out with a stop at the Green House?"

The prospect of antiquing cheered her. "I'm game. Maybe I'll find a Valentine figurine or something similar for my future home."

I suppressed a smile. "Wrong holiday. Look for Easter bunnies."

Forty-four

Like the bakery, the Green House of Antiques was dressed for Easter with fanciful baskets at every turn. Some of them, filled with treats such as chocolate eggs, bunnies, and jelly beans, were wrapped in pastel cellophane and ready for gift-giving. Others were empty—all sizes, shapes, and colors.

Surprisingly, we were the only customers, and Lola was the only salesperson on the floor. She wore a beaded flapper's dress with a long string of pearls, and, rather incongruously, brandished a feather duster as she wove her way through aisles of antiques. She seemed truly happy to see us, which was understandable. It must be unsettling to work alone amidst all this vintage furniture.

"Good afternoon," she said with a smile of recognition. "Earrings and old books? Right?"

Annica returned her smile. "It's better to be known in an antique shop than a bakery, I guess."

Lola frowned. "A bakery?"

"Inside joke."

"We have some lovely spring jewelry," Lola said.

I wished I could discuss the music box's odd behavior with her, but if I did, she would think I was delusional. Or maybe not. She'd told me a story about it, but I couldn't recall the details.

Ask her.

I said, "I don't suppose you remember, but I bought a music box from you around Valentine's Day. It had an unusual history."

"I remember. The little Cupid box. Are you enjoying it?"

"Very much, and it works now."

"How on earth did you get it going?"

"I didn't do anything special. One day, it just started playing." I didn't add that I hadn't wound it up at the time.

"If I'd known it wasn't broken, I would have bought it myself." She paused. "Would you like to sell it back to us?"

"No, but what was the story connected to it again?"

"I remember that, too. The music box was a lover's gift. Somehow it became involved in betrayal and murder, but the lady who owned it kept it all her life. Sorry, I don't know any other details."

"How did you find out that much?" I asked.

"From the woman in charge of the estate sale. For some of the antiques, she jotted down notes. That story stuck in my mind."

"I wonder where she heard it."

"That I can't tell you, but I assume from a family member, probably the heir."

The facts didn't agree with Evanora's story as I knew it. Still, could there be a grain of truth in it? The music box had been a lover's gift. And murder, yes. Ned was killed. But betrayal? Did that fit Evanora's tale?

"Who was the heir?" I asked.

"All these questions!" She twisted the rope of pearls around and around. "How would I know that? You'll have to talk to Ms. Zara."

"Could I?"

"I don't see why not, but not this week. She's out of town on a buying trip. Ms. Zara is the one who attended the sale. Anyway, what does an old story matter? It's probably not even true."

I glanced toward Annica, who was trying on earrings at the jewelry counter. When she'd worked at Past Perfect, she had taken pleasure in spinning outrageous yarns about the shop's merchandise.

"It adds to the ambience," I said.

"You like old series books, don't you?" Lola asked. "Are you interested in the Campfire Girls? We acquired an entire set last week. They're in tip-top condition."

"I'll look at them," I said, but my mind was still on the music box. Did the heir know it worked occasionally and without the aid of a key?

Lola swirled her feather duster over a two-tier side table and moved away. "I'll see if your friend found anything to her liking."

~ * ~

Toward the back of the shop an Easter bunny doll decked out in a pretty pink gingham jumper presided over a jumbo-sized basket filled with children's books, many of them tiny, just the size to fit into a small hand.

Lying on top of the stack was a timeworn copy of *The Velveteen Rabbit*. At the Green House, one could find treasures in even the darkest corner.

The collection wasn't all children's fiction, nor Easter-themed. Although my main interests were Judy Bolton and Beverly Gray, I paused for a moment to examine the contents of the basket.

Underneath a vintage edition of *Little Women* with a beautifully illustrated cover was a small blue book. As I reached for it, my heart gave a great leap forward. Could it be...?

Yes! Eagerly I opened it to see that the pages were covered with writing in a familiar hand. Finally, when I had all but given up, I'd found another diary.

But wait! Was it a record of events that had taken place before or after Evanora's fateful summer?

I turned back to the first page. The heading 'Falling Leaves' gave me my answer. Coincidence had blessed me again and led me to Volume II of Evanora's diary.

If there were a Volume III, I didn't want to leave it behind in the basket. Hastily I looked, but the rest of the books were simply that. Books.

I took my find to Lola, who was helping Annica decide between two pairs of earrings.

"I found this in the basket back there," I said. "It's an old diary."

Annica's eyes lit up. "Is that what I think it is?

I nodded.

"Someone must have put it there by mistake." Lola reached for the diary. "I'll take it."

No you won't. I held onto it.

"There was one just like it in a box of books I bought in February," I said. "I'd like to buy it."

"But it's a mistake," Lola insisted.

"How much?"

"Well…" She gave her necklace a twirl. "Nothing. If I'd known it was there, I would have discarded it. Just take it and you don't have to mention this to Ms. Zara."

I wondered how Lola couldn't have noticed the diary but didn't intend to ask. All that mattered was that it was mine now. I slipped it into my shoulder bag.

"What do you think?" Annica asked. "The Easter eggs or the chocolate bunnies?"

It took me a minute to realize she was referring to the earrings.

"The bunnies," I said. "Or both."

She glanced at the price tags and did a quick mental calculation.

"I'll take the bunnies," she said.

Lola turned to me. "Did you find the Campfire Girls books?"

I'd forgotten about them but felt I should make a purchase.

"I'll need a minute to decide," I said.

Just a minute. I couldn't wait to go home and continue reading Evanora's story.

Forty-five

A vintage white Plymouth with green fins was waiting for me when I turned into the driveway. Brent sat inside, his hand resting on the head of a large ferocious looking dog who resembled a wolf. Good grief! *Was* it a wolf?

As I parked, Brent exited the car, taking care to slam the door quickly. I peered through the window. The beast scrambled into the driver's seat and stared back at me with sad dark eyes. Instead of a collar, he wore a thick rope around his neck.

"Have you been hunting?" I asked.

"Very funny." He strolled over to the trunk and brought out a shopping bag from Pluto's and a yellow tulip plant. "It's another throwaway dog."

"How can you tell he isn't a wolf?"

"He's dog-like. When I went up to him, he raised his paw to shake. Wolves don't do that."

"He may be a wolf-hybrid. You don't hear much about them anymore."

I knew that hybrids often lacked the temperament to live in harmony with humans and other pets. I couldn't see the advantage of deliberately crossing a dog with a wolf, but where did that leave the ones who were already here?

"He's some kind of mix," Brent said. "I see a little husky in him. He acts like he lived with people. He must have been cute as a puppy, but look at him now."

"He's wildly majestic," I said as I took the plant. "For me?"

"For the house. I don't want the sheriff to get jealous."

The collies were yipping behind the door, and the wolf dog was howling in the car. All the scene needed was a scrawny coyote at the edge of the woods across the lane.

As soon as we stepped inside, the collies advanced on us, tails wagging, eyes fixed on the shopping bag. They knew that whatever was inside was good, and it was for them.

"Back, girls!" I set the plant on the counter and, because the dirt was dry, gave the tulip a drink.

"I have good news," Brent said.

"So do I. You first."

"I'm fed up with all these dogs being dumped, so I got my men on it. They've been driving all over Foxglove Corners, Lakeville, and Maple Creek, looking for an old silver Honda with a sticker on the window."

He pulled a paper out of his pocket. "Jeff found it this morning parked in a driveway on Elmsdale Street in Lakeville. Another car, same make and color, was parked in front of it. Both cars had stickers on the rear windows."

"Great! You found Carrot Top. Let's celebrate with tea. Or coffee."

"Whatever you're having." He eyed the loaf of banana-nut bread on the counter. "And some of that."

I put water on the stove to boil and brought mugs and dessert plates down from the cupboard. "What do we do now?"

"I have a plan," he said. "I'll let it be known that I have too many dogs. I have to get rid of a couple of them, but I'm too chicken to do it myself, so I'll contact this woman. The rest will be history."

"That's entrapment," I said.

"Call it whatever you like. This woman probably left dozens of dogs on country roads to starve to death. She deserves to be entrapped. Besides, she threw a plate of food at Annica."

"How are you going to get in touch with her?" I asked.

"I'll call the number on the sticker."

"When I called, I got a 'not in service' message," I said.

"Maybe you copied it wrong."

"It's possible."

I'd done it quickly, writing through falling snow, anxious to go inside and confront Carrot Top.

"I was thinking," I said. "If Relocations, Inc., is a business, how do they attract their customers? They can't just place an ad in the paper offering to dispose of unwanted pets."

"I don't know. Word of mouth? Al's Source? Maybe they park in lots, hoping the curious will call them."

"Then they'd probably get requests from people looking for movers."

"When we get our hands on that woman, we'll find out," he said.

I could hope she didn't run a legitimate moving company. I was ninety-nine percent certain she dealt with moving pets.

I set the loaf of banana bread on a carving board and began to cut it into thick slices under the watchful eyes of eight collies. They knew sooner or later crumbs would fall to the floor and the red-haired bringer of treats would slip them hand-outs when I wasn't looking.

"It'll never work," I said. "No one will believe you're the kind of man who would throw a dog away."

"I'm a good actor."

I smiled. "Since when?"

"I've proved myself lots of times."

That was true. "All right. What part do I play in this scheme?"

"All you have to do is testify that you saw her dump a dog on Jonquil Lane and four collie puppies, too."

"The person who abandoned those puppies was a man," I reminded him.

"Her husband or partner, then."

"I'll do it," I said. "Gladly. And she'll deny it. When I cornered her at the gas station, she swore she didn't own a dog."

"She was telling the truth. Her mission in life was to get rid of other people's dogs."

"I need evidence."

Brent's enthusiasm was catching. In my mind, Carrot Top was already apprehended and behind bars. The abandoned dogs were properly avenged and so was Annica. Peace reigned in Foxglove Corners again, and all the dogs had homes.

"Are you taking Wolf to the new shelter?" I asked.

"That's my next stop. Hey! Wolf! That's the perfect name for him."

"As long as no one thinks he's a real wolf."

He helped himself to another slice of banana bread, unmindful of the fact that Candy was practically sitting beside him at the table. "You said you had good news, too?"

"Annica and I went antiquing today, and I found another one of Evanora's diaries."

Which I couldn't wait to read. I was as eager to learn more of Evanora's story as Brent was to set his entrapment plan in motion.

~ * ~

Not wanting to spend time cooking an elaborate dinner, I brought two steaks out of the freezer, threw a salad together, and let the dogs play in the yard. Before long, Candy and Misty began to worry me with their strange behavior. They kept running to the edge of the lane and looking into the woods. Misty was whining.

Not knowing what they were sighting or sensing was troubling, and I soon brought everyone inside.

Misty alone refused to settle down, stationing herself at the window where she had a good view of the woods across from Jonquil Lane.

Coyotes? They'd be fools to come closer to a house where eight large collies lived. After a while, I sat in the rocker and took the diary out of my purse. Misty lay at my feet, her head on her paws, and closed her eyes. Looking forward to a long uninterrupted block of time, I began to read:

EVANORA'S DIARY

FALLING LEAVES—The woods have burst into spectacular color. Leaves keep falling as I make my daily pilgrimage to the house in the woods. By rights, I should be in school, but I decided to skip the fall semester. I wouldn't be able to concentrate on my courses. All I can think about is Ned.

These days I'm always restless. I'm not interested in getting clothes together for a baby that doesn't seem real to me. Mother is sewing a layette. She made a baby blanket.

"It's your favorite color, Evanora. Mint green."

"Yes," I said. "It's nice."

How can I care about a baby when I don't have its father?

If I had attended Ned's funeral, I would know that he is truly gone. But I couldn't make myself go, and after his body was buried, I discovered he isn't gone at all. He lives on in Cecily's playhouse. Once I felt his presence there. Only there. Only once. He never goes near the stream where he was killed.

I talk to him at the house. One day, he'll answer and tell me what to do and maybe, maybe, he'll tell me who murdered him. After all, there are stranger things in heaven and earth than are dreamed of...

One day I'll see him again.

Forty-six

SPECIAL REQUEST—My family is very nice to me these days, but they don't understand my desire for solitude. They don't know why I still walk in the woods, sometimes with my lunch in a paper bag. I tell them I'm giving Honey the exercise she needs. They don't know that I can't wait to reach my real home.

I asked Dad if we could give the heart on the playhouse a fresh coat of paint.

"We?" he said. "You never painted anything in your life, Evanora."

"Okay, you."

"It isn't our property," he said.

"Why would the owner object to our taking care of it?" I asked. "Who would even know?"

"But no one will see it," he said.

"I will."

Finally he agreed.

As I said, everyone in my family is nice to me.

NAMES—Mother keeps sewing and knitting and crocheting. It looks like she's creating a doll's wardrobe, like she used to do when Sara and I were little girls. She showed me a tiny dress she'd made, or maybe it was a nightgown. Like the blanket, it was mint green. Most of the clothes she makes are mint green. "It's a color for either a boy or girl," she said.

She asked me if I'd given any thought to names.

I looked up from my book.

"For your baby," she said.

"It's too soon."

"No, it isn't. You need to be prepared."

I didn't want to have a discussion about baby names. "Okay" I said. "If it's a boy, I'll call him Edward. Ned for short."

"And if you have a girl?"

"Nora," I said. "Or Eva."

Anything to make her stop talking about the baby.

SARA—"Why are you spending time in that old house?" Sara asked this morning. She saw me making my usual lunch: a peanut butter sandwich, a banana, and a thermos bottle of tea. I guess she assumed I was going to eat in the playhouse.

"I'm taking advantage of the good weather," I said. "Pretty soon it'll be too cold to go out walking."

"People will start calling you the mad woman of the woods," she said.

"What people?" I asked.

"Anyone who sees you."

I wasn't worried. I don't think anyone in our neighborhood is monitoring my activities. If they are, they'll see a girl walking her dog. There's nothing unusual about that. Besides, I don't care what people think.

"I need exercise," I said, "and so does Honey. No one else around here takes her for walks."

"Do you want company?" Sara asked. "I don't think it's safe for you to wander around in the woods alone."

I definitely did <u>not</u> want company. Ned might not appear if Sara was with me. But I couldn't hurt her feelings. She's been supportive of me, acting like a real sister at last.

"You can join me someday," I told her. "But not today. I want to be alone today."

OUT OF THE FOG—Something strange and wonderful and also terrible happened today. I was eating my sandwich in the little house and looking out the window at the stream, remembering other lunches and other days. It had been foggy when I'd entered the woods. It was still foggy, and the half-opened window let the fragrant fall air blow inside. In spite of what had happened at the stream, it was a beautiful view.

I was thinking how soon the trees would be bare when I saw a figure in blue step out of the fog. He stood at the edge of the stream, looking toward the house.

I knew it was Ned even though I couldn't see his face clearly. Like you can't see a face in a dream, but you know who it is.

Only why didn't he come closer? Did he see me? I didn't think so. Then why had he come?

I called his name. He didn't move. But I could. I got up so fast I tore my sleeve on the edge of the table.

I dropped my sandwich and hurried outside, but as I started to run to the stream, he vanished.

There was nothing to see but fog and water.

REFLECTIONS—I didn't sleep well last night. I tossed and turned endlessly and thought about Ned. If he had returned to earth, why didn't he appear in the house where I was? Was his coming and going dependent on the fog? Why stand beside the stream where he was slain? Most of all, I wondered why he disappeared before I could go to him.

One more question. Why didn't Honey react to Ned's appearance? He was one of her favorite people. I always thought dogs had a way of knowing when there are ghosts in the area, but that must be an old wives' tale.

When I came back to the house, I found my sandwich gone, every last crumb. Honey had left the banana alone and obviously didn't drink tea. She didn't look the slightest bit guilty. That's my Honey.

I wasn't hungry anymore.

No one can know I've seen Ned. They'd think I was mad for sure.

I told Mother I'd do the shopping today, and afterward, I drove to the cemetery to visit Ned's grave. It's at the end of a winding country road. I was the only one there. I don't know if Ned is there or if he rises to walk with the fog, but this was the best I could do. I laid a grocery store bouquet on his grave. There's no headstone yet, only a small statue of a praying angel.

"Come again," I whispered. "Please Ned. I can't do this alone."

A woman in black walking by with a small child looked at me, then quickly looked away.

DREAM—Last night I dreamed I turned the hands of my clock backward to the day before Ned was shot. I didn't see him that day, or the day before, but if I could live that time over, I would find him, wherever he was.

"Don't go into the woods tomorrow," I would tell him. If he asked me why, I would say I had one of my premonitions. Something bad was going to happen to him if he didn't heed my warning.

I would tell him that I inherited the ability to foretell the future from my Aunt Nora. That's sort of the truth. Aunt Nora did have the ability, but she didn't pass it on to me.

I would make him believe me, whatever it took, and he wouldn't be at the stream when the assassin came looking for him.

At that moment, in the dream, a shot rang out. The sound came from the woods.

I was too late.

I woke and listened to the ticking of the alarm clock on my nightstand.

For heaven's sake, who dreams about a clock that doubles as a time travel device? My life isn't a science-fiction novel.

But suppose, just suppose, there were a way to make time run backward. If only I'd known what was going to happen that day, how different everything would be.

JUSTICE—I read that they questioned a man who had bragged about making Ned pay for shooting his brother in an attempt to stop a robbery in progress. He denied even knowing Ned, claiming he was just entertaining "the boys in the bar." So I guess that's a dead end. They never found that man, Jimmy Redmond, who robbed Maybelle and shot her. Every road in this investigation leads to a dead end.

I thought Ned came back from the dead for me, but maybe he's waiting for his killer to be apprehended.

Forty-seven

"Anyone home? Jennet?"

Crane's voice and a pack of barking dogs broke the spell Evanora had cast on me. I had lost myself in her tale, and no wonder. It had become a ghost story, my favorite genre.

"In here." I marked my place in the diary and set it on the coffee table.

In the kitchen, the collies pranced and danced around Crane. Candy and Velvet followed him to the gun cabinet and back to the kitchen.

"Dinner will be a little late," I said.

"That's okay."

It wouldn't take long to broil a steak and bake potatoes. The salad was already made, and we had chocolate cake left from yesterday.

He opened a can of Vernor's for himself and one for me. I sat beside him at the table, happy to be living my own life again rather than Evanora's.

"I ran into Fowler today," Crane said. "He has a plan to trap the lady you call Carrot Top. It might work. He made contact with somebody at Relocations, Inc., and is trying to decide which of his dogs to sacrifice."

"He won't let her get her hands on them, I hope."

"They'll be the lure. He hasn't worked out the details, yet, but you know Fowler. He won't put his precious dogs in harm's way."

"What do you think of his plan?" I asked.

He shrugged. "It might work, but he'll need solid evidence before we can charge her."

"Won't an offer to dump dogs for a price be evidence?" I asked.

"It should be, if she takes the bait."

"If I'm right about her turning dog abandonment into a business, she has to be stopped. Relocations, indeed."

"Brent's new shelter is filling up fast," Crane said. "We always had strays, but it didn't used to be like this when the Woodville sisters were in charge."

"Then Carrot Top came to town. I hope Brent will be successful."

He usually was. Brent had a hunter's instinct and an impressive sense of what could best be called stick-to-it-ivity.

Crane finished his drink and went upstairs to shower while I put the steaks on to broil, thoroughly confusing Candy who didn't know which one of us to shadow. Where food was concerned, she looked more like a wild thing than an elegant tricolor collie.

I wondered if anyone would adopt a dog who looked like a wolf.

~ * ~

The night was filled with noise, not the kind that was conducive to sleep like the splattering of rain on windows, but the kind that makes you wonder if the neighbors are having an all-night party.

Annoyed at being awakened yet again, I listened. The coyotes were howling. Nothing new about that. From downstairs in the dining room, Evanora's melody played to the end and started again. Out on the lane, a motor hummed, a sound which was practically unheard of in this place at this hour.

Suddenly the humming stopped, and other sounds shattered the stillness. A gunshot! The crackling of breaking glass.

What on earth?

One of the dogs gave a high-pitched bark. Misty? In another moment, she was at the side of the bed, her paws on the comforter. Halley, still in the doorway, growled softly.

Crane, who could sleep through any upheaval, woke in an instant. "What was that?" he demanded. "Did you hear that?"

"Is it our house?"

I turned on the light. Crane was already out of bed, striding through the doorway, the dogs leading the way.

It sounded as if a hundred agitated canines were barking at once. Sounding the alarm. My heart was beating almost as loudly.

I followed Crane to the first floor where there was no apparent damage. Light streamed in through the window, turning the familiar furniture shapes into grotesque shadows. The collies, annoyed at the disruption in their peaceful night, flew into protector mode and clustered around me.

I glanced out into the darkness. The yellow Victorian was ablaze with light. Every lamp on both floors appeared to be burning.

"It's at Camille's!" I cried.

Crane stopped at the gun cabinet. I hurried to the closet and grabbed his jacket. Slipping it over his pajamas, he threw open the door.

I could hear Twister and Holly barking from across the lane. As I hastily donned my parka, I was vaguely aware of the music box still playing.

"Stay here!" Crane ordered.

I followed him out the door, thinking to close it on the curious collies, but Misty was too fast for me. She slipped through, determined to accompany me.

The lane was peaceful enough—now—slumbering under a full moon. But there had been that untoward humming. A car on Jonquil Lane in the dead of night. Gone now.

A gust of cold wind whipped my nightgown around my bare legs. I pulled my hood forward and crossed the lane, catching up to Crane at the walkway.

One of the windows had been broken, leaving a square of jagged edges. I climbed the stairs and reached for Misty's collar, then remembered she wasn't wearing it. None of the dogs wore collars at night.

"Stay!"

She pressed her body to mine as I stared in horror at the shattered window. Such violence was practically unheard of in our town. Why would anyone shoot at the house of the quietest, most innocuous couple in Foxglove Corners?

And more important, were Camille and Gilbert all right?

Gilbert flung open the door. In the living room, Camille, clad in a long flannel nightgown, sat on the sofa, cradling an anxious Holly. Twister, the Belgian shepherd, older and braver, stood beside them, his dark hair bristling.

Crane's voice was sharp, his expression grim. "Is anyone hurt?"

Camille's voice trembled. "We're all right. They broke our window. Why would anyone do that to us? We never hurt anybody."

Gilbert placed his hand on Camille's shoulder while Misty nudged Holly. "We'll find them, Camille," he said.

How? I wondered.

Camille wiped her eyes with the back of her hand. "The shot woke us up. The bullet went through my painting of the dogs. It's ruined."

"Thank heavens it didn't go through one of the dogs," I said. "Or you or Gilbert."

Because that could have easily happened. Such atrocities were all too frequent, but they always occurred in other places.

Crane was no longer with us. He had gone outside, likely to investigate, but whoever had fired the shot was long gone, and the shooter wouldn't have left a trail.

"I heard a motor," I said. "Just before the shot. Not that it helps."

I sat beside Camille, stroking Holly's head, knowing that nothing I could say would make Camille feel better. The shock had torn away her reserves.

"Shall I make you a cup of tea with a lot of sugar in it?" I asked.

"No, dear. That won't help."

"It won't hurt."

"How about a brandy?" murmured Gilbert.

"I want my painting back the way it was," Camille said. "And my window whole again. This has been my home for years and years. My safe place. I want that back."

"It'll be safe again," Gilbert assured her.

I wondered. A shot in the night. A car that disappeared. No witnesses except perhaps for the coyotes.

Desperate for something to do to help, I rose and headed to the kitchen. "I'll get you that cup of tea, Camille. You may think you don't want it now, but it'll help a little."

"And I'll pour myself and Crane a brandy," Gilbert said. "I, for one, won't sleep any more tonight."

What time was it? Three in the morning by the microwave clock. The night was as good as over for all of us.

My hands shook as I filled the teakettle. How would the yellow Victorian ever be Camille's safe haven again? For that matter, how safe were Crane and I and our collies in our house across the lane? I'd thought Foxglove Corners was the most desirable place on earth, the embodiment of country peace and quiet. I couldn't bear to think I'd been wrong.

Forty-eight

I looked from the bed to the closet, wondering if I should try to sleep for two hours. It was too early to be moving around the house, too early to cook breakfast and get dressed.

Back to bed, I decided. Tomorrow was a school day, and after the night we'd had, I needed all the rest I could get. If only I could convince my heartbeat to regulate and my brain to quit flashing images of the yellow Victorian in ruins.

Crane was already asleep as were the dogs, with the exception of Misty, who waited to see what I was going to do. Halley lay in the doorway, her usual sleeping place. As I smoothed the crumpled sheet and lay down, the blanket pulled up to my chin, Misty stationed herself at the side of the bed.

I'm here. I love you. You're safe now.

But every time I closed my eyes, I imagined I heard the sinister hum of an engine out on the lane. A drive-by. Any moment a bullet would come crashing through our wall. Finding its mark. Crane. One of our precious collies. Myself. If I allowed myself to fall asleep, was there a chance I would never wake up?

In the morning, I would have to be reasonably bright and alert in order to teach my classes. And good luck with that.

Maybe I should take another sick day?

But the only sickness was lodged deep in my heart. I grieved for Camille's fright and loss, and for something that had been taken from me. My security.

You live with an armed deputy sheriff, I told myself. *Crane is strong and resourceful. He'll do whatever it takes to protect his family.*

But the strongest of law enforcers could be gunned down. Case in point: Evanora's Ned.

A remembered line from the diary came to mind. Evanora had heard a shot while lying in bed. Could she have heard the shot that took Ned's life?

From across the lane, I had heard the shot that broke the window of the yellow Victorian. Another weird connection between Evanora and me.

Was it relevant?

I closed my eyes, felt the heaviness of my lids and the burden of Evanora's grief and...

The alarm went off, a pleasant enough little refrain, but I was heartily tired of it. The smell of pancakes and coffee overrode my aggravation at being so rudely awakened.

I found Crane in the kitchen making breakfast. "Good morning, honey," he said.

"Morning. It came too soon."

Through the kitchen window, I had a good view of the yellow Victorian. A nailed-on board covered the gaping space cut out by the bullet.

Bullets can travel through boards...

In another window, a single lamp burned. Camille and Gilbert were awake. I doubt if they'd gotten much sleep.

"Tea or coffee?" Crane asked.

"Both," I said.

Coffee to help me wake all the way up and tea to soothe the knots in my stomach that sleep hadn't been able to untie.

"The coffee's ready," he said. "I'll make you a cup of tea."

"I can do it." I started to rise, but he waved me back down again.

Thank heavens for our familiar routine: Breakfast on the stove, collies gobbling their kibble, the sun trying to rise, Crane already dressed for his patrol of Foxglove Corners. Everything the same.

Everything different.

"I wonder if Gilbert will call the police," I said.

"*I'm* the police" Crane reminded me.

"It isn't likely they'll catch the shooter, is it?"

"Not likely. He didn't leave a trace. But you never know."

I then asked the impossible question, the one that had chased me through my dreams. "Will it happen again, do you think? To our house the next time?

He didn't answer in words. How could he? His touch and his kiss would have to suffice.

~ * ~

Marston High School came to slow life under a weak sun. Car doors slammed. Friendly shouts fractured the morning silence. A snatch of truly nerve-shattering music shrieked out from a boom box.

"I really needed quiet time today," I said as Leonora and I entered the building.

"You came to the wrong place."

I resisted the impulse to yawn and rubbed my eyes instead until I realized I was smudging my eye makeup.

"I wonder what's happening back home," I said.

"I'm guessing nothing. The shooter made his statement and took off."

We picked up our mail in the front office, junk mostly, and walked to our rooms through halls that were rapidly filling up with students, everyone in a rush.

"I wish I knew what kind of statement he thought he was making."

"Poor Camille," Leonora said. "She's such a gentle soul."

"I'm worried it'll happen again." I didn't have to add 'at our house.'

Leonora sighed. "You'd think we were living in the city. No place in the world is completely safe."

That was especially true of our school. I would never forget the day a disturbed student had opened fire in my classroom, nor the boy who had died. To the young people in my World Literature class, the incident had long since receded into the past. Most were likely unaware of it, but for those who had been affected by it, the memories would never go away.

Why did peace have to be so elusive?

"You need a nice long rest," Leonora said. "We all do. Luckily, we have Easter vacation to look forward to."

"There's that." I pulled my room key out of my purse. Three girls were waiting outside my classroom door.

"What are we going to do today?" asked Cecile, her tone verging on boredom.

"Mmm," I said. "Something good."

At the moment, I couldn't remember the day's lesson. Thank heavens it was written in my plan book.

They followed me inside, going to their desks while I hung my coat in the closet.

"You look nice today, Mrs. Ferguson," Cecile said.

I thanked her, glad I'd made the effort to wear my emerald green jumper with a ruffled blouse and my Valentine locket from Crane. If I looked my best, maybe I'd feel better.

More students drifted or burst into the room. More noise. Shuffling feet. The first bell.

And the school day began.

~ * ~

During the next several hours, I was so busy that the events of the previous night fell back into the past. Leonora and I bought roast beef and potato take-out dinners at Clovers, and as soon as I tended to the collies, I crossed the lane to visit Camille.

Gilbert had arranged for a glass company to repair the broken window. Camille had taken the damaged picture down from the wall and spent the day baking, which was her way to cope.

But she wasn't coping that well. Her eyes were haunted, and she seemed to be listening for a shot that, thankfully, never came.

"Take these home for you and Crane," she said, packing a half dozen strawberry muffins in a bag. "And don't let the coyote get them."

Happy that I had a ready-made dinner and a blueberry pie from Clovers for dessert, I sought escape to the best place I knew. Evanora's diary lay on the coffee table where I'd left it. I opened it and began reading.

EVANORA'S DIARY

MUSIC—At night I wind my music box and listen to a song I've never been able to identify. I call it 'Ned's Melody.' I've listened to it so often I can hear it in my dreams. I wish I knew its name because I'm afraid one day the music box will wear out. Nothing lasts forever.

I feel that my life is spinning toward an end. I'll never be happy again. Every day is a carbon copy of the day before. Fall has a tight grip on the land. The trees are almost bare, and walking in the woods is dangerous because the wind has brought down so many branches, and leaves cover them. The ground is slippery in places.

Sara warns me to look where I'm going, not to trip. She says a fall at this time could be deadly. I tell her I'm always careful.

Every morning, I take Honey and go for a walk in the woods. I don't bring a lunch but take a thermos of hot chocolate and sit in the little house waiting for Ned to come back. It's so cold. So different from the way it was in the summertime when Ned was with me.

He never comes, and I don't sense his presence anymore; neither there nor by the stream. But I won't stop waiting for him and hoping, someday, I'll find him.

Sometimes I'm disturbed by heart-wrenching thoughts. Could it be I never saw him that foggy day? That I conjured him out of my grief and longing?

I'm not going to believe that, because if it didn't happen, then I have nothing left to live for.

LOSS—Now the baby is gone, too. It would have been a little girl. Stillborn. What a sad word. Mother called her Nora as soon as she knew of her existence. She even embroidered her name on pillowcases and little pinafores and dressed a doll for her.

The baby never seemed real to me. To be truthful, I never wanted to be a mother. I wanted Ned, and a house of our own with trees and flowers in the yard and a picket fence. Then, and only then, we could add children. I couldn't see myself raising a child alone. Now I don't have to.

It's funny, though, sometimes I wonder what it would have been like to have a daughter. And she would have been part of Ned. For a time, I didn't think about that. Now, it's too late.

Mother wept as she gathered all the clothes she'd sewed for little Nora. So many tiny garments, most of them mint green.

"Some other baby girl will wear them," she said. "They'll keep."

I didn't say anything. What could I say?

I'm trying to think about college now. English courses. New worlds to conquer. Another future so different from the one I thought I was going to have.

But my heart isn't in it.

Forty-nine

ANOTHER YEAR—I haven't written in my diary in a long time. I've been busy reading for school and, besides, there's been nothing in my life worth writing about. That changed last night.

Ever since Dad had his heart attack, he's been going downhill. I was too absorbed in my studies to see how much he had aged.

"He may not have much longer to live," Sara said. "He's on medication, and we can pray for a miracle, but...I don't know what we'll do without him."

I didn't know what to say. My father always seemed invincible to me. I suppose I thought he would live forever.

Last night I took him a cup of weak tea and sat with him. We talked about school and my plans for a career. I don't really have any plans. I'll graduate and look for a job nearby. I don't have any desire to leave this part of the state. My happiest and saddest memories are here.

Dad took my hand in his and held it. "I have something to tell you, Evanora. I should have told you before. I wish I had. But what's done is done. Now it's time."

"Just rest," I said. "Drink your tea. We can talk later."

"That young man you cared for...Your child's father..."

I looked at him.

"I was the one who killed him."

The words fell into the silence, each one like a stone falling on my heart. I didn't know what to say. Words are so important. When they fail you, you're left with nothing.

"Aren't you going to say anything?" he asked.

"You can't mean it," I said.

"I didn't intend to shoot him. I only planned to threaten him. I didn't want him to hurt you, and he was going to. He had other girlfriends, girls you didn't know about. I just pointed my gun at him and told him to stop seeing you, to leave you alone, or I would make him regret it. He laughed at me. I pulled the trigger, and he died instantly."

"Ned <u>had</u> other girlfriends," I said. "Past tense. Had. He loved me."

"I don't think so, honey."

I tried to pull my hand out of his grasp. He held on tightly.

"What happened then?" I asked.

"I left him there, by the stream where he fell. I went home and put the gun away and pretended that nothing had happened. It wasn't easy for me to see how you were grieving."

"You would have let another man pay for your crime?"

"There was no other man. No other real suspect. I'm sorry it happened. I didn't mean to do it, but it happened, and there was no undoing it. What was the point of stirring up trouble for your mother and Sara—and you? We won't tell them about this. There's no need for them to know what I did. Nobody has to know. Just you."

His voice faded. I saw the glisten of unshed tears in his eyes. My father never cried.

"Can you ever forgive me?" he asked.

"I don't know," I said.

It was the only answer I could give him. But I hated myself for not saying the words he wanted to hear. Soon he would be gone, and I would never able to say them.

"I did it for you, Evanora," he said. "You would never have been happy with him. Ned Douglas wasn't the man for you."

"That isn't true. I loved him."

But I loved my father, too. And what would it cost me to say the words he wanted to hear?

"If it was truly an accident, then I forgive you," I said.

But would God forgive him?

That was between my father and his maker.

MY LAST WALK—Winter came early this year. I wore my snow boots and my warmest coat for my walk today and wondered if I would ever come this way again. The stream has practically vanished under the fallen leaves, and the little house is freezing inside.

There is nothing of Ned here, and I am suddenly certain there never will be. Maybe that presence I felt and the sight of Ned standing by the stream were all I will ever have.

I stayed longer than I should have, sitting at the table, sipping hot chocolate from my thermos, and remembering, and it seemed that I saw his face again and felt his touch on my hand, and his kiss.

He was here with me. Some of him, anyway. For a few seconds, anyway.

"Don't go," I told him. "Don't go, don't go, don't go. I have so much to tell you. I love you, Ned. So very much."

He didn't answer, and, gradually, the feeling dropped away from me, like a velvet cloak falling to the floor.

I was sitting in Cecily's playhouse drinking chocolate that had cooled and shivering in the cold while the wind ripped the last of the leaves from the trees and scattered them in the snow.

I am alone.

FAREWELL—to my diary. It served its purpose. I have a record of my love for Ned and his for me. I have the story of my last happy summer on paper. I can reread what I wrote and relive those days whenever I like. Nothing can ever take the written word from me—or the memories.

But sometimes I wonder if I captured everything we said. What if I forgot something? Did whole conversations drain out of my mind?

Did Ned ever say he loved me? I don't remember. But he must have.

One day it'll come back to me, and I'll open this book again and write 'Epilogue.'

But not today.

Fifty

The rest of the diary, more than half, consisted of blank pages. I turned each one, hoping Evanora had written her epilogue, but finally had to accept that she had ended her story. In all likelihood, there was no Volume III. She would have had plenty of room to record future events in this little book.

I had no way of knowing what happened afterward. Had Evanora managed to salvage some happiness in the future, which was, from my perspective, the past? Did she ever see Ned's spirit again? Was it the memory of her love affair with Ned that tied her spirit to the Valentine House?

And would I ever again be aware of her presence in that place of enchantment?

With a sense of deep loss, I closed the diary and slipped it into my shoulder bag. Tomorrow was Saturday. I'd stop at Clovers and lend it to Annica.

~ * ~

The next morning, I found Brent at Clovers sitting in my favorite booth eating what looked like a triple order of bacon and eggs. Annica hovered over him with a coffeepot. It shouldn't take long to pour a refill, but she was doing it in slow motion, as if she never wanted to leave his side and tend to her other customers.

She wore a new spring dress, pale lavender in color, with the Easter bunny earrings she'd bought at the Green House of Antiques, and she looked happy—even radiant. The rift between her and Brent must have been a figment of my imagination. Or they had just made up.

Brent looked up from his breakfast spread. "Hey, Jennet! Just the lady I wanted to see."

Annica turned that radiant smile on me. "Morning, Jennet. Coffee or tea?"

The rich aroma of the coffee made the decision for me. "Coffee," I said, "and a muffin. Blueberry, if you have it."

"We do, and they're still warm from the oven."

"Did something happen?" I asked Brent.

"Yes and no. I made contact with someone at Relocations, Inc., and explained that I had two dogs to relocate. We agreed on a price and a place and time to meet. Today at nine."

"Great! Carrot Top fell for it."

"Not so fast. I was there with Napoleon and Chance. She didn't show up. I waited an hour. She must have caught on to me. I have no idea how."

Annica returned with two blueberry muffins and poured my coffee. Then, nodding to Marcy who was always happy to cover for her when she wanted to visit with one of her friends, she set the coffeepot down, sank into a seat, and pushed runaway strands of red-gold hair behind her earrings.

"It's early, and I'm already tired," she said. "What are you two talking about?"

"Our plan to trap Carrot Top and put an end to her vile business went awry," I said.

"Oh, no. Well, you'll come up with another one."

I handed the diary to Annica. "Here's the rest of Evanora's story. Be warned. It's a tearjerker."

The clover chimes rang.

"Carrot Top…" Brent began.

Annica started and glanced toward the door, but it was only a family party coming in, two adults and two whiny children. Marcy led them to a table.

"False alarm," Brent said.

"What about Carrot Top?" I asked.

"She's smarter than I thought."

"But we're smarter still," Annica said.

The chimes rang again, delicate fairy notes welcoming another customer.

I turned to look. Colton Reeves stood in the doorway surveying the room, a fake cowboy with a Stetson hat on his head, an arrogant expression on his handsome face, and in his hands a bouquet of roses. Red. The color of blood.

"Your boyfriend," Brent said.

"Not mine." Annica reached for the coffeepot and started to get up. But Colton had seen her. He strode up to the booth before she could make her getaway.

"Good morning, Miss Annica," he drawled. "Or should I say 'Miss America?' I picked these flowers just for you."

With this outrageous speech, he tried to hand her the bouquet. She held on to the coffeepot with both hands. "You shouldn't have, Colton."

"I wanted to. You should have roses in your life, not dirty dishes."

"Really, you shouldn't have. I told you—"

Brent let the strip of bacon he'd been about to eat fall into the eggs. He rose, towering over the Texan. His glare was deadly, his voice loud enough to bring all sound in the restaurant to a sudden halt.

"Just a minute, Tex. You're in Michigan now. You can't just waltz into town and start bringing flowers to another man's girl."

Colton's blue eyes turned glacial. "I think it's up to Annica to decide whose girl she is. Annica?"

He waited, but Annica had turned to Brent. "Did you mean what you just said? That I'm your girl?"

"Sure I did. I thought you knew it."

Apparently not getting the message, Colton said, "The last time I looked, the lady was free. Tell him, Annica. You make your own decisions."

For the first time since I'd known her, Annica was speechless.

"Why don't you move along?" Brent asked. "Go back to Dallas and leave us alone."

Colton fixed a cold stare on Annica and let the roses drop to the floor. She remained silent. Marcy gave a cry of alarm.

"Maybe I will," he said. "I'll find a friendlier place."

So saying, he stomped his way to the door.

The chimes rang again. They sounded like tiny, tinny jeers.

"Good riddance," Brent said.

Marcy stooped to pick up the bouquet. Still wrapped in cellophane, they were no worse for the rough treatment they'd received at Colton's hands. Their rich fragrance filled the air.

Annica frowned. "I don't want them. Take them away."

"Well, I do," Marcy said. "I'm going to put them in water. Poor things. I don't think Mary Jeanne would like you ordering customers out of Clovers, Mr. Fowler," she added.

"He wasn't a customer," Brent said. He retrieved the fallen strip of bacon and dipped it into a yolk. "He only came for Annica. He was a…You all know what he was. I hope he drowns in the Gulf of Mexico."

"I think he came from San Antonio," Annica said.

"Same difference.

The little restaurant had never been so quiet. I glanced at the other diners. Our little drama had captured their interest.

"The show's over," I said in a loud voice. "You can go back to whatever you were doing."

Annica still stood as if frozen in place, holding onto the handle of the coffee pot as if it were a lifeline.

Brent said, "Annica, would you get me another glass of orange juice, please?"

Remembering that she was a waitress, Annica murmured, "Coming right up."

As she moved back to the kitchen, I noticed her step had acquired a definite spring.

"Well…" I smiled at Brent as he scooped a spoonful of egg into his mouth. "That was fun."

"It sure was," he said, "and no one's bleeding."

Fifty-one

Back home, I took Halley, Velvet, and Misty for a walk up the lane, destination Sue Appleton's horse ranch. Maybe she could help us come up with a Plan B to stop Carrot Top in her tracks. But as we passed the abandoned construction site, the desire to veer off the intended path began as a tiny spark and grew until finally it was irresistible.

The spell of spring weather would have made the woods easier to navigate. I could imagine the red heart on the Valentine House calling to me. The bright sunshine, the gentle breeze, and the scent of flowers wafting on the air all conspired to overwhelm me.

One last visit couldn't possibly hurt. Was Evanora there even now, anxiously waiting for Ned to appear?

By the time we reached Squill Lane, I had made my decision. A visit to Sue could wait for another day. When our walk was over, I would come this way again with Misty and see if we could find Evanora.

Or her spirit.

~ * ~

Misty entered the abandoned development with her tail wagging and her nose to the ground, happily sniffing all the wondrous scents that had lain under the winter snow. It doesn't take much to entertain a canine.

I allowed her to lead the way, taking my time to savor the signs of spring, like the purple crocus-like plant that grew amid exposed roots and rocks.

The first walk of spring is sheer magic, and it was so quiet in the woods, so gloriously silent, that I could hear my slightly labored breathing as I trudged over the uneven ground. The air was moist, and a light fog began to form around the trees.

Ghost fog?

The silence was tangible, practically a living thing. And why weren't the birds singing? Surely it wasn't too early in the season for them. Perhaps Misty had frightened them away with her exuberance. I imagined all wildlife must seek cover at the approach of our kind.

The red heart on the house swam out of the mist. It appeared to speak to me in a voice no one else could hear.

I frowned, noting that the door was ajar again. I was certain I'd closed it after our last visit. Of course, the house was old; the door didn't close properly. Any animal could have opened it. Or a vagrant. Or even the wind.

It didn't matter as long as the house was currently empty, and it was. Otherwise, Misty would have known.

Still, she sat in the entrance as if anxious to communicate a warning: *Danger alert! Go back!*

"It's all right, girl," I said, knowing that whatever or whoever dwelled within meant us no harm. "Come. We won't stay long."

She moved at a gentle tug on her collar. As I crossed the threshold, the temperature seemed to drop at least twenty degrees. I snapped my spring jacket shut and stood in the middle of the room, shivering in the frigid air, waiting and listening. For what? A heartbroken plea, 'Don't go'? The music box's ghostly melody? A muffled sob?

"I know your story, Evanora," I said softly. "I'm sorry it ended the way it did, and I hope you found peace. Somewhere."

Silence.

Well, you didn't expect an answer, I hope.

A sudden sound took me by surprise, a hollow voice, a whisper: *Move! Hide!*

Misty growled. Wrenching the leash out of my hand, she dashed to the door. In the same moment, a shot fractured the silence.

I fell forward and made a grab for the leash, but it was gone, still attached to my collie's collar.

Why was I on the floor? The shot had missed me. Hadn't it?

A second shot rang out, and the world shuddered back into silence.

As I attempted to push myself up, I felt a sharp, burgeoning pain in my arm. Blood soaked through the sleeve of my jacket, my life blood draining away.

I wasn't going anywhere.

I lay on the floor, still and stunned. In a moment, clarity returned.

What do you mean you're not going anywhere? You have to. You can't let the shooter get away. You have to find Misty. Move!

All I could do was watch blood soaking through my sleeve. Red on yellow, yellow on red. The world seemed to pull back from me. The pain was an iron band burning my flesh, squeezing it. I was going to be sick...

You have to get help. The bullet didn't strike a vital organ. Did it?

I needed something I could use to pull myself up. A table, a chair, anything. But the house was empty. In my time, it had always been empty.

Thoughts careened through my mind, colliding with half-formed plans, struggling with my awareness of the pain.

No one knew where I was. Only Misty. And where was she?

Noise erupted in the woods. Ungodly screeching from a female throat. Furious barking. Ominous echoes. Barking!

Misty had escaped the bullet. She was near. Close to the house. They both were, she and the shooter.

I tried to sit up again and became aware of a strange sensation. Something was pulling me upward, supporting me with strong and solid arms, encouraging me with a barely discernible voice that sounded slightly human: *You're going to be all right, Jennet. Now go. Find your dog.*

With help that had come out of nowhere, I rose and moved away from the widening spill of blood.

On my feet now, I stumbled to the door, leaving a trail of blood in my wake; and all the way it seemed that unseen arms kept me upright and moving forward.

At the doorway, I held onto the frame, standing on my own power, seeing the woods and the stream in somber sepia tones. I closed my eyes and opened them again. The scene returned but in pale color.

A black-clad woman lay on her side facing the stream, held in place by the paw of a growling white collie. The woman's knitted cap had fallen off, revealing a bird's nest of carrot red curls. She lay so still. She must have fainted. I hope Misty hadn't frightened her to death.

As I stumbled toward Misty and her captive, I almost stepped on the gun. I thought about picking it up, then decided it was out of the reach of the woman, assuming she regained consciousness.

Instead, I fished my phone out of my pocket with my good hand and took two pictures. One of the shooter and one of the gun. Now I had all the evidence I needed.

Misty looked over her shoulder at me. *See what I did?*

"Good dog, Misty," I said. "You saved the day."

Now to save myself. Leaning against the nearest tree, I dialed nine-one-one.

"I need help," I said in a voice that sounded unlike my own. "I've just been—shot."

The dispatcher asked where I was, and I gave the answer that hovered on the edge of my mind.

"In the greenwood."

"Where is that again?"

Realizing what I said, I amended my response. "I'm in the abandoned development on Jonquil Lane, about twenty minutes into the woods, going north."

Fifty-two

The aftermath of a confrontation with evil can be monotonous if repeated often enough. With me, it was becoming overly familiar. Sirens, an ambulance, long hours in Emergency, a diagnosis—flesh wound—and home where Misty waited anxiously for my return.

For the woman in black, it must have been the same, except instead of home, her destination was custody. Not for dumping dogs, not yet, but for attempted murder.

To keep myself calm while Crane went in search of my doctor, I replayed the moments that followed immediately on my call for help. The crackle of stamped-on leaves, the snapping of branches. And a familiar voice calling my name.

Brent had emerged from the woods carrying a rifle. "Jennet! What the hell are you doing, sitting on the ground?" He broke off as his glance fell on my bloody jacket.

I'd managed to shrug it off and wind it clumsily around my arm. "You're hurt!"

"That horrible woman shot me," I said. "I think it's a flesh wound. I hope it is. But should it bleed so much?"

He avoided my eyes. "All gunshot wounds bleed. I'll call nine-one-one."

"I already did."

He extended a brawny arm to help me up, bringing to mind the hand that had supported me in the house. I stood shakily, leaning on him while the woods slipped into their sepia tones again.

"What about Carrot Top? Shouldn't she regain consciousness? Misty must have knocked her over."

"Good for Misty. We should leave her here."

"We can't do that," I said.

And we didn't. The police and paramedics saw to it.

The memory floated away as Crane joined me in the narrow room. "I can take you home, honey. We just have to wait for the paperwork."

I'm not sorry to say I was happy that the woman who had shot me didn't have that option.

~ * ~

When she heard what had happened, Camille baked a ham and a banana cream pie. She believed every celebration should be accompanied by food. Because she didn't want to risk running into the coyote, Brent carried our dinner across the lane and, naturally, stayed to enjoy it with us.

Over ham, potato salad, and rolls, we broke our rule about banning serious conversation at the table. I had several questions, but few answers. After claiming that her husband had forced her to form Relocations, Inc., the woman refused to talk except to say she only meant to scare me, to convince me to keep out of her business.

I knew her name now. It was Delia Blackwell, far too pretty a name for a she-devil.

I passed the potato salad to Brent. "How did you know where to find me?"

"I didn't. I was on my way to your house for Sunday dinner when I saw that Honda with the sticker on the window and a woman behind the wheel. I trailed it—all the way to Jonquil Lane. By the time I caught up to it, no one was inside. I figured she'd gone into the woods, so I followed her. When I heard the shots, I knew it was too late."

Crane set his fork down and frowned. "You could have notified me, Fowler."

"There wasn't any time."

"Lucky I heard it on the police radio."

Lucky was the watchword. We were all lucky, except for Delia Blackwell and her husband.

"That woman...She'll pay for her crimes now, won't she?" I asked.

"For attempted murder, yes," Crane said.

"Her relocations and money were more important than my life," I said.

"She must have thought you were behind the attempt to shut her down," Brent said. "Sorry, Jennet, I wish she'd come after me instead of you."

I could follow her reasoning as I was the one who had challenged her in the gas station, and I was the one who'd witnessed her abandoning a dog on Jonquil Lane. To my knowledge, she had never set eyes on Brent.

I could also understand why she had targeted the yellow Victorian. She wouldn't know which house I lived in and, unfortunately for Camille and Gilbert, she chose the wrong one. Perhaps she'd seen me on the lane today. But I hadn't heard the hum of her engine behind me.

Well, not every mystery can be solved.

Which reminded me of the help I'd had that could only have come from Evanora.

"After I was shot, someone gave me a hand, helped me to stand and walk to the door," I said.

"Someone?" Crane asked.

"Evanora's spirit. I'd like to make one more trip to the house. Maybe take her some flowers."

"You want to leave flowers in an empty room to die?" Brent asked.

"I'll put them in water and leave them on...The table?"

Uh no. The table was in Evanora's time—and in my dream.

"I don't want you to go back to that place," Crane said. "Especially if you think it's haunted."

"She's a benevolent spirit," I said. "I'd like to express my gratitude to her."

"Then write her story in that book you're working on."

He referred to the collection of stories I'd compiled on the ghostly experiences I'd had since moving to Foxglove Corners. It was almost finished. Evanora's tale would complete it.

"I can do that. Then I think I'd like to write a mystery. I'll call it *Rescuing Dogs Can Be Murder*."

"I like that title," Brent said. "You write it. I'll read it."

"If you want to thank her, find out where she's buried and leave flowers on her grave," Crane said. "By the way, what are you going to do with the diaries?"

At present, Annica was still reading them, but soon she'd return them to me.

"I'm not sure," I said. "The Green House doesn't want them back. I don't know whether Evanora had any descendants who'd like to have them."

"You can bury them or burn them." That was Brent's idea of a practical solution. Neither one appealed to me

"That's no way to treat the written word," I said. "Evanora had definite ideas about the enduring power of words."

"Then she went off and died and left her diaries behind," Brent said. "I reckon they're yours. You paid for them."

"You're right. I'll keep them. We have lots of storage space."

"Let's hope she won't want them back," Crane said. "I've had my fill of ghosts for a while."

"So have I," I said.

But I didn't mean it.

~ * ~

Easter recess gave me plenty of time to search for the missing details of Evanora's life. On the first day of my vacation, I returned to the Green House of Antiques and was able to speak to the new co-owner, Zara.

She didn't know anything about a girl named Evanora or the diaries. All the items from that particular estate sale had been sold, and there were no small blue books lying around.

I had no choice but to believe her. However, the next day, with the help of Miss Eidt and her outmoded vertical file, I discovered a yellowing clipping of the obituary of Evanora May Sherbourne's obituary. It gave the year of her death as 2000, and the name of her only survivor, her sister, Sara. She was buried in the cemetery at the end of Huron Court. My next step was to visit her grave.

Because of the danger of being thrown into another time while traveling on that bedeviled roadway, I asked Crane to go with me. He agreed to accompany me on his lunch hour.

First, we stopped at a flower shop for a memorial bouquet and also bought a blowsy but beautiful blue hydrangea plant.

"I think she liked blue flowers," I said. "She never found the plant in the woods that smelled like lilacs."

Crane nodded. "I'm sure she will be happy to have them, honey."

To my surprise and relief, nothing untoward happened on our way to the cemetery. As expected, Huron Court lay silently in a veil of light mist. Ghost weather.

We found Evanora's grave in the old section beyond an ancient iron gate. It was a pleasant location, if one had to be buried. A mature weeping willow tree near the grave provided shade and, it seemed to me, comfort. The headstone bore Evanora's name and the dates of her birth and death. Nothing more. She had lived for a half century.

"Rest in peace, Evanora," I said. "And thank you for your help."

I laid the plant and the bouquet on her grave and reflected on the indifference of nature to human life. We all had our moments in the sun. Then we moved on into the darkness while seasons changed and life on earth went on. Evanora's time in the sun with Ned had been short, but nonetheless glorious.

"If you're ready, we should leave," Crane said. "It feels like rain."

I was a little disappointed. I had half-hoped to see a young girl in a mint green dress slip out of the mist to wander among the graves in a never-ending search for her lost lover. According to a line in the diary, Ned Douglas had been buried in this same cemetery beside his Aunt Maybelle.

But Evanora wasn't here. Mist aside, I wasn't going to see a supernatural apparition today.

It occurred to me then. If Evanora was anywhere on earth, it was in the woods of the abandoned development, in the Valentine House where she had once been happy. That stretch of godforsaken acreage was tailor made for a spirit to haunt.

As for myself, my fascination with the little house was over. I didn't plan to set foot in it again. Ever.

With a last silent prayer for Evanora, I took Crane's arm and we went back through the iron gate to find our own sun.

Meet Dorothy Bodoin

Dorothy Bodoin lives in Royal Oak, Michigan, with her blue merle collie, Layla. Dorothy worked as a secretary for Chrysler Missle Corporation, two years of which were spent in southern Italy. A graduate of Oakland University with Bachelor's and Master's degrees in English literature, she taught English in a Michigan high school. On retiring from teaching, she began her second career as a writer. She is the author of the Foxglove Corners mystery series, six novels of romantic suspense, and one Gothic romance.

Other Works From The Pen Of

Dorothy Bodoin

Treasure at Trail's End (Gothic romance) - The House at Trail's End seemed to beckon to Mara Marsden, promising the happy future she longed for. But could she discover its secret without forfeiting her life?

Ghost across the Water (romantic suspense) - Water falling from an invisible force and a ghostly man who appears across Spearmint Lake draw Joanna Larne into a haunting twenty-year-old mystery.

Darkness at Foxglove Corners - Foxglove Corners offers tornado survivor Jennet Greenway country peace and romance, but the secret of the yellow Victorian house across the lane holds a threat to her new life. (#1)

Winter's Tale - On her first winter in Foxglove Corners Jennet Greenway battles dognappers, investigates the murder of the town's beloved veterinarian, and tries to outwit a dangerous enemy. (#3)

A Shortcut through the Shadows - Jennet Greenway's search for the missing owner of her rescue collie, Winter, sets her on a collision course with an unknown killer. (#4)

Cry for the Fox - In Foxglove Corners, the fox runs from the hunters, the animal activists target the Hunt Club, and a killer stalks human prey on the fox trail. (#2)

The Witches of Foxglove Corners - With a haunting in the library, a demented prankster who invades her home, and a murder in Foxglove Corners, Halloween turns deadly for Jennet Greenway. (#5)

The Snow Dogs of Lost Lake - A ghostly white collie and a lost locket lead Jennet Greenway to a body in the woods and a dangerous new mystery. (#6)

The Collie Connection - As Jennet Greenway's wedding to Crane Ferguson approaches, her happiness is shattered when a Good Samaritan deed leaves her without her beloved black collie, Halley, and ultimately in grave danger. (#7)

A Time of Storms - When a stranger threatens her collie and she hears a cry for help in a vacant house, Jennet Ferguson suspects that her first summer as a wife may be tumultuous. (#8)

The Dog from the Sky - Jennet's life takes a dangerous turn when she rescues an abused collie. Soon afterward, a girl vanishes without a trace. Ironically she had also rescued an abused collie. Is there a connection between the two incidents? (#9)

Spirit of the Season - Mystery mixes with holiday cheer as a phantom ice skater returns to the lake where she died, and a collie is accused of plotting her owner's fatal accident. (#10)

Another Part of the Forest - Danger rides the air when a kidnapper whisks his victims away in a hot air balloon, and a false friend puts a curses on a collie breeder's first litter. (#11)

Where Have All the Dogs Gone? - An animal activist frees the shelter dogs in and around Foxglove Corners to save them from being destroyed. Running wild in the countryside, they face an equally distressing fate and post a risk to those who come in contact with them. (#12)

The Secret Room of Eidt House - A rabid dog that should have died months ago from the dread disease runs free in the woods of Foxglove Corners, and the library's long-kept secret unleashes a series of other strange events. (#13)

Follow a Shadow - A shadowy intruder haunts Jennet's woods by night, and a woman who can't accept the death of her collie asks Jennet to help her find Rainbow Bridge where she believes her dog waits for her. (#14)

The Snow Queen's Collie - A white collie puppy appears on the porch of the Ferguson farmhouse during a Christmas Eve snowstorm. In another part of Foxglove Corners a collie breeder's show prospect disappears. Meanwhile, the painting Jennet's sister gave her for Christmas begins to exhibit strange qualities. (#15)

The Door in the Fog - A wounded dog disappears in the fog. A blue door on the side of a barn vanishes. Strange wildflowers and a sound of weeping haunt a meadow. The woods keep their secret, and a curse refuses to die. (#16)

Dreams and Bones - At Brent Fowler's newly purchased Spirit Lamp Inn, a renovation turns up human bones buried in the inn's backyard, rekindling interest in the case of a young woman who disappeared from the inn several decades ago. As Jennet tries to solve this mystery, she doesn't realize it may be her last. (#17)

A Ghost of Gunfire - Months after gunfire erupted in her classroom at Marston High School, leaving one student dead and one seriously wounded, Jennet begins to hear a sound of gunshots inaudible to anyone else. Meanwhile, she resolves to find the demented person who is tying dogs to trees and leaving them to die. (#18)

The Silver Sleigh - Rosalyn Everett was missing and presumed dead. Her collies had been rescued, and her house was abandoned. But a blue merle collie haunts her woods and a figure in bridal white traverses the property. (#19)

The Stone Collie - Jennet's discovery of a collie puppy chained in the yard of a vacant house sets her on a search for a man whose activities may threaten Foxglove Corners' security. Meanwhile, horror story novelist Lucy Hazen is mystified when scenes from her work-in-progress are duplicated in real life. (#20)

The Mists of Huron Court - The house was beautiful, a vintage pink Victorian in a picturesque but lonely country setting, and the girl playing ball with her dog in the yard was friendly, suggesting that she and Jennet walk their dogs together some time. Jennet thinks she has made a new friend until she returns to the house and finds a tumbling down ruin where the Victorian once stood and no sign that the girl and dog have ever been there. ((#21)

Down a Dark Path - What hold does the pink Victorian on Huron Court have on Brent Fowler who is determined to re-create the home of long-dead Violet Randall? When he disappears, could he have been cast adrift in time? (#22))

Shadow of the Ghost Dog - An invisible dog grieves inside the house chosen as a setting for the movie based on Lucy Hazen's book *Devilwish*, and a landscaper unearths a human skeleton in the backyard while planting shrubs. (#23))

The Dark Beyond the Bridge - The discovery of a secret ghost town in a densely rural area of Michigan's lower peninsula leads to mystery and danger for Jennet Ferguson and her friends. (#24)

The Deadly Fields of Autumn - An antique television set that airs an obscure Western at random times and a woman who disappears with her newly-adopted rescue dog draw Jennet into a puzzling mystery. (#25)

The Lost Collies of Silverhedge - Collie breeder Madselin Rivard was dead, leaving her prized, valuable collies uncared for in their kennel. Jennet and her friends rescue five of them, but eight remain unaccounted for. (#26)

All the Pretty Little Collies - Danger stalks the collies of Foxglove Corners when an unknown villain begins tossing poisoned meat into their yards, and a girl with a winning blue merle collie is warned via threatening messages to withdraw her dog from competition or risk the consequences. (#27)

Phantom in the Pond - Brent Fowler's plan to open a house for geriatric collies goes awry when strange things begin to happen in his newly-purchased country estate. (#28)

Challenge a Scarecrow - Scarecrows that guard a dangerous secret and a woman who believes she has brought her dog back to life add up to a frightening and deadly month for Jennet Ferguson.

Letter to Our Readers

Enjoy this book?

You can make a difference

As an independent publisher, Wings ePress, Inc. does not have the financial clout of the large New York Publishers. We can't afford large magazine spreads or subway posters to tell people about our quality books.

But, we do have something much more effective and powerful than ads. We have a large base of loyal readers.

Honest Reviews help bring the attention of new readers to our books.

If you enjoyed this book, we would appreciate it if you would spend a few minutes posting a review on the book's ***Amazon page*** or on its Wings ePress, Inc. webpage ***at www.wingsepress.com***

Thank You very much.

Visit Our Website

For The Full Inventory

Of Quality Books:

Wings ePress, Inc
https://wingsepress.com/

Quality trade paperbacks and downloads

in multiple formats,

in genres ranging from light romantic comedy

to general fiction and horror.

Wings has something for every reader's taste.

Visit the website, then bookmark it.

We add new titles each month!

Wings ePress Inc.
3000 N. Rock Road
Newton, KS 67114